THE BORZOI KILLINGS

Also by Paul Batista

Death's Witness

Extraordinary Rendition

THE BORZOI KILLINGS

PAUL BATISTA

LONGBOAT KEY, FLORIDA

ISBN 978-1-60809-206-2

Published in the United States of America by Oceanview Publishing
Longboat Key, Florida

www.oceanviewpub.com

10 9 8 7 6 5 4 3 2

PRINTED IN THE UNITED STATES OF AMERICA

To my sister, Susan Becker,
and the memory of our beloved parents.

1.

BRAD RICHARDSON'S OFFICE AT the estate was a light-filled room lined with glass walls overlooking the lawn that led to the dunes. Whenever he stood, he saw the Atlantic Ocean over the low, reedy expanse of Egypt Beach and the silver crests of the waves collapsing onto the shore.

He loved the office, as he loved the sprawling house itself, in late October when the trees started to change colors and the lawn, no matter how well-watered and tended by Juan Suarez, stopped growing. Around the house were the flat potato and corn fields that had dominated this whole area when he was a boy and his parents owned a saltbox summer house on Main Street in East Hampton. Now, even all these years later, large tracts of farmland were still here near the Atlantic shore, along with some new houses, all large, rising out of the distant fields.

The house was quiet on this Tuesday morning. His wife Joan was in the city at their Fifth Avenue apartment, Juan had the day off as he did every Tuesday, and Brad had told the cooks not to bother coming to work since he intended to go into East Hampton and pick up food for lunch. He looked forward to driving on the village's broad Main Street lined by ancient trees and stately houses. In October the famous village was largely empty; the restless crowds of the summer were gone; and on this day, under a flawless autumn sky, it was one of the most beautiful places on earth.

Brad also looked forward to a quick tour of the new construction at the public library on Main Street. He and Joan had donated several million dollars to the renovation of the cozy seventy-five-year-old building. The outer shell of the library—the tasteful framework of walls and roof—was preserved by the restoration of the original exterior brick, wood, and shingles. But the interior was gutted, and beautifully crafted rooms, shelves, and floors were being installed. Ultimately the names of Joan and Brad Richardson would appear on a discreet marble plaque over the new fireplace.

He visited the construction site each week. He made an effort to learn the names of most of the carpenters, masons, and plumbers. They knew him. Brad Richardson was, after all, one of the richest men in the world, ranked tenth on the *Forbes* list of the wealthiest Americans. He was slender, likable, engaging. One of the organizers of the annual World Economic Forum at Davos, Switzerland, he had that rare gift of making other people feel comfortable and respected. Some of the workers at the construction site called him Brad.

Not only did the quiet of his Tuesday world soothe him, but he still managed to feel that rush of pleasure like a drug whenever he stayed ahead of the European and Asian stock markets. Years earlier, when he came into the world of finance, even a hundred-dollar gain on a trade made him giddy. Now, when the numbers involved were infinitely larger, a sensation like euphoria, but quieter, more secure, still came over him. He had heard serious marathon runners talk about the body's soothing reaction to the endorphins their bodies released during the 26.2-mile race. A day's success in trading flooded him with "endorphins," as he would say, "even though I don't know whether there really is such a thing as an endorphin. I'm the only guy in history ever to flunk Biology 101, the legendary gut course, at Harvard."

Brad was a dedicated, powerful swimmer. As on most Tuesdays from late April through late October, he left the house at noon and walked barefooted over the lush lawn to the dunes and Egypt Beach, the southern border of his property. He wore a bathing suit and a loose-fitting white bathrobe. Sunlight glittered on the vast expanse of the Atlantic.

The dogs—Felix and Sylvia, fawn-colored, almost mirror images of one another—kept pace with him as he ran across the deserted beach, shedding his bathrobe. The Borzois, too, were powerful swimmers, and they plunged into the waves with the same grace, speed, and skill as Brad.

After ten minutes of intense swimming, he rolled onto his back. He stretched out, his arms spread. His face was in the benign sunlight. Near him floated the dogs, sleek as eels. Sometimes in the gentle swell of the waves their warm bodies touched his.

Brad Richardson's world was utterly quiet now. The ocean waters sustained him. The sky was pure blue. Three seagulls, far overhead, wings open, were suspended on some invisible flow of wind. And, above the dazzling white birds, parallel contrails from two invisible jets spanned the upper atmosphere for miles and miles.

Sun, air, water. Brad Richardson had the sense that he had lived for thousands of years. And that he had thousands more ahead of him.

Just as he was deciding to end his day at four (it was late in Europe, early the next day in Hong Kong), Brad Richardson found himself doing something he had always vowed not to do because he thought it was pretentious: he talked into two cell phones at once, seamlessly handling the information he received in Japanese and French and responding fluently in both languages. He stared through the panes of glass toward the ocean. Sylvia and Felix, still tired from their ocean swim, slept in the warmth of the sunlight near the glass doors.

Brad heard footsteps behind him. Somewhat surprised at the sight of the man casually approaching him, he said, "Be with you in a second." He was too distracted to smile.

The Borzois rose to their feet. Normally edgy, they walked together in the direction of the man in the yellow raincoat. Their hard nails clicked on the floor. As Brad gradually brought his dual conversations to an end, he thought that it must have started raining because the man wore not only the raincoat but knee-high green boots as well. Brad turned again in his old banker's swivel chair to look at the lawn and the dunes. There was no rain.

Brad wore a collarless sweater. The freckled back of his neck was exposed. The man in the rain slicker, focusing on the middle of Brad's neck, swung a machete as if it were a baseball bat, striking that vulnerable area of the neck. It was a flawlessly directed swing.

Making a sound like a human wail of grief, cowering, Sylvia and Felix moved closer to the man in the raincoat as if looking for safety. Two perfectly executed, back-to-back strokes from the machete struck both dogs. The bodies of the Borzois still quivered powerfully, uncontrollably, as he left the light-filled room.

2.

His real name wasn't Juan. It was Anibal. When he casually mentioned that to Joan Richardson as they drank iced tea during one of his work breaks, she said, "Really? I've never heard of that name." She wore a white tennis visor that shaded her eyes and nose. Her intensely blue eyes glinted in the visor's shadow. "It sounds Arabic, doesn't it?"

Juan wasn't sure he understood the word "Arabic." He said, "Not to worry about it, Mrs. Richardson. I like Juan better."

Three months earlier, in late spring, she'd made him indispensable to the way she and Brad Richardson lived. Their gray-shingled, twenty-room house on the ocean at Egypt Beach near the understated and elegant Maidstone Club offered up endless projects on which Juan could work.

Juan was bright. He was a gifted mason. There was a complex weaving of New England-style stone walls throughout the two acre estate. Juan could make the brick and the stone pristine again after the steady erosion from seasons of ocean winds and rains, snow and late winter fogs, as well as the dry days of hot sunlight in June, July, August, and September.

He was also a skilled gardener. The house the Richardsons called the *Bonac* was built in 1925 by a branch of the Vanderbilt family. Unlike the gaudy and overblown homes of the newly wealthy investment bankers, the house had gardens that were carefully designed and planted decades earlier. Juan knew the secrets of restoring and maintaining a garden's freshness, symmetry, and style. He was a plumber, too. And he could easily control the crafty, childlike play of the bizarre floating machine that devoured and neutralized the algae that sometimes floated on the glinting surface of the Olympic-size pool.

From her kitchen Joan Richardson often watched Juan, his shirt off, navigate the strange device through the pool's water. He was over six feet tall, so strikingly different, she thought, from the many Mexican, Nicaraguan, and Costa Rican men who had settled in this far eastern end of Long Island. There was a relaxed, muscular tautness to his shoulders. Every lean contour of his body was framed against the grassy dunes and the bright Atlantic beyond him. *He could be a model*, she thought. It was a guilty pleasure to watch him, like glancing as she sometimes did at Internet porn. At night, even with slender and immaculately clean Brad Richardson asleep next to her, she touched the most sensitive places of her body as she thought of Juan. In the eleven years of her marriage, she had never once conjured up her husband's image in the long and luxuriant prelude to sleep.

She first saw Juan Suarez on a chilly day in April as she and Brad opened the house for the first time since Thanksgiving. They discovered Juan when they hired blue-eyed, sandy-haired Tom Golden, who ran an expensive nursery and landscaping company, to bring a crew to the estate to trim and shape the high hedgerows, always green, that blocked the view of the sprawling house from the road.

Tom Golden had arrived, as usual, in his new steel-gray BMW just after one of his trucks pulled up to the hedgerows. There were at least six immigrant men, Juan among them, standing in the open trailer attached to the truck. Thirty minutes earlier,

Golden had found them on the side of the Montauk Highway in Wainscott where as many as twenty men gathered just before dawn every morning to wait for the owners of nurseries, painting companies, and contractors who stopped quickly, almost furtively, as if buying drugs, pointing at the men they wanted for the day. Strong, swift, Juan vaulted into the back of the trailer as soon as Tom Golden pointed at him. As he always did, Juan held out his hand to help the smaller men clamber up.

It was an overcast day. Golden made the assignments for work at the Richardson estate—the hedgerows needed to be trimmed and boxed and dead leaves raked and pulled by hand from the plants in which they had been tangled since the fall. There was the scent of ocean water and thawing earth in the air. Juan sensed that he and the others would work only half the day, and receive half a day's wages in cash, because the darker areas of the clouds seemed to carry rain. There was already a mist, chilly and damp. Juan wore only a thin sweatshirt.

Golden, always in a hurry, knew that Juan was meticulous with the gasoline-powered pruning saw. It was as though Juan could create topiary from any bush. Speaking in rudimentary but understandable Spanish, Golden assigned Juan to trim the tall roadside hedgerows. Juan immediately turned to the corner of the truck's flatbed where the gas-driven trimmer was stored, opened the cap, put his finger into the well, and found that the fuel rose only to the tip of his index finger. He unscrewed the top of the ten gallon gas drum and poured gasoline through a funnel into the trimmer. Then he unfastened a tall, two-legged ladder. Carrying the ladder and the heavy trimmer, he jumped from the back of the truck.

Almost miraculously, the overgrown hedgerows, swept carefully by the powerful saw, were groomed under Juan's graceful motions as he stood at the top of the ladder. He inhaled the odor of the exhaust fumes together with the earthy smells of the cut leaves, twigs, and branches. Under him, a man he knew only as Paz, slightly over five feet tall, raked the fallen cuttings while Juan moved steadily down the hedgerows, feeling the heaviness in his arms and shoulders but still able to keep sweeping carefully at the tall bushes.

Juan never came near the owners of the houses where he worked. Sometimes there was a glimpse of men, women, and children around a distant terrace and swimming pool, and sometimes he saw people playing tennis on clay courts. And sometimes in the distance he could see thin women sunbathing, naked. They had that aura of moneyed privilege Juan had first seen only when he had migrated from Washington Heights in upper Manhattan to the Hamptons, which he had always heard described by men from Honduras, Nicaragua, and Guatemala as the place where everyone could find work, the promised land.

Juan was surprised when he saw a man walk out of the house carrying bottles of Pepsi in a plastic bag. Juan was the first crew member to notice him, and it took several seconds before he realized the man was bringing the Pepsis to them. Brad put the bags on the ground at the foot of Juan's ladder.

"Time to take a break," Brad Richardson said in Spanish. "They're cold."

Juan said in English, "Thank you, Mister," as he reached down from the ladder to take the chilled bottle that Brad handed up to him.

Releasing the bottle, Brad looked directly at Juan's eyes. "No problem," Brad said in English.

As Juan slowly drank, he kept the heavy saw balanced on the highest step. He stared out over the dunes to the open ocean water. To his right, the immense shingled roof of the Maidstone Club rose in the distance from the slopes of the seaside golf course. The small triangular flags on the course flapped crazily in the intensifying wind, colorful agate against the rolling slopes of the golf course. The wind became more and more chilly.

3.

THE RAIN STARTED AT just after eleven. It came in cloudlike sheets, driven on tall gusts of wind. The ladder shook. By the time Juan climbed down, gripping the precious saw, he was drenched. He jogged to the rear of the truck. On the open trailer the other men already crouched under a dirty tarpaulin. They held their hands aloft to keep it in place. Juan draped the edge of the tarpaulin over his head, clutching the stiff fabric at his neck. But the gusty rain continued to drench him. Stirred by the incoming wind from the sea, the tarpaulin on the unprotected flatbed often lifted off of them. They grabbed it to bring it down to make it a secure tent, not just a loose cover. It was futile. The tarp billowed and snapped, almost out of control. In obscene Spanish, they kept asking when the fuck Tom Golden would arrive in his BMW to tell them they could drive back to the edge of the Montauk Highway where they had gathered four hours earlier and pay them whatever cash he decided to hand out. Juan gazed down the straight country road in the direction from which the BMW would come. The sheets of swirling gray rain would make it impossible to see Tom Golden's silver car until it was nearby. The other men, trying to control the flailing tarpaulin, repeatedly asked him in Spanish where the motherfucker was. Some of the sounds from the flapping tarpaulin were as sharp as the resonance of small firecrackers.

Suddenly Juan saw something he never expected. From the house, a woman in an orange raincoat came running across the lawn, holding the hood over her head in the same way Juan held the tarpaulin's edge over his head. The woman was quick. Stopping on the white gravel driveway near the truck, she shouted, barely audible above the torrents of wind and rain, "Why don't you all come inside the house? You'll catch pneumonia out here."

More fluent in English than the other men, Juan translated. They jumped off the trailer, leaving the tarpaulin to blow away heavily, with a slapping noise like a huge wet flag, onto the road. It flew into a barren potato field. The men ran. Juan was first, jogging behind her in disbelief that she was about to take them into her home. Noticing that she had thin, curved, elegant ankles, Juan hadn't yet seen all of her face. He assumed she was the wife of the kind man who had brought out the Pepsis.

Just as they walked through the entrance to the vast kitchen, a small Mexican-Indian woman, whom Juan had sometimes seen when he brought the weekly laundry to the laundromat at the end of Main Street in Sag Harbor, passed out towels to the men. She laid more towels on the floor as she told them to gather around the tall chairs that surrounded the kitchen's central marble-surfaced island. On that table were silver urns and china cups and plates with cookies and cake. The men took their seats, towels draped over their shoulders and heads like shawls.

When Joan Richardson removed her slicker and handed it to Leanna to be hung in what she called the mud room, Juan and the other men—all of them acting demure and ill at ease and shy— saw that she was beautiful. Blue eyes, blonde hair, full breasts, slim legs in slacks. And she was kind, Juan thought. She instinctively appeared to know that Juan—by far the tallest, the one who most calmly looked at her, the obvious leader of the smaller dark men around him—knew more English and would interpret for her.

She said, "I should have called Golden this morning and asked him not to bring you all here. I heard it would rain. I guess I hoped for the best."

"It's okay," Juan answered. He didn't know her name. He never knew the names of the people at the houses where he worked. The small, tasteful signs at the entrances to the long driveways in East Hampton, Sagaponack, and Southampton had the numbers and names of the streets and roads, never the names of the owners. "We get wet all the time."

"Go ahead, have your coffee. Leanna? Can we also give them tea?"

"Nobody drinks tea, Mrs. We drink coffee."

"My name is Joan." She began pouring hot coffee into cups and pointed to the milk and sugar in ceramic bowls. "And my husband's name is Brad."

"He's nice. Nobody ever gave us soda before."

"Really? I'm surprised. No one ever? Brad's thoughtful."

Juan wasn't sure he knew the meaning of "thoughtful." He was sure that the other men noticed that this blonde woman with the dazzling smile was spending a great deal of time talking to handsome, black-haired Juan Suarez. He knew he would later take merciless ribbing from them.

Joan asked, "Where do you all live?"

Juan hesitated. Like the others at the table—and like every illegal immigrant he knew—Juan was leery about that question. It was men in uniforms or suits who always asked the question, and no one ever answered it accurately. He said, "Hampton Bays."

Hampton Bays was twenty miles to the west, a far less attractive, working class area of the legendary Hamptons. In fact, Juan lived in a rundown ranch house with at least ten other men, women, and children in the desolate woods along the Sag Harbor-Bridgehampton Turnpike, the ancient road that for more than two hundred years had been the place where generations of local black families lived in frail, ramshackle houses.

Joan Richardson, regretting the question, recognized the evasion. She smiled and changed the subject. "I don't know your name."

"Juan."

"What about the others?"

Juan hesitated. For the most part he knew these men by names that were Spanish words referring to parts of their bodies or their habits: Victor the Pineapple, Julio the Dick. Juan told her that three of the other men were named Juan as well. "Like John," he said. "John and Juan. They're the same. Lots of men are Juan."

She laughed. It was a gutsy, big laugh for such a slim woman. Then she asked, "Do you always work together?"

"No, it depends on who gets picked."

"Gets picked? That doesn't sound fair."

"It's okay. It's the way it is."

More than an hour passed before Tom Golden, running through the sheets of rain without an umbrella, came through the kitchen door. He glanced first at the cowed Mexican men. Clearly he'd expected to find them still in the rain under the tarpaulin on the open trailer. When the storm started he had been three miles away in Amagansett, where another, more skilled crew was working on the renovation of several interior rooms.

Tom Golden had never imagined that Joan Richardson or any of his elite, moneyed customers would let a yard crew into the house because of rain. His orders were that they never wander away from the truck or the specific work areas he assigned them. There was the detritus of mud and leaves, footprints and puddles of water, spread over the marble floor. Wind gusts pelted rain against the seaward-facing windows.

Ignoring the watchful men, Tom said, "God, Mrs. Richardson, I'm sorry for this." He waved his muscular, hairy arm in the direction of the men. They were now quiet, expectant, watchful, like children about to be disciplined at school.

"Why so?" she asked.

"They've made a mess in here. The leaves, the dirt."

"I asked them to come in. Brad thought it was a good idea, too."

For the first time, Juan glanced down a long hallway, at the end of which was a room with glass walls where Brad Richardson sat at a gleaming computer terminal. He was leaning backward in a wooden swivel chair, speaking into a cell phone. He waved and smiled at his wife and the other people in the kitchen. He continued with his conversation.

"I've told them, Mrs. Richardson, that in bad weather they should stay in the truck until I get there."

She laughed. "Tom, you're a busy man, obviously. You've been gone for more than an hour since it started raining. They'd be drowned by now."

"It didn't start raining where I was until fifteen minutes ago."

She laughed again, that full-throated laugh: "Were you in bed with the sheets over your head?"

"I was at a job in Amagansett, over on the Montauk side. Must have taken the rain longer to get further west. Weather travels west to east out here."

"Is that so?" Joan Richardson asked. "What a surprise." She looked directly at him. *Dumb bastard*, she thought, and then said: "But no harm, no foul. They've enjoyed their cookies and coffee. And Juan is a wonderful translator."

Juan's full head of black hair was still wet, almost gleaming, curling over the collar of his sweatshirt, as though he'd been swimming. He was taller than Tom Golden by at least a head. His arms, covered with sleek black hair, were even more muscular than Tom's. Juan had the exhausted, happy look of a Spanish tennis champion who had just won a tournament, and Tom Golden looked like an entitled fraternity boy from Ohio State.

"Juan's a talented guy," Tom said. "The pick of the litter."

Joan Richardson rolled her striking blue eyes upward. "The pick of the litter?" She feigned a shudder of disgust. Then she said, "Brad thinks that maybe we better call it a day. He's been on calls to Europe all morning, but he said a few minutes ago that the day is a washout for these men. You'd better get them home. If it clears up tomorrow, Brad said come back or wait another day or two. It's your call."

He saw that he had annoyed Joan Richardson. He didn't want to lose the Richardsons as customers. They were his most important clients by far. He ranked his customers by their status on Google. Brad Richardson was not only one of the richest men in the world, he was influential in other ways as well. He wrote articles on economics and politics for the Op-Ed page of the *New York Times* and the editorial page of the *Wall Street Journal*. He recently had lead articles in two editions of the *New York Review of Books*. Tom recognized that all of this was a really big deal: Brad was not only immensely wealthy, he was emerging as an intellectual, a man of ideas and vision. There were news articles that said Brad Richardson was high on the President's list to be the next Secretary of the Treasury.

But Brad's wife was even more of a presence on the Internet. She was the golden daughter of George Cabot, who still reigned, at 77, as the bishop of the Episcopal Diocese of Washington, presiding as a liberal icon over the National Cathedral, and of Catherine Bybee, once an actress who before her marriage in the 1980s was called the Grace Kelly of the Reagan era. And Joan over the last five years had become legendary for running the

Richardson Foundation, a charity that funded relief for hundreds of thousands of displaced children who were refugees from wars in Syria, Somalia, and South Sudan. A cover story in *Elle* ranked her with Melinda Gates as the leading female philanthropist in the world. In the picture of her on the cover of *Elle* she was depicted as what she was in real life: blonde, striking, elegant, smiling, a woman who loved life.

And Tom Golden knew something else about her. She was an easy touch, a babe, hot. In the bar at the American Hotel in Sag Harbor and the grill room of the Noyac country club, local men and women—the native aristocracy of people born in East Hampton and Southampton who owned the landscaping companies, the fancy stores, the architectural design firms, the real estate companies—shared stories about Joan Richardson's multiple affairs. Brad traveled the world. Joan didn't. She spent long summers on the East End, and word circulated about the men. Tom Golden, who knew one of the men who had been her lover for a week last fall, once imagined he could reach her. Why not?

But Joan Richardson was said to be unpredictable, with diverse tastes in men. Tom soon saw that her range didn't encompass him. By now he was more interested in keeping her business and the prestige that brought him than he was in screwing her for a week or two and then losing her as a client. He cultivated the image of a stud, and word had spread among the rich ladies that he was endowed.

"Don't worry about it, Mrs. Richardson," he said. "They're well taken care of."

Juan was one of the four men who rode in her SUV to the roadside woods in Wainscott. He was in the back seat. The fallow corn and potato fields through which they drove were as wide and flat as the nearby ocean. Rain still fell so densely that the sky and the fields appeared to merge into the drenched air. From time to time she glanced into the rearview mirror, pretending to keep in sight the lumbering truck behind her SUV, but really to see Juan—the high cheekbones, the deep eyes, black eyebrows, thick hair. In her glances she saw him only in profile, since he was gazing at the fields.

Tom Golden's car was already idling several hundred yards from the isolated Post Office building on the Montauk Highway, the road that ran through and linked Southampton, East Hampton, and Montauk and ended at the lighthouse at Montauk Point. The truck pulled in behind the BMW. Joan brought her SUV as close to the truck as she could. Three men clambered out of the crowded cab of the truck. The men in her car, including Juan, said, "Thank you," in English as they opened the doors and got out.

She remained in the front seat, listening to the rhythmic rubbing of the windshield wipers while she watched each of the men walk up to the window of Tom's car. He handed cash through the half-closed window to each of them. She couldn't see how much, but not one of the men, quickly looking at the bills to count them, was happy with what Golden had given out. She had no idea, she realized, how much he paid them, although she did know that Golden's bills to her and Brad for a small crew working all day on their estate was almost two thousand dollars. At last, with a transparently ingratiating smile for her, Tom Golden closed the window and sped away in his silver car, its tires flinging wet stones and dirt from the unpaved shoulder of the road.

There were no other cars parked in the woodsy, unsheltered area by the roadside. There was a small shopping mall on the other side of the highway—a Starbucks, the upscale Citarella food store, a fish outlet, and a place selling cheap wicker furniture. The men just stood in the rain. One of them unlocked an old bicycle from a telephone pole and rode west along the highway. The other men, Juan among them, moved far back from the road so that they could find some shelter under the taller, thicker branches of the leafless trees.

Joan Richardson stepped down from her SUV. Again pulling the hood of her yellow coat over her head, she walked toward them.

"It's still pouring," she said, raising her voice over the rain and wind. "Who's coming for all of you?"

Suddenly they weren't focusing on her. When she turned, she saw an East Hampton police cruiser. As it slowed, the car tossed up sheets of dirty water from its oversize tires. Every one of the men was intent on the cruiser. They obviously felt menaced, they were leery and quiet and intense. Then the cruiser accelerated and sped away, hissing through the rain.

She asked again, "Who's coming for you?"

Juan said, "People come to pick us up."

"How does anybody know you're here?"

One of the men had a cell phone. He lifted it for her to see.

"Friends," Juan said. "We have friends. We called. They're coming soon."

"I can drive you all home," she said. "The car's big."

"Thank you, Mrs., but our friends will be here soon."

"You can all wait in my car. There's room."

"It's okay, Mrs."

"All right," she said. "Take a long bath when you get home. Get warm."

Imagining Juan naked, powerful, and sinuous as he took a bath, she went back to her SUV and drove off, waving to them while they huddled under the dripping bare trees. It was a cold early spring, and the terrain of woods and underbrush in which they stood looked dismal.

Fifteen minutes after Joan Richardson left, Hector, one of the shuttle crew drivers hired by Tom Golden and other contractors who used day-laborers, pulled up to the edge of the woods. The men climbed into his fifteen-year-old Ford station wagon. In the oversize car, they counted their cash: they had each received thirty dollars in five-dollar bills from Tom Golden. They swore at the cheap motherfucker. Each of them had to give five dollars to Hector for carfare.

Inside the fetid car, one of the men teased Juan. "Mrs. wants to fuck Juan. Juan, when are you going to fuck Mrs.?"

Everyone in the car laughed. Since Juan wanted to get along with these men, he laughed too, but said nothing. He thought about Joan Richardson's ankles.

4.

It was Brad Richardson who drove to the work gang on the Montauk Highway in Wainscott at six-thirty on Thursday morning. From the open window of his Land Rover, Brad waved Juan over. He remembered the kind man who earlier that week had carried bags of Pepsis to the crew before the rainstorm. A clear dawn, with just a slight chill, was rising through the stark branches of the trees at the roadside. Tom Golden and the other contractors hadn't yet arrived.

"Juan, good morning," Brad called out through the open window.

Pointing at his chest, Juan asked, "You want me?" Then he walked to the Land Rover's open window.

"Juan, my wife and I were talking. We thought about having you come to work for us full-time for a while."

Juan hesitated. "I don't understand."

"Do you work for Tom Golden every day?"

"No."

"Good. We need a full-time caretaker and handyman. Do you want to work for us?"

"You sure?"

"Of course. Otherwise I wouldn't ask. Gardening, pruning, some carpentry, raking, whatever you know. Just raking and cleaning up, if that's what you want to do. If you don't like it, you can quit, no hard feelings."

Brad was an efficient man. He told Juan that he and his wife would pay him one thousand dollars each week. After three years in America, Juan knew what that number meant. "You sure?" he mumbled.

Brad ignored him, saying his driver would pick him up at seven each morning wherever he lived. All Juan had to do was tell the driver where that was. The same driver would take him home. Brad and his wife would buy comfortable work clothes for him. The clothes would be cleaned and pressed so that he could start each day fresh. They would first be tailored for him. His name would be stitched over the left pockets and the name of the estate—the *Bonac*—over the right pockets.

All that Brad and Mrs. Richardson expected of Juan was that he would in the first days walk around the buildings at the estate—the house itself, the ancient potato barn mostly buried in the earth with its roof just above ground-level, the tennis court, and the gardens. Juan was to decide what needed to be done. It was important to Brad that Juan be a "self-starter." Juan knew, and had been in America long enough to appreciate, that a self-starter was a guy who made up his own mind about what needed to be done, how to do it, and how to get it done, quickly.

"And," Brad said, smiling, "we want you to spend some time each day with the dogs."

Juan remembered two sleek dogs trotting from time to time down the hallway that connected Brad's office with the gleaming kitchen. Their toenails had clicked on the burnished wooden floors.

The dogs were Borzois. Juan had never before seen or touched, fed or groomed, a Borzoi. In fact, he'd never heard the name of the breed. But he knew that no matter how elegant or inelegant a dog's coat, muzzle, ears, legs, and tail were, all dogs responded the same way to love, discipline, attention and play—they became attentive, loving, obedient, sweetly dependent. Within a week, Felix and Sylvia, both of them benignly neglected during the two years they had lived essentially as trophies in the Richardsons' homes, became Juan's dogs. They followed him, waiting for him to play with them or feed them. They stayed near him as he worked inside or outside the house. He loved them.

And Juan also loved his work. He easily fell into the patterns of the Richardsons' home—the treasures of the carefully constructed estate, the sloping expanses of the grounds so much like the nearby undulating golf course at the Maidstone Club, the needs of the seawalls, and the endless, repetitive sibilance of the ocean surf.

He also quickly fell into the patterns of the Richardsons' lives. They lived with largesse and generosity, not just to their friends and Juan but to the furtive, cautious population of immigrants from Guatemala, Mexico, Honduras, and Costa Rica. They learned through Juan that there were houses and small warehouses that collected donations of cash and food and clothes for the men, women, and children, a kind of underground support system designed to elude the surveillance of the immigration police. The Richardsons bought large quantities of clean, durable clothes—jeans and sweatshirts and Nike and Adidas sneakers for the men, shirts and blouses and slacks for the women, sweatshirts with popular names like Ecko and A&F for the kids. The Richardsons bought food. They even paid for doctor visits. Many of the people among whom Juan lived knew that he worked for a generous man and woman. Some people admired him for that. Others resented him.

There were other aspects of the Richardsons' lives that Juan soon came to love, including the parties. Joan and Brad gave parties almost every weekend, some small, most large. Brad even

called the Borzois—so sleek, so clean, so perpetually groomed—
"party animals."

And Juan became a "party man." At the start of the summer,
Brad Richardson asked Juan to work at the weekend parties as a
greeter at the front door, in a tuxedo. Together with Brad, Juan
even made a one-day visit to Manhattan, to the corner of Madison
Avenue and 45th Street, to buy the tuxedo at the muted, elegant
Paul Stuart store where Brad's father had started shopping in the
late 1940s when it opened and to which he started bringing Brad
when he was nine and already a well-mannered preppy. When the
other Mexican men Juan had once worked with learned that he
now sometimes wore a tuxedo, they ribbed him that even more
of the white women in East Hampton and Southampton would
take Juan to bed. "You get rich someday, Juan," they said. "You
give it hard enough to them you get rich."

During the party season, Mariana, a dark, comely woman
with two kids with whom Juan started living just a week after
he arrived in Sag Harbor, served food and drinks and helped to
clean in the quiet hours of early Sunday morning as the parties
slowly dissolved after hours and hours of music, dancing, conversation, drinking, and cocaine-inhaling by the Richardsons'
guests. Mariana was paid five hundred dollars in cash each time
she worked. This was a staggering amount. And it was made
even more staggering because Juan was given seven hundred
dollars each time he, in his beautifully tailored tuxedo, acted as a
greeter and guide, Felix and Sylvia quietly roaming around him.

5.

THE PARTY ON THE Fourth of July weekend was the largest and the most festive. Blond boys—boarding school and college-age children of the Richardsons' friends—worked in white shirts and black slacks as valet parkers. From his vantage point at the main entrance, Juan watched them hand chips with numbers engraved on them to the guests arriving in their Mercedes, BMWs, Bentleys, even old MGs and Triumphs. So many guests came that the quick boys, always running and laughing, high on marijuana, had to park many of the cars on the richly green lawns Juan knew he would have to re-sod and groom after the weekend.

As Juan passed dozens of guests along to Brad and Joan Richardson, he witnessed and heard the never-quite-touching air kisses, the quick hugs, the hand-shaking, and the endlessly repeated words, "How wonderful to *seeee* you!" He heard some men referred to as "Senator" and "Congressman." Juan knew that Senators and Congressmen worked in Washington and that they spent time with President Obama. He even thought that from time to time he recognized people whose images he and Mariana had sometimes seen on the television they shared with all the other people who lived in the crowded ranch house.

Brad Richardson was a generous host. Dressed in a blue summer blazer, white shirt, and linen slacks, Brad saw to it that the guests had drinks and food in endless supply. He introduced Juan as his "friend and assistant." Always somewhat shy, Juan had learned that a few soft words and a smile could bring him successfully through every brief conversation he had in a noisy, diverse crowd.

Toward nine, Brad asked Juan to urge people to move in the direction of the terrace overlooking the Atlantic. Fireworks soon began to fly skywards from the dunes. They were reflected on the sparkling surface of the ocean water. It was a thunderous, exciting show, with several rockets unfurling the American flag over the Atlantic before its image gradually decayed. Voices shouted "wow" or "oh" or murmured "my God" as the half-hour-long fireworks display boomed from crescendo to crescendo and then gradually dissolved. Smoke from the explosions drifted and faded.

Joan Richardson had spent increasing amounts of her time speaking with, and standing near, a tall man with blond-and-gray hair everyone called the Senator or Hank. As Joan and the Senator walked toward the pool at three in the morning, she told Mariana and the other waiters and waitresses, cooks and caterers to start the process of cleaning the detritus and debris that crowds of partying people created: the used glasses smeared with lipstick and greasy fingerprints, desiccated lemon and lime peels, plundered dishes and plates with the remnants of food, empty bottles of wine and champagne, ashtrays blackened with cigarette and cigar butts and stumps of joints. Juan's job was to guide weakened guests, debilitated by alcohol, drugs, or endless cocktail chatter, outside where the still-quick valets retrieved their cars. Juan was also, Brad told him, gently to persuade the remaining guests to come to the realization that the party was winding down. The objective was to be finished before dawn.

As the cleaning went on, Juan walked by one of the college girls (slim, fully developed, yet seemingly new to the world as if freshly minted). He overheard her talking to a boy with blond streaks in his hair who was almost as slim and attractive as she was. She held in her hands a book whose bright, arresting cover bore a drawing of what Juan recognized as the United States Capitol Building. Just below the image of the Capitol the name "Hank Rawls" was printed in slightly raised, iridescent letters.

The girl was laughing, rolling her eyes as she said to the boy, "Another new novel by Senator Rawls. There's life after, like, runs for President. Did you, like, know that he once ran for President, you know? Like, that was until he got his picture taken on a sail boat with a girl. Like who was not his wife. They were naked. Like, end of campaign, end of Senate, beginning of a writer's life."

"No shit," the boy said.

"No. Like it really did happen."

"Must have been before we were born, you know."

"Or maybe when you were like in kindergarten at Collegiate and I, you know, was in first grade at freakin' Brearley."

The girl noticed Juan and lifted her right hand, waving him toward them. As Juan and the boy stood on either side of her fragrant body, they looked at a full-page color picture of Senator Rawls, with his halo of sandy hair and the taut smile lines that made him resemble Clint Eastwood, but gentler, more refined.

The girl read aloud: "A graduate of Choate, Princeton, and Stanford Law School, Hank Rawls served in the United States Senate from Wyoming for two terms. After leaving the Senate, he returned to his Wyoming ranch. He is the author of four previous novels, all *New York Times* bestsellers. *Congressional Privilege* is his fifth novel. He has also performed in several recent major films directed by Ang Lee and Sofia Coppola. He lives in Wyoming and Washington. He has three grown children."

Juan heard the boy laugh. "The Senator might live in Wyoming, but his spurs are like buried right here in East Hampton."

The nubile girl closed the book and held it aloft before giving it to Juan. Although he couldn't read English, Juan loved to touch and feel the school books Mariana's children brought home from the Bridgehampton elementary school. He drew his index finger over the printing of Hank Rawls's name on the cover; it was like touching braille. Then he put the book on a glass table and wandered away from them. He understood the meaning of the words *The Senator's spurs are buried right here in East Hampton.* He was disoriented. He now knew Joan Richardson was Hank Rawls's lover. This disturbed him. He felt a wave of hurt and jealousy.

Juan searched through three rooms for Brad. There were still men and women all over the place—rooms, hallways, even in bathrooms with open doors. In one of the airy, high-ceilinged rooms he saw Brad, a happy man, seated on a sofa. Joan Richardson wasn't in the room. But there were several other men and women listening to Brad's slow, deliberate, slightly Southern-accented voice. Juan stopped behind the sofa. Brad's right hand rested on the wrist of another man, who had the broad shoulders and neck muscles of an athlete. Like many of the young men at this Independence Day party, he also had blond streaks in his hair. Brad, still speaking, didn't remove his hand from the man's wrist even when he saw Juan. In his gentle voice, Brad said, "Juan, you look better than anybody here. You're the only sober one in the room. Sit down. Rest. Join us."

The man with Brad said, "You hit the A-List with Juan. He's gorgeous!"

Brad laughed. "He has a wife and little kids, Trevor."

"Jesus Christ did, too. But that robe got all those boy disciples to fall in love with Jesus, and Juan's tuxedo does the same."

Juan had not only a ravishing smile—one that guided him through many of the new places and scenes in his life—but a stoic patience. He listened without speaking as he heard Brad, who had barely drank during the evening and was much more focused than his remaining guests, say, "Juan is a man for all seasons. Stonemason. Gardener. Landscaper. Grass cutter. Tree sculptor. Host."

Trevor said, "And dog trainer, too, because those two skinny bitches were once just beasts."

"He has a way," said Brad, "with dogs."

"That reminds me of a snide comment about Shakespeare's wife, Anne Hathaway, who was much older than the Bard of Avon. She seduced him: people whispered, 'Anne-hath-a-way.'"

Brad said, "Trevor, enough with the literary allusions. You spend too much time learning useless things."

The discomfort the half-understood conversation caused Juan was broken by Sylvia and Felix as they suddenly trotted off in the direction of the pool. Juan took the dogs' movement as his cue to walk toward the doors that opened onto the pool terrace. He was exhausted. He'd learned that maintaining the patience and dignity he desired in this world of new words, people, meanings, inflections, and gestures could make him more tired than building a stone wall. He decided to sit down for the first time during the long, noisy night on one of the patio chairs near the luminous pool lit from submerged lights. He was also unsettled by the image, etched in his mind, of Brad resting his hand for so long on Trevor's wrist. In Mexico, men who touched for that long did so furtively, letting go as soon as they thought someone saw them. Had Juan misunderstood, or not completely understood, Brad's grace and generosity toward him? Did Brad Richardson want to touch his hand?

Sitting near the gently illuminated pool, Juan thought he was alone. The Borzois stretched quietly on either side of him. He rubbed the bony base of Sylvia's ears. Stars filled the clear sky—no haze, no clouds, just utter blackness surrounding the stars. Nights in Mexico, in the desert village where he was raised, were often this clear and with a sky alive with stars. As a teenager, he sometimes lay on his back on the ground and gazed at the faintly glowing stardust of nighttime skies.

And then Juan heard a sound, a voice, a moan of pleasure. Across the blue-and-green illumined water of the pool, Joan Richardson stretched out on her back on a long lounge chair at the far end of the terrace. On his knees between her spread legs kneeled Hank Rawls. Joan Richardson's face was raised to the sky, her neck and upper back slightly arched.

The Senator's right hand was between her open legs. Juan, who had first made love to a woman when he was 14 (she was 32), knew exactly what was happening. The cadence of Joan Richardson's moans told Juan that this caressing, this climaxing had been unfolding for many minutes and that Hank Rawls was very skillful in making that happen.

Juan rose, soundlessly, from his chair. In unison, Sylvia and Felix got up and followed him. Although their paws clicked on the terrace, there was no way that either Joan Richardson or the man stroking her could hear Juan's footsteps or the dogs' nails. Juan slid the glass door to the terrace shut. Brad Richardson was still sitting on the sofa and talking. Trevor was still next to him. They weren't touching. There was laughter from the people on the sofa opposite them.

Brad caught Juan's eye. "What's it like outside, Juan?"

"It's pretty chilly, getting chilly, I think," answered Juan.

He left the room with the dogs trailing him.

6.

JUAN OFTEN FELT THAT the only thing he owned in the world was the Schwinn bicycle he had found months earlier ditched in the woods off the Montauk Highway. It was the fleeting, distinct silver glint of the wire basket amid the green leaves that caught his eye. He had plunged into the tick-infested brambles and undergrowth. The closer he approached the silver glint, the more certain he became that it was an abandoned or stolen bicycle. It was intact but dirty. It was a girl's bike—there was a curved metal bar fusing the front column to the rear column of the chunky frame—and when he yanked it out from the briars and shrubs he saw it must have been recently stolen because the fat tires still contained so much air that he could ride the bike to a nearby gas station and fill the tires completely at the air pump. It had only one gear and one speed. The brakes were in the pedals. He had to push back and down with his feet to stop this machine he loved.

Juan was a prodigious rider. On Tuesdays, after he saw Mariana's kids climb into the yellow school bus for their trip to the handsome brick elementary school in Bridgehampton, he took his bike out of the living room (the only secure place in the ranch house) and began his long rides. He wore no helmet. He wouldn't have worn one even if he had one. He was free. He didn't have to return to the house until almost four in the afternoon, when the children, tired and hungry, would jump down from the yellow bus. On Tuesdays, as on five other days of the week, Mariana worked at the old supermarket on Sag Harbor's pretty Main Street at the end of which were Long Wharf, the windmill, and the marina where whaling ships once left for the oceans of the world. The wings of the windmill never turned.

Juan found it irresistible to ride to the ocean beaches. They were to the south, just three miles from his house. He crossed the intersection of the old turnpike and the Montauk Highway at the eastern end of Bridgehampton's Main Street. There was a Civil War monument at the intersection—a stone sculpture of a Union soldier so old that the soldier's features were almost effaced, and the gray surface of his uniform looked porous. Just beyond the intersection, the landscape changed suddenly from the woodsy clutter of the old road where he and the other immigrants lived into a classic country lane. The lawns became spacious. The widely spaced, shingled houses were handsome. The huge old trees lining Ocean Drive formed a canopy over the road. In the sky was light so radiant that the edges of the overhead leaves appeared to be on a fire that never consumed them.

He arrived at the beach at high tide. The powerful, flashing waves almost reached the dunes. As a wave receded, the sand was swept clean and flat until the next surging wave foamed up the beach, creating a different perimeter of gleaming flat sand as it slipped back into the ocean.

Taking off his sneakers and tying the shoelaces to the handlebars, Juan walked eastward on the beach, pushing his bicycle and staying close to the grassy dunes to avoid even the farthest-reaching incoming waves. He was concerned that the touch of salt water on the bike would create rust. The first time he had tasted, seen, or touched salt water was when, after thousands of miles of riding with seven other stinking men in the windowless rear of the rented Hertz truck, he had arrived in New York. On his fourth day in the city he walked downtown to look at the harbor. He was awestruck: the expanse of water in New York Harbor, the far shorelines of New Jersey and Staten Island, the distant Statue of Liberty, the innumerable tankers and boats criss-crossing the harbor. There had been one geography book in his village school in Mexico. Although it had pictures taken from satellites of the land masses of the world and the much vaster blue spaces of the ocean, he'd never imagined that the living ocean glittered so vibrantly to a far horizon. His teacher told him that salt water not only instantly corroded metal but had miraculous power to cure hurt or bruised bodies. *Holy water, giver of miracles.*

As he often did on these Tuesday afternoons, Juan decided to make his way to the East Hampton beaches three miles to the east of Bridgehampton. He rode the quiet old roads—which were once wagon trails and footpaths—from Bridgehampton through Sagaponack to East Hampton. Most houses in sight near the shore were large, shingled, sprawling, on several acres of land. Some were more modern: cubes of wood and windows piled on each other like the bright Lego pieces Mariana's kids stacked on the floors. There were also acres of flat farm fields with rows of ripening cornstalks. It was late August. The cornstalks rustled drily in the afternoon heat.

As usual, Juan's destination was Egypt Road, which ran between the Richardsons' estate and the rolling golf course of the Maidstone Club. After he climbed the wooden steps that led from the beach to the road near the house, he walked his bike on the shoulder next to the hedgerows he maintained so well. He had cleaned the windows of the house on Saturday, Sunday, and Monday, and today they glinted like clear jewels in the sunshine and clean air.

Earlier in the week he had mowed the lawns, riding on the small tractor whose blades were like thousands of small shearing scissors grooming the grass as they cut. As always, even after the fragrant mowing, the lawns were lush. Not far from the *Bonac*'s front door, the American flag snapped from its white pole, all those vivid colors against the blue sky. Brad Richardson must have raised the flag, normally Juan's job, since, as Juan knew, Joan Richardson was in the city and Brad had rewarded everyone who worked at the house by letting them take the day off.

Brad's friends often worried that on these sacred Tuesdays he was alone. Unlike other extraordinarily wealthy men, he had no security guards. He never felt vulnerable in the immense house, or on the sometimes empty roads, or on the streets of East Hampton where he had walked on the weekends as a teenager and now as a 47-year-old man. He saw himself as a native of the seaside village, a local, with no need for a palace guard.

But after the financial collapse in 2008, menacing messages had been left on the voice mail of the office telephone system on Park Avenue. For several weeks Brad had been accompanied by the muscled-up, shaven-headed men, both black and white, of a security detail. Two black SUVs with tinted windows followed Brad and Joan wherever they went. Always in black suits and ties, the men were also stationed at the estate.

Brad disdained the ostentation of security details. Among the people he knew the presence of security had become yet another symbol of wealth. Joan, too, felt uncomfortable with the security. One night Brad said, "This is silly, don't you think?"

Joan laughed. "This might make Nancy Reagan and Kim Kardashian feel important and impressive, but not me."

And they dropped the security service.

Now, as Juan pushed his heavy bicycle near the estate, he noticed a black SUV, immaculately clean, on the fine white gravel of the circular driveway. He slowed his pace, wondering why the car was there, and then jumped on the bicycle. Its chunky

tires left tracks in the roadside sand. It was a five-mile ride to
the run-down ranch house on the Sag Harbor-Bridgehampton
Turnpike.

On these long rides Juan had come to enjoy stopping at the
Starbucks on the Montauk Highway. At first these stops were uncomfortable for him. He'd never known anyone who went into a
Starbucks even for a take-out. The shops had tables, chairs, and
sofas in them, and the people who had coffee and cakes and used
their laptops and iPads there were for the most part young, white,
and oblivious to what was happening around them.

The first time he left his Schwinn near the door and walked
into the Starbucks he stared straight ahead at the girl behind the
counter. Juan ignored the menu of drinks displayed on the wall
and simply said, "Black coffee."

She asked, "Grande, venti, or trenta?"

Confused, Juan stared at her. She was a local girl, her face
littered with acne. He was certain she couldn't speak Spanish,
although she had just uttered three Spanish words. She pointed
to the smallest cup. He nodded.

In the overheated shop redolent with the odor of crushed coffee beans, he took the hot container to a chair near the front
window, watching the traffic on the Montauk Highway and the
cars—mainly gleaming and expensive German cars—parked in
front of the store.

After that first stop Juan became more relaxed. He tried other
coffee drinks. He smiled at people. Usually he sat for fifteen or
twenty minutes, enjoying the coffee and the music. There was
even a young woman with stylish brown hair, pretty face, and
warm demeanor with whom Juan exchanged smiles but never
words. He was happy when he saw her there and slightly let down
when she wasn't.

He had discovered another world—companionable, comfortable, warm.

"Anibal." The familiar voice was behind him.

Startled, Juan turned. Oscar Caliente always dressed like a Brooks Brothers preppy: chinos, blue or gray blazer, button-down shirt. He was a handsome man who looked like a slightly darker version of George Clooney. He wore old-fashioned glasses with flesh-colored frames.

Juan, like everyone else who knew Oscar Caliente, was afraid of him. Oscar ran a crew of at least twenty men. It had taken less than a year for him to gain total control of the East Side of Manhattan from 86th Street to 125th Street between Fifth Avenue and the East River; his men wiped off the streets even the smallest competitor, including freelance punks who thought they could make a few bucks selling weed and cocaine for extra cash. Oscar Caliente had a zero tolerance policy about other drug dealers in his territory. In addition to the twenty full-time crew members, Oscar had at least thirty other men and women who had the contacts with customers—Oscar actually called them clients—in the territory. The runners delivered the cocaine, heroin, opium, weed, Vicodin, and any and all other drugs the clients wanted. Oscar was an entrepreneur: he ran a full-service business capable of filling any need any customer had, even for peyote and mushrooms.

Juan stood up. Oscar embraced him. Juan said in English, "Oscar, how are you, man?"

In Spanish, Oscar answered, "I'm always good, thank God."

With his left hand Oscar gently guided Juan into his chair as he pulled a chair for himself from another table. The pretty girl already seated at the table didn't even glance up. Juan felt a surge of fear: he had hoped never to see Oscar again. He had always been straight with Oscar. Because of fear, Juan had never skimmed a single dime from the cash the customers had given him even though at the end of a night that could be as much as four thousand dollars. Juan had heard that other runners who held back even small amounts of cash were beaten, stabbed, burned with cigarettes and kicked in the balls by the full-time members of Oscar's crew.

"We miss you," Oscar said in Spanish.

"I had trouble, man."

"I heard. Why didn't you come to me? I could have helped you. I don't let anybody screw around with my people. You gave those guys who jumped you what they deserved. You kicked the shit out of them. I'm proud of you, man."

"The cops were looking for me all over the place. I didn't want to get arrested. If I got arrested I'd be gone."

"You know better than that. Fucking cops. I could have made a call to get them to stop. You're one of my best boys. I take care of my boys." Juan had heard that Oscar Caliente controlled the police commanders who supervised the two precincts in Oscar's territory.

Oscar was leaning forward so close to Juan's face that he could smell and feel Oscar's breath. Oscar never smoked or drank. He had clean, mint-freshened breath. He never touched the millions of dollars in drugs that were distributed in his territory.

Oscar placed his right hand on the back of Juan's neck and gently pulled him even further forward. Their faces were within inches of each other, as if they were brothers about to share secrets. Juan trembled: the tendons in his neck vibrated like cords drawn very tight.

"You're working for a rich guy, right? I've been thinking about you. You see, you were a great worker and I asked around about you. And they told me you were meeting lots of rich guys out here. Really, really rich."

The grip of the hand on his neck was not strong. It was not Oscar's own strength that Juan feared. Oscar was not strong. His hands were small. He was vaguely effete. It was his ability and his willingness to get ruthless men to act for him that caused the fear. "I'm just raking leaves," Juan said. "I washed dishes in New York, remember? Raking leaves and washing dishes. That's all I know."

"Bullshit, that's not true, man. You're special. Christ, I had you wash dishes so no one would figure out who you were and who you worked for. Very special, very good at what you do. And it isn't washing dishes and raking leaves."

In the months in New York when he worked for Oscar Caliente, Juan's special assignment was to range late at night out of Oscar's established territory on the Upper East Side and East Harlem to the downtown after-hours clubs. There were at least seven clubs throbbing with music and wild dancing on West 14th Street and West Houston Street and in the old warren of streets between them in the Meat Packing District near the Hudson River. The clubs were open from eleven at night until six or so in the morning. Juan was soon so well recognized by the bouncers at the velvet ropes at the entrances and the owners inside that he had free passage, like a Hollywood celebrity or the mythic *Smooth Operator* in the Sade song. He even brought with him an entourage of two or three men and women who carried what Oscar always called the "dry goods."

"I rake leaves," Juan said.

"Come on, Anibal, cut that shit. You look like Antonio Banderas, you know, that guy in the movies. It lets you get all over town. You love that, I know. The parties, the girls. You love it. I saw it in you."

Staring at Oscar's close face, Juan said, "Really, man, I don't want to do it."

Oscar smiled. "Sure you do. Think about it. You can get out of that shack in the fucking woods with all those Honduran and black guys. I saw your beautiful mama and her babies. She won't have to work any more in the supermarket. Or you can dump her and play around."

Juan stared at him. It was no surprise that Oscar knew where he lived, who Mariana was, that she worked at the grocery store, and how many kids she had. And it was no surprise that Oscar Caliente knew that Juan worked for the Richardsons. All that made Juan even more afraid and also angry at this small, well-dressed man who had grown up in Mexico City in a wealthy family, attended a private school in Massachusetts where he learned to speak flawless English, returned to Mexico, and sought out and within three years became one of the key leaders in the Sinaloa cartel. Oscar could move seamlessly between Mexico and New York. Dressed in his blazers and button-down shirts—the type of clothes he had worn at the school in Massachusetts—he quickly established Sinaloa in the city. His instructions now were to expand the Sinaloa domain to the Hamptons.

Still smiling, Oscar Caliente said, "I need you to come work for me again. But out here. I'm new here. Now we're selling to the punks in the streets and the college kids. We don't make any real money when our clients are punks and kids. You can get to the rich guys. They love you, I know it, I've heard all about it. I can start to sew it up out here. And we both get big."

On the table in front of Juan was a sleek iPhone Brad Richardson had given him. The only other cell phones he ever had were the single-use disposable ones Oscar gave him each time Juan went downtown to the clubs.

Oscar picked up Juan's iPhone. He manipulated it as rapidly and deftly as a teenage girl, found Juan's number, and entered it in his own contacts list. Before standing, he said, "I'll give you a call."

Five days later Juan Suarez made his first delivery. It was to Trevor, the man who had held Brad Richardson's hand at the party. Trevor lived in a pretty carriage house on a quiet back street in Southampton Village. Juan had no idea his first client would be Trevor. Oscar had simply given him an address, a large order, and a time for the delivery.

"Lordy," Trevor said, embracing Juan at the door. "What a wonderful surprise."

Juan hesitated. "You live in a nice place."

"You're welcome here any time. Why don't you stay for a little while?"

"Not today. I have to get to Water Mill."

"Busy, busy boy," Trevor said, taking from Juan the plastic Duane Reade bag in which Juan had carried two shoe boxes.

"Thanks," Juan said. He smiled at Trevor. He didn't want to antagonize a customer because word of that might get back to Oscar Caliente.

"I'll be in touch soon," Trevor said.

And then briefly, glancingly, he kissed Juan's lips.

Juan stepped back but didn't flinch. Trevor could not gauge this handsome, exotic man's reaction. Juan was cool, motionless, waiting. Finally, he said, "The money."

"Of course." Trevor picked up a brown envelope on a table next to the door. "This is for you."

In the back seat of an Audi driven by a man he knew only as Jocko, Juan counted the two thousand dollars in hundred dollar bills that were in the envelope. He had just earned three hundred dollars for five minutes of work. And this was just the first of four drops on this hot night.

7.

JOAN RICHARDSON WAS WITH Senator Rawls at the party for major donors to the Metropolitan Museum of Art when her cell phone, deep in her purse, started vibrating. Attended by three hundred people, the party was closed to the public. The grand museum was suffused with soft, flattering light. Torches burned. On the mezzanine above the entry hall a tuxedoed quartet played Boccherini, Mozart, the Beatles. Because of the sounds of the voices and the music, she could barely hear the ringing cell phone. She was reaching for her second fluted glass of champagne, as was Senator Rawls. She ignored the cell phone. She knew it was Brad Richardson because the ring—the steel guitar portion of the original James Bond theme—was unique to him.

Hank Rawls had spent the entire afternoon at her Fifth Avenue apartment. For hours they had touched each other everywhere, licked each other, and had sex on her bed, in the kitchen, and in the room-sized shower before they dressed for the party. But at this glamorous party they hadn't even touched hands.

Within thirty seconds of the first ringing, her cell vibrated and rang again. More than a hundred miles away in East Hampton, Brad was being more persistent on the cell phone than he had been in years. It rang as many as six times while she and the Senator spoke with the aristocratic, perfectly dressed, dulcet-voiced

Phillipe de Montbello, who for twenty-five years had been the director of the museum. He was more a connoisseur of fund-raising than of art. He made a donor feel as if he were granting a favor by accepting the gift. Again she ignored the faint, persistent ringing from her sequined purse.

As soon as de Montebello glided to a group of people that included Bill Clinton and Caroline Kennedy, Joan made her way to the bathroom. Other than the bathroom matron in a blue uniform, no one else was there when her cell phone rang again. Exasperated, she snapped open her purse, composed herself to sound calm and neutral, and evenly said, "Brad?"

An unfamiliar man's voice asked, "Is this Joan Richardson?"

She was startled. "Who's this?"

"Detective Halsey, Suffolk County Police Department." Halsey was a common name in the Hamptons. Some of the original settlers in the 1600s in Southampton and East Hampton were named Halsey. By now there were dozens of Halseys on the East End—plumbers, electricians, policemen, lawyers, teachers.

"Oh, hello. Has there been a break-in?" The *Bonac*'s state-of-the-art security system was linked to three police stations in Suffolk County.

"Is this Joan Richardson?" he repeated.

"Yes, it is. Has there been a break-in?"

"No, no break-in."

"Are you in my house?"

"We are."

"Why are you using my husband's cell phone?"

"We used it to find you."

"Where is my husband?"

"Mrs. Richardson, where are you?"

"Has there been an accident?"

"Where are you, Mrs. Richardson?"

She was now very nervous, confused. She pressed her left index finger into her left ear and leaned forward, as if to reduce the level of noise in the quiet bathroom. Raising her voice, she said, "Where is my husband?"

"Your husband is dead, Mrs. Richardson."

Sensing that all the blood in her body had instantly drained away, she said, "That can't be true. You can't be who you say you are. This is a sick joke, isn't it?"

"No joke. He is dead, Mrs. Richardson."

She leaned against the marble counter, bending forward because her stomach was suddenly painful. "My God, how?" Her voice shook.

"Murdered."

"What?"

"Someone killed him earlier today, probably this afternoon."

"How do you know that?"

"We got an anonymous 911 call about half an hour ago. We got here as soon as we could. The front door was unlocked. We found him in his office. There was cold coffee in a mug in the kitchen, so we think he was dead for a few hours when we got here."

"My God." Joan Richardson noticed the women's room matron staring at her, a questioning and sympathetic look on her face. "How did it happen?"

"I don't want to talk about it on the phone." The detective paused. "Is there any way for you to get back here tonight?"

"Yes." And then she repeated, "Yes."

"Please do it as soon as you can. We don't want to disturb the crime scene until you have a chance to look around."

"I'm at a party in the city. I'll find my driver and get out there."

Even in the marble, stainless steel bathroom, she heard the murmur of hundreds of people and the tinkle of glasses from the party. And the Mozart music, that empty, cocktail party music.

"When can I expect to see you?" he asked.

She hesitated. "I don't know. Four or five hours."

"Can't you do it faster? Our forensic people are already here. Things are getting stale."

"I'll try. But I've got to change first. I'm at a party."

"Whatever," he said. "Do what you can. We'll be waiting."

Lightheaded, trembling, Joan Richardson went into one of the stalls and sat on the toilet. Her mind felt as though it would burst. She was so profoundly distracted that she couldn't urinate. She reached through her purse for the brown bottle of Valium she always carried. She called out to ask the bathroom attendant to pass her a cup of water under the stall door. She swallowed three of the always neat, miraculous pills. Gradually, even as she washed her hands and ran her wet fingers through her hair, the pills began working their magic. She took a twenty dollar bill from her purse and handed it to the bewildered Malaysian woman.

In the vaulted entryway to the museum, where hundreds of candles cast their glow from candelabras, Joan Richardson roamed for almost five minutes as she searched for Hank Rawls. She smiled tautly and brushed past the many men and women who tried to engage her—Michael Bloomberg; Jamie Dimon; the pudgy, oval-faced Steven Cohen; and ancient, owlish Felix Rohatyn.

Surrounded as always by people, Hank stood near the hallway that led to the Temple of Dendur. He was happy. He was in his element. He was now sipping scotch. He always enjoyed himself. When he saw Joan wave at him, he slowly disengaged from the men and women around him. Taking his hand, Joan Richardson led him to one of the unoccupied alcoves not far from the coat-room. A statue of a Roman goddess, with robes of gauzy marble draped over her shoulders, rose above them in the alcove.

She said, "Brad is dead."

"Come again?"

"I just got a call from the police. Brad is dead."

"Brad is dead?"

"Killed."

The Senator repeated as if he didn't understand, "Killed?"

"I have to get out there," she said. "We have to get out there. Davey will drive us."

"We? That's not a great idea, Joan. I'm staying here."

She stared at him, her expression a strained mixture of surprise, fear, and resentment. But then she said, "Of course. You're right. You stay. I'll be okay."

She took out her cell phone. Cupping her hand over her suddenly very dry mouth, watching the Senator finish his scotch and swirl the leftover ice cubes at the bottom of his glass, she called Davey. The driver was just outside the grand flight of stairs at the front of the museum. He was one of the dozens of chauffeurs allowed to park their SUVs and limousines on the brick-inlaid plaza that stretched for three city blocks in front of the museum. The long and narrow fountains cast up walls of water in which festive lights shined.

"Davey," she said, "I need to drive out to East Hampton tonight. Now."

"Sure thing, Mrs. R.," he said good-naturedly. It was as though she had told him she wanted to drive around the block. Large, beer-bellied, although sober for years, Davey still had an almost attractive, winsome Irish face. He was obedient, unquestioning, charming. "The car's right here."

8.

"We're home, Mrs. R." She didn't stir. "We're home," Davey repeated.

Drugged by the champagne and Valium, she had slept for the last fifty miles of the one-hundred-twenty-mile drive. Davey had noticed, when he glanced from time to time into the rearview mirror as the Mercedes raced late at night along the empty Long Island Expressway, that when she slept Joan Richardson didn't look as put-together and well cared for as she usually did: her head leaned too far back against the head rest, her mouth was wide open, her legs were splayed out.

"We're home," he said again, louder. Waking, disoriented, she pulled her hair back off her face, squeezing her eyes shut and opening them. For a moment, she didn't seem to know where she was or have any sense of what was happening. But then she focused: the country road in front of her home was blocked by yards of glistening yellow tape with the words "Police Line" repeated endlessly.

She opened the rear window of the Mercedes. Chilly air laden with mist washed over her face, a wave of relief. All around her were police cars with lights crazily revolving. Floodlights starkly illuminated the lawn like a movie set at night. Everything was ash white, a moonscape. It was well past midnight.

The tiny eyelets of at least a dozen digital cameras pulsed brightly as soon as she stepped out of the car. The cameras stunned her. She raised her hands defensively. With Davey trying to fend off the reporters from *The East Hampton Star*, *Southampton Press*, and local television and radio stations that had already been alerted to the killing of Brad Richardson, she hesitated at the police tape that surrounded her home.

Soon a man in a sports jacket and regimental striped tie, an identification tag hanging from a ribbon draped around his neck, walked toward her. "Mrs. Richardson?" he asked. She nodded.

He raised the gleaming tape high enough for her to walk under it. "I'm Detective Halsey. I'm the guy who called you." His head was completely shaven.

Following her, Davey bent to pass under the tape. Halsey's voice was not pleasant: "Wait a minute, fella. And who are you?"

"The driver."

"You stay here."

Joan Richardson glanced at him. "It's all right, Davey."

As soon as she entered the house, she saw men and women in police uniforms and emergency worker garb crowding the wide entryway. For her it was chaotic, almost otherworldly.

"Don't touch anything," Halsey said. "And keep walking right behind me." His voice had an edge of rudeness, not at all deferential.

When she realized they were walking through the long hallway toward Brad's office—his sanctuary, his special place, the center of his world—she sensed her knees and legs weakening, as though her bones were turning to dust.

From the open doorway to the office she saw what first struck her as black oil spread over the bare wooden floor. It took the beat of a moment or two until she recognized, to her right, lying uncovered side by side, the bodies of Felix and Sylvia. They were not, she saw, whole bodies. Their heads were gone.

Joan Richardson threw up: she tasted the now-vile canapés, shiitake mushrooms, and sushi she had eaten four hours earlier in the civilized interior of the Met. Instinctively she bent forward so that her vomit wouldn't spill over her dress and shoes. At the sight of what had come out of her, she vomited again; her body shook uncontrollably. A sweet-faced black woman in a green uniform, an emergency worker, handed her a towel. Joan Richardson wiped her mouth and face. The woman extended a bottle of water toward her. She waved it away. She wanted never to put anything in her body again.

As if other people's vomiting was an everyday event for him, Halsey said, "He's over there."

Alongside the old-style wooden chair Brad always used—it was now tipped over, utterly transformed—was his body. She saw the white slacks, leather shoes, no socks, and his thin virtually hairless ankles. A white canvas was spread over the rest of his body.

Halsey said, "That's your husband's body, isn't it, Mrs. Richardson?"

Joan Richardson put her hands over her face, bent forward, and vomited again. This time she couldn't keep her dress or shoes clean: the vomit spilled over them.

She was struggling to cover her face while she threw up. Tears streamed from her eyes as if stung by tear gas. Her face was red, contorted. When she ran her hands through her hair they left trails of vomit and spit. Halsey didn't move. Finally, the woman in the green uniform began wiping Joan Richardson's face and hair with a wet towel, using the practiced gestures of a mother cleaning a five-year-old who has taken a fall into dirt and bruised herself. Joan let herself be cleaned, even comforted.

After Joan had settled somewhat—her crying stopped, her face was as clean as wiping with towels could make it—Bo Halsey said, "Can you follow me, Mrs. Richardson, for just a second?"

She nodded, speechlessly, and walked behind him to the door. She felt stripped down and utterly vulnerable. There was no artifice to her. Appearances didn't matter. She stumbled slightly. Halsey turned. He took her arm. It wasn't a gentle grip. In the hallway just outside the office, he stopped. "I know this is hard," he said.

She shook her head up and down, a quick gesture relaying the unspoken words, *It is, it is.*

"Let me just cut to the chase right now for a second. I need to know some things right now. The guy who did this might not be far away, understand? Can you tell me anything about how this happened?"

Her whole body was shaking, as if overcome by a sudden fever. "Everybody loved Brad."

He repeated, "Do you know anything about how this happened?"

Her eyes were wide open, the same startling blue as always, even though there were jagged red streaks all converging on the irises. She was struggling to understand, as though Halsey were speaking an unknown language. "What do you mean?" she asked, hearing the tremor in her own voice so unlike the confident, clear resonance it usually had.

"What do I mean? Your husband is dead, Mrs. Richardson. Do you know anything about how that happened?"

Now she understood. She quickly shook her head, the universal signal for *no, no, no.*

"Has anyone threatened him?"

"No, never."

"Who has access to this house? Who can get in?"

"Many people. Brad makes friends with everyone. This is like an open house."

"Can you think of anything that's valuable that anyone might have wanted to take from the house?"

She waved her right arm, a gesture that meant *Everything, everything is valuable.*

"Think about money," Halsey said. "Money was taken from his pockets. They're ripped open, some change was spilled over the floor, with one or two dollar bills. All the drawers in his desk were ransacked. All the furniture in the room is broken because whoever did this thought there was cash."

Suddenly she became alert and tense. "Brad always kept cash in one of the closets upstairs."

"How much?"

She said, "A great deal."

Brad was heedless with cash. Even though he was neat about everything else, he dropped crumpled cash on tables, countertops, shelves, just as many men have places where at the end of every day they drop change, keys, cufflinks, dollar bills—the dumping ground of objects they carry in their pockets.

"How much?"

She said, "He might have had two or three hundred thousand dollars in cash upstairs."

Even Bo Halsey, with more than twenty years of experience as a homicide detective, was taken aback. He was uncertain that he'd heard correctly.

"Two or three hundred dollars?"

"No, no," Joan Richardson answered. "Hundred thousand. Two or three hundred thousand dollars."

Halsey glanced over Joan's right shoulder into Brad's office, where at least eight people were videotaping, taking pictures, or placing objects into transparent bags with tags tied to them. "Cerullo," Halsey called out, loudly.

Joan watched as Dick Cerullo, a tall, awkward man in an inexpensive sport jacket and a red-and-blue striped tie, approached Halsey. Whispering to each other, they walked away from her.

During these seconds while she was utterly isolated, she felt terror, wildly imagining that the killer might still be in her house, waiting for her. From a distance, she watched Halsey, appearing almost bored, point at another man standing in Brad's office. Shorter than Cerullo by a head, the other man joined Halsey and Cerullo. He wore the same style of ill-fitting sport jacket as Cerullo, but at least two sizes smaller. As if in a huddle, the three men whispered, even giving hand signals.

Halsey finally turned to her. "Mrs. Richardson," he said, "these are Detectives Dick Cerullo and Dave Cohen. They're veteran homicide detectives. They worked with me for years on the NYPD before coming out here. They're going to help me find the man who did this."

Joan's moment of isolation and terror lifted. She stared at Halsey and the other men, thinking that together they looked like the Three Stooges and had as much chance of finding the man who had killed her husband as Moe, Larry, and Curly. They were not confidence-inspiring. "I hope so," she said quietly.

"Where is that cash?"

"He kept it in the bedroom at the top of the stairs." She gestured to the staircase on which she had walked thousands of times over the last eight years and on which, she now thought, Brad would never walk again. "Just to the right."

Cerullo and Cohen had never seen such an opulent bedroom. They were both basketball fans. "My fucking word," Cerullo said, "this place has got to be the size of a court." The bedroom's floorboards shined in the muted light as if they were waxed and polished in the same way a professional basketball court would be.

Cohen was more efficient than Cerullo. With a video camera hanging on a strap from his left hand, he glanced calmly around the entire room. He learned long ago that it was important and possibly life-saving to first assess everything in a room before focusing on anything specific. He walked toward a finely crafted sliding door in one of the walls. He rolled the door to the right, revealing a row of very orderly drawers and, to the left, the even more orderly rows of hanging suits, jackets, and slacks. He picked up a clean poker from the fireplace next to the closet. Handling the poker like a scalpel, he used its curved point to pull out two drawers.

Cohen called out to Cerullo, "Dick, get over here."

As Cerullo approached, Cohen handed him the bag in which he carried the clunky, ten-year-old video camera. Cerullo started the camera while Cohen began narrating and describing who they were, where they were, the time, and the date. His hands in plastic gloves, Cohen displayed the first drawer to the camera. It was empty. He repeated the same scene with the other drawers. They too were empty. Cerullo turned the camera off.

Cohen went to the windows that faced the ocean. He opened another sliding closet door. Inside was a dazzling array of women's clothes. He reached through some of the dresses to look for drawers in the back wall. There were none. He started to turn away. It was in that moment when he was about to slide the door closed that he saw stacks of cash simply lying on the floor. They were tightly bound in red elastic bands. He pulled forward one of the packets. It was the size and shape of a brick. The elastic bands held the bills so tightly that the stack weighed as much as a brick.

At the top of the packet were hundred dollar bills; that meant, Cohen was certain, that the rest of the bills in each packet were hundreds. He quickly counted the number of neatly stacked packets: there were at least thirty. "Holy Mother of Jesus," Cohen said. "Look at this shit."

Cerullo, who was at the other side of the bedroom, was startled. He was certain that Cohen had just discovered a body. Despite fifteen years with the New York Police Department and another five as a homicide detective in Suffolk County, he had never passively reacted to the sight of dead or wounded people. He walked warily toward Cohen, who motioned with his head for Cerullo to look into the closet. Cerullo saw the cash immediately. He wasn't distracted by the elegant clothes.

Cohen whispered, "Check for security cameras in here?"

Most people, they knew, didn't have security cameras in their bedrooms. Neither of them saw anything like a camera in the places in which they were usually concealed, such as the corners of the ceilings or the tops of picture frames.

Dick Cerullo had noticed in the bathroom a small door in the wall near one of the two showers. He had been in big houses before, so he knew it was likely to be a door to a crawl space in the attic where the machinery was located that controlled the bathroom's air-conditioning, steam room, and sauna.

Picking up the first brick of cash, Cerullo whispered to Cohen, "Let's get this shit into the attic." Since they were homicide detectives, they would have free access to the house for at least three days at any time they wanted, even when no one else was there, and there were bound to be times when no one else was there. After all, they had a license to investigate.

Cohen, the smaller man, slipped into the crawl space, and Cerullo handed the packets to him. When they closed the door, Cohen whispered, "This never happened, right? Oscar doesn't know, right?"

Cerullo chuckled. "Oscar who?"

"Oscar, like in Felix and Oscar."

When they came downstairs, Dave Cohen saw Bo Halsey talking to three technicians. When he had Halsey's attention, Cohen said, "There's nothing up there, Bo. The money's gone."

9.

IT WAS WEDNESDAY. JUAN was in the kitchen. He washed by hand the bowls and spoons that Mariana and her kids had used to eat breakfast. The brown dishwasher was broken; it was stuffed with paper and plastic bags. With a small checkered towel he dried the bowls and spoons and carefully put them in the area of the brown cabinets that was reserved for the four of them.

Just as he closed the cabinet door, he heard the siren. From the kitchen window he saw beyond the yellow and orange trees the revolving red lights of the first of three police cruisers. In that instant he had no doubt that they would stop in the cluttered driveway. Juan ran to the broken deck behind the house. The screen door slammed behind him. There were woods nearby—the deep groves of yellowing leaves that finally led, almost a mile away, to the town dump. He heard the first cruiser squeal to a stop, its sirens now emitting a shrill *beep-beep* sound. He glanced around the edge of the ramshackle house. The cruiser stopped on the driveway's broken tar. He thought he saw Joan Richardson in the back seat. There were two men in uniforms in the front seat. More cruisers abruptly stopped in front of the house, lights flashing.

When he heard the cruisers' doors open, Juan vaulted over the deck's wooden railing and dashed across the weeds and fallen branches of the back yard. Juan heard the insane bedlam of the multiple sirens at full volume and the loud, excited voices of the cops.

Juan was a fast runner. He cruised easily through the woods, dodging the rampant branches and the fallen limbs. Behind him angry voices shouted: *Stop, stop, stop. The motherfucker's over there. Get him.*

Juan was in another world: he imagined he could outrun these heavily uniformed, clumsy men and make his way over the small hills of the dump and speed through the woods toward the ocean three miles away and then swim in the Atlantic to his real home thousands of miles to the south. He had the advantage, he thought, of strength and speed and fear and dreams.

But then he stopped. He was afraid. His blood throbbed. He shouted, "Here, here I am."

An angry voice screamed: "Don't move. Don't move. Let me see your hands!"

Juan saw the shapes of at least six men twenty yards away in the chaotic undergrowth of the woods, all converging in his direction. He saw, too, the glint of sunlight on pistols and rifles. The branches cracked under their feet.

"Show me your hands! Show me your hands!"

Juan held out his hands.

Two of the men rushed at him, knocking him to the ground. His face was pushed into the newly fallen leaves. His hands and arms were pulled up behind him. Pain seared his back and chest. One of the men held a pistol against his temple. He smelled the odor of dirt and fallen leaves. Plastic handcuffs locked around his wrists. He was yanked to his feet. Pieces of leaves and dirt hung from his face and nose. Stumbling, he was pushed from behind toward the police cruisers, their lights flashing regularly, swiftly, all bedlam.

As he approached the lead cruiser, he saw every feature of Joan Richardson's rigid face. The window was open half-way. There was no curiosity or hatred or concern in her expression. She was impassive. For a moment, he expected her to help him, given all that had happened between them over the last half-year—the times when they drank iced tea on the pool terrace or when she worked with him in the garden, and the quiet hours inside the house when Brad and everyone else were away.

He wasn't able to look at her for long, or to find out whether she would help in some way, because as he was pushed toward the cruiser a truncheon struck his back near his kidneys, forcing him against the door of the car. His nose and mouth smashed into a window and began to bleed. He tasted the blood. A man with red hair, his hat off, leaned near him and shouted in his ear, "You have the right to remain silent. Anything you say can and will be held against you. You have a right to a lawyer. If you can't afford a lawyer, you'll fucking get one for free, you spic."

Juan's head was pressed so forcefully against the window that he couldn't say anything. He was choking. He was less than a foot away from Joan Richardson. A cop yelled, "Is this him?"

She shook her head up and down: the silent *yes.*

Juan was jerked away toward another cruiser. It had a wire mesh between the front and rear seats. The rear door opened. A powerful hand on the top of his head pushed him down and into the cruiser. A woman in uniform sat to his left. She held a wet towel and wiped his face to clean off the blood and dirt. She didn't want his face smeared with blood or visibly bruised when he was led into the red brick Southampton police station, where television news trucks would be filming him on the short walk from the cruiser to the door of the station. The police had already announced his arrest and he had already been endowed with a name.

Juan the Knife.

10.

Mariana's favorite work at the supermarket was stacking cans. With the gift of her agile hands, she loved removing them from the cardboard boxes in which they were delivered and placing them in gleaming, colorful rows along the shelves for all the world to see. They formed a bright mosaic.

Mariana was in the second aisle arranging the oval-shaped cans of sardines when Alfonso, a man with a limp whom she sometimes jokingly rebuffed when he tried to kiss her, approached. He spoke in Spanish: "Juan's been picked up." Fear washed over her like a sudden infusion of cold water. *Picked up*: to her and all the people she knew, the words meant you disappeared, you entered the endless maze of prisons and detention centers. No one ever returned from a *pick up*.

Mariana walked to a storage room at the rear of the store, put on her hooded sweatshirt, and picked up her small knapsack. She left nothing behind; she knew she would never return. In the clear autumn air, she made her way through the curving, quaint heart of the village, passing the Sag Harbor Cinema with its big 1930s-style marquee, the antique stores, the stone-and-brick library with its green dome, and the stately houses along Main Street. At the end of the Village, where Main Street became the old turnpike and the houses became more and more run-down, she broke into a trot. The ranch house was less than a mile away.

Mariana stopped when she came close enough to see the house. Three police cruisers and a large van were in the driveway. She was afraid, almost panicked, as she had often been when she sensed that immigration police were poised to arrest her. As soon as she saw men carrying Juan's bicycle out of the house, she knew what she had to do. She walked back to the village, went into the library, found the bathroom, and stayed there for the two hours until her children would arrive on their school bus at three. It was the first day of school in the new year.

When the bright yellow bus came to a halt at a corner several stops before her children's usual drop-off place, Mariana held the door open and said to the woman driver, who recognized her: "I want my kids. We walk today. It's nice out."

The boy and girl strapped on their colorful knapsacks, looking happily at their mother. They were smart, outgoing kids, well-liked in the pretty grammar school in Bridgehampton. When Mariana told them they were not going home, they became quiet. She said they were going to Celia's house. They referred to Celia, a 65-year-old kindly Salvadoran, as "aunt" even though she was not related to them. Celia's house was closer to Bridgehampton and the Montauk Highway than Mariana's now-abandoned ranch house.

Over the next three days, Mariana and her children stayed inside Celia's neat home. Mariana kept the newspapers away from her children, who read English fluently. The radio and television were turned off. Every time they asked about Juan, Mariana said that he had returned to Mexico. They, too, she said, would soon be in Mexico. It was home. Their grandmother lived there. It was always warm, she said, you never needed any winter clothes. Life would be better there.

The old Buick station wagon stopped in the driveway of Celia's house. Clutching an oversize leather bag, Mariana and her children climbed into the third row of seats because the first two rows were crowded with Mexican men who were also on their way to New York. Wide-eyed, the children stared at Main Street in Bridgehampton, where some of their young friends lived, as they passed through the beautiful village.

The windows of the car were tinted so darkly they were almost black. They drove cautiously west toward the city, never above the speed limit and never below it. The driver wanted to avoid the attention of state police cruisers.

11.

"MRS. RICHARDSON, I NEED you to help us more."

Detective Halsey stood on the other side of the marble counter in the middle of the kitchen. Two other men, who she remembered were Dick Cerullo and Dave Cohen and who she thought of as Larry and Curly, the Stooges who followed Moe, the leader, stood behind him. Twelve hours earlier, during their solo, late-night visit to the crime scene, Cerullo and Cohen had taken the stacks of hundred dollar bills—they called them "Benjamins"—from the crawl space in the attic to their car.

Joan Richardson was impatient. It was now three days after her husband's death. She was about to leave for New York for the funeral service at St. Bart's, with its ornate dome that gave the whole church the look of a mosque. Six hundred invited guests were expected, among them Alan Greenspan, three former Secretaries of the Treasury, Warren Buffett and George Soros. At night she had stayed in East Hampton in the sprawling Hunting Inn during the three days in which other people made the funeral arrangements because Bo Halsey had asked her to stay. She'd become shaken, irritated, and distracted by his frequent although brief visits to ask her questions.

"I don't know how else I can help you. I gave you Juan's name and helped you find him. I'm not a detective, and I've had a very, very hard time."

Halsey said abruptly, "We would have found him soon enough, Mrs. Richardson. People knew he worked here and that he had a big old Schwinn bike. People knew he rode around on it. And we found the tire tracks from his bike in the sand near the hedgerow. There aren't many old-style bikes like that out here. Single-speed, push-down pedal brakes. And a woman who was out on the beach came forward right away to tell us that she'd seen a tall, good-looking Mexican pushing an old bicycle near the dunes the day your husband died. A movie star, she said. Most Mexicans out here don't look like a movie star. So it wasn't really that hard to figure out who he was."

"All right," Joan responded, waving her right hand dismissively. When she was tense, a barely visible pattern of veins rose to the surface of her skin near her temples. "So I wasn't any help. I thought I was helping. I didn't need to bother, I guess, when I drove out to his house with you."

Ignoring her haughty tone, Bo Halsey gazed at her for five seconds. "Let's talk again about your day in New York on Tuesday."

"Again?"

"Your shopping day."

"Yes, my shopping day. I'm sure Mrs. Halsey has shopping days, too."

"There is no Mrs. Halsey."

He looked into her eyes, that extraordinary blue, as if by silence he could elicit more from her. He knew that Joan Richardson had lied to him earlier and was still lying. Cerullo and Cohen had gone to the city and, accompanied by three NYPD detectives, asked the doormen at her Fifth Avenue building how often they had seen her that day. The doormen on the morning shift said they didn't see her leave the building. What they had seen was the familiar face of Senator Rawls arriving at noon. And the doormen on the afternoon and early evening shifts saw them leave the building

at seven-thirty in sleek evening clothes to walk the two blocks
uptown to the private party in the Museum, where Halsey had
reached her hours later on her cell phone. Video surveillance tapes
in the lobby showed the Senator arriving and, many hours later,
the glamorous couple leaving.

Halsey knew that the Senator and Joan Richardson had had
more than seven hours of uninterrupted time in her apartment.
A vigorous guy like Senator Rawls and a very beautiful woman
like Joan Richardson could have easily gone at it, Halsey thought,
again and again in the course of such a long afternoon and early
evening, especially if the 60-year-old Senator used that magical
blue pill.

"When did you leave to go shopping?"

"I'm not certain, Detective. Ten, eleven? I didn't keep track."

"Did Davey drive you around?"

"No, I got a cab off the street."

"Where'd you go?"

"Really, Detective, how can I remember that?"

"When did you get back to the apartment?"

"Three-thirty? Four? I had to get ready for the party."

"Any cell or telephone calls after you got back?"

"Probably not. I might have turned the cell off. There are days
when I really don't want to talk to anyone."

"Did you use email?"

"I might have. But so many things happened that night, Detective, that I can't remember much about the day."

"Did you go to the party with anyone?"

"I answered that yesterday, didn't I? My friend, Senator Rawls,
picked me up."

"We haven't been able to reach him. Where is he now?"

"I believe he's in Paris."

"He hasn't returned our calls."

"He is a busy man, Detective. He must get fifty calls a day. And he's in Paris, he told me, rehearsing for a movie. I'm sure he'll get back to you."

"When you speak to him, please be sure to ask him to give me a call. You have my card."

Joan Richardson glanced at the large clock above one of the sinks. There were Roman numerals on its face. "I have to leave now, Mr. Halsey," she said.

"No problem, Mrs. Richardson."

"Thanks." Her voice was sardonic, as it sometimes was when she was irritated, impatient, or afraid.

Halsey, wanting the last word, said, "We'll see you when you get back."

Joan Richardson was used to having the last word, but this time she let it go.

12.

JUAN WAS NEVER COLDER in his life. He had been taken before dawn from the prison on the outskirts of Riverhead, where he'd spent three nights in an unheated concrete cell in isolation and without visitors. Dressed in green prison fatigues under a bullet-proof vest that fit rigidly and tightly over his chest, back, and arms, he waited in a holding pen just behind one of the closed doors to the courtroom. It was just as cold here as in his concrete cell. The guards, their weapons in their hands, wore Eisenhower-style bomber jackets.

At last, the iron gate to the holding pen slid open. A slim Asian woman came in. She carried a briefcase. She had absolutely black eyes and black hair.

She said slowly, uncertain whether he spoke English, "Mr. Suarez, I am your lawyer."

Not speaking, Juan nodded. He was uneasy with Asian people. He had never seen one in Mexico. And, when he arrived in New York, he found work washing dishes by hand fourteen hours a day at a dirty Chinese restaurant on First Avenue just above 96th Street. The abrupt, unfriendly man and woman who owned the restaurant never once asked his name, and he knew them only as Mr. and Mrs. Wan. They never said hello or good night. They paid him in cash, handing it to him as if they were reluctant to let it go. In the hot, noisy restaurant, Mr. and Mrs. Wan made slashing hand gestures to relay instructions to him. With the same hand gestures and a few explosive words, they threatened to fire him if he took one minute more than the ten minutes allotted to him during the two breaks in each fourteen-hour shift.

She asked, gently, "Do you speak English?"

"Some, not much."

"My name is Theresa Bui."

He nodded.

"I'm your lawyer. Do you understand? I'm a public defender. Do you know what that is?"

"Yes."

She smiled. It was a kind smile. She said to one of the nearby guards, "I need privacy for a few minutes with Mr. Suarez."

The men stepped back no more than a foot, no more out of earshot than they had been. They weren't about to listen to a 34-year-old Asian woman with a briefcase.

Theresa Bui decided to ignore them. She explained that Juan was about to enter the courtroom with her; that she would be handed a paper; that the paper was an "indictment"; that he was accused of the murder of Brad Richardson and the stealing of more than $200,000; and that he would have to say *not guilty* to the judge.

"Mr. Suarez, you do understand me, don't you?"

"I do. Yes." He saw, or wanted to believe he saw, patience and sympathy in her eyes.

"Do you want to tell me anything?" she asked.

He whispered, "I didn't hurt Mr. Richardson. He was my friend. Good to me. I never take any money. I don't need his money."

Theresa Bui gazed into his face. *Such a handsome man*, she thought. "I understand," she said. "We're going to plead not guilty."

"Yes, not guilty."

"And then I will come to visit you soon. To talk more. To help."

He was close to her. He was ashamed of his odor: he hadn't been allowed to shower in all the time since his arrest and he knew he smelled of sweat, of fear. "Where is my wife?"

"Mr. Suarez," she whispered, "I didn't know you had a wife."

"And my kids?"

Kids? she thought. *My God.* "You have children?"

"Two—a boy and girl. Where are they?"

"I'll try to find out," she said, knowing that she had no way to do that.

A harsh buzzer sounded above the door. It was shrill. It startled her. Reacting instantly, a guard unlocked the door of the holding pen. Juan walked between the guards into the beige courtroom. He was dazed by what he saw. The ceiling was very high. There were rows of wooden benches arranged like church pews. And there was an immense bench behind which sat Judge Helen Conley, a severe-looking woman whose gray hair was pulled into a bun. Three lawyers stood at a table in front of the judge's bench. A television camera, with a small red light glowing, was trained on Juan. He glanced fleetingly at the people on the benches. Mariana and her children weren't in the courtroom. Had the world, he wondered, swallowed them up?

Her voice amplified by a microphone, Judge Conley said, "I understand there is some uncertainty as to who this man is."

"There is, Judge," Margaret Harding answered. She was standing at the other table. She was tall. She had black hair. She was dressed in black except for an elegant green scarf draped over her shoulders. "We believe the defendant is an illegal immigrant. A counterfeit Social Security card was found when the search warrant was executed."

The judge looked at Theresa Bui. "Give us a hand here, coun-selor. Does the public defenders' office know who this man is?"

"I'm not sure," Bui answered. Her voice quavered. Juan saw a slight tremor in her hands.

"You're not sure? How can you not know your client's name?"

Bui said, "I didn't think his name was an issue."

Judge Conley glanced over her half-glasses at the prosecutor. "Ms. Harding, why do you think his name is not the name on the indictment?"

"A confidential informant told us that he may in fact have a different name."

"Ms. Bui, ask your client what his real name is."

Theresa Bui turned toward him, whispering, "Do you have another name?"

Juan understood what was happening, but a sense of defiance suddenly replaced his fear and wonder. He recalled that the furious cops who arrested him had screamed that he had the right to re-main silent. *The right to remain silent.* Juan, staring at the judge, didn't answer Bui's question.

Judge Conley, her eyes shifting from Juan's steady, almost un-nerving stare, said, "Well, Ms. Bui?"

"He won't answer me, Judge."

Conley said, "I've had enough. We have the defendant's body. The *corpus*, as in *habeas corpus*. So he's been indicted under the name we have."

"If we learn his real name," Margaret Harding said, "we'll ask the Grand Jury to supersede the indictment."

"Very well then," the judge said, sounding curt and impatient. "Let's proceed with the indictment we do have. Ms. Bui, do you want me to read the indictment? As I assume you've told your client—whoever he is—the indictment in effect alleges the mur-der of Bradford Richardson, the theft of more than $200,000 in

cash, and obstruction of justice in light of the defendant's flight
and his assault on two police officers when he was arrested. Now,
do you want me to read all the exact words of the indictment or
will the defendant waive the reading?"

Without speaking to Juan, Theresa said, "Waive."

"Then how does the defendant plead?"

"Not guilty," Theresa said, signaling to Juan that he should
repeat the same two words.

Instead, he said, "*No culpable.*"

"I take it that means '*not guilty*,'" Judge Conley said. "Is that
correct? Does he understand that?"

"He does," Theresa answered.

Peering at Margaret Harding, Helen Conley said, "I assume
there is no issue about bail because the defendant is plainly a flight
risk as well as a danger to the community, to put it mildly."

"Clearly," the black-haired woman said.

Juan sensed even more tension in Theresa Bui. She seemed to
inhale for strength. "Your Honor," she said, "do you really think
you should say things like that?"

The judge glared at her. "Such as?"

Theresa Bui stood down from the challenge. "Nothing, Your
Honor."

Speaking with a tone of calm assurance, Margaret Harding
said, "Not only is the defendant a flight risk and a plain threat to
the community, but the case against him is overwhelming. Our
detectives located hair samples from the room where the killing
took place. DNA from a hair clipping was taken from the defendant at the time of his arrest and appears to match a hair found in
the Richardsons' bedroom, where we believe the theft took place."

"I appreciate the comments, Ms. Harding, but I just denied
bail. I assume these statements are for the benefit of the cameras.
I won't tolerate that, now or at any other point. This is a court

of law, not a television studio." She took five seconds to look at Margaret Harding, challenging her to react. When it became clear Margaret would not take up the challenge, she continued: "I think the only other business that remains today is to fix a date for our next appearance."

Pressing her BlackBerry, Harding said, "Does November twenty-one work?"

Glancing at her iPhone, Theresa Bui said, "It does."

Juan immediately calculated that the date was a month away and that he would somehow have to find a way to pass hundreds of hours with absolutely nothing to do. He had used his hands every day for years: he had laid brick with them, cut grass, lifted stones, washed dishes, cooked, and touched women in their most sensitive places. He would not be able to do any of that.

As she flipped through papers, Judge Conley asked, almost casually, "Ms. Bui, does your client waive the speedy trial act?"

Again, without speaking to Juan, who knew the meaning of the word "speedy," Theresa said, "He does."

"Very well. See you all on November twenty-one."

As if acting on a signal from the judge, two guards grabbed Juan's arms. Held by the guards, Juan was hustled to the door from which he had entered the courtroom. He looked at the gallery again, searching for the faces of Mariana and her children. Nothing. All he saw was the rush of reporters out of the courtroom.

In the parking lot just outside the rear door of the drab courthouse, as Juan was pushed into the back seat of a police cruiser, he saw people with cameras jostling to get close to him. He recalled the time in July when a picture was taken of him and Joan Richardson, both in bathing suits and just out of the water of the Olympic-size pool. Joan herself had taken the picture with her cell phone, extending her glistening arm and saying, "Smile for the camera."

Using one of the printers in the Richardsons' home, Joan had printed out that picture—two beautiful people gleaming with water, laughing, their lithe bodies in full view. She gave it to Juan. He took it to his ranch house and slipped it for safe-keeping in a plastic bag under a moldy rug in the basement, the only secure place he could find. At night, when Mariana and the kids and the other people who lived in the house were sleeping, he had often gone down to the basement and taken the picture out to stare at it. The glorious picture made him happy.

Bo Halsey now had that picture.

13.

RAQUEL REMATTI WASN'T CERTAIN she remembered Theresa Bui. Raquel had taught hundreds of law students during her fifteen years as an adjunct professor at Columbia. Attentive to every one of them, she was the most popular member of the faculty. She led and entertained the students in her seminars, which were limited to twelve with a waiting list of fifty. Her lectures on trial practice, at which she spoke fluently and without notes, were held in the largest classroom at the school. She was refreshingly different from most of the dour, awkward men and women on the faculty.

Even though she was busy with her own law practice in midtown, Raquel stayed at her office at Columbia when she taught on Tuesdays and Thursdays until she had seen every student who wanted to speak with her. She carefully read and made written comments on their papers, all limited to five pages because, as she told them, trial lawyers had to be succinct and only short messages were persuasive. Raquel was a gregarious woman who had met an uncountable number of people since she started practicing law in the mid-1980s. She liked to believe, although she knew it wasn't possible, that she recognized the faces and names of every person she had ever met, particularly her students.

And people remembered her. She was almost six feet tall yet she carried herself with the balance of a dancer. Her face was striking: the dark skin of her southern Italian heritage, a somewhat aquiline yet beautifully shaped nose that no plastic surgeon had ever touched, large brown emotive eyes, and high cheekbones. Raquel's hair was naturally black; it was now streaked with a single trace of white, Susan Sontag-style.

There was another reason people recognized her. As soon as televised trials started to become popular in the early 1990s, Raquel Rematti was a regular guest on national networks, and that had continued without interruption. She'd even been offered a show as one of the television judges, and declined it. She had no interest in becoming the Italian Judge Judy.

When her secretary Roger mentioned that Theresa Bui, who said she had once been a student in Raquel's trial advocacy class at Columbia, had made an appointment, Raquel asked him to do a computer run of her name. Raquel had made it a practice to preserve the names of all her students over the last fifteen years, at first in a handwritten journal and later in a computer, so she would never be at a loss to have some information about them—date of graduation, even grades—in order to make any of them who visited her feel welcome. Roger, a 35-year-old with spiky orange hair and silver studs piercing each ear, had returned to Raquel's office within five minutes. He said, "Columbia, Class of 2007. Was an undergraduate at Vassar. And that, as they say, is all she wrote."

When Roger led Theresa Bui into her office at noon on the bright, fall-sharpened day, Raquel didn't recognize her. There had been more and more Asian men and women in her classes over the last few years, as the bright children of ambitious Chinese, Korean, and Vietnamese immigrants finally migrated from fields like computer science and medicine to the raw terrain of the law. Raquel gave Theresa Bui a welcoming wave as she continued to listen to someone on her cell phone. She pointed at the sofa, signaling Theresa to sit.

As Theresa waited, she looked at the array of pictures on the walls. She recognized some of the men and women with whom Raquel had been photographed over the years. Except for slight shifts in her hairstyle, Raquel hadn't really changed since the first pictures taken of her in the mid-1980s when macho Oliver North, just after she graduated from Yale Law School, hired her as one of the small cadre of lawyers to represent him in the Iran-Contra trial. He was crazy—one of those men who wanted the world to believe he was the go-to guy for clandestine assignments vital to what they saw as the security of the United States—but despite the profound differences in their politics, she liked him. He was charming in a goofy, self-deprecating way. There were a few times over the years when, as a gentle spoof, he had her as a guest on his radio show. He also had a sense of humor: he called her *Jane Fonda* and *Hanoi Hannah*.

There were other faces Theresa Bui recognized in the array of pictures of Raquel's clients—Manuel Noriega, Michael Milken, Robert Blake, Darryl Strawberry, Roger Clemens. There were also pictures of her with famous people who had never been her clients Hillary Clinton, Jessie Jackson, Oprah. And, on the wall near the floor-to-ceiling windows overlooking Park Avenue were pictures of her with some of the men she had dated: Jack Nicholson, Jesse Jackson, Mortimer Zuckerman, Philip Roth. She had never married, she had no children.

Raquel Rematti was that rarest of all lawyers: the only woman among the six or seven most famous criminal trial lawyers in the country.

"Theresa," Raquel said warmly when the call ended. "Sorry, some clients like to talk on and on. I've never learned the fine art of dumping them when they start repeating themselves. How have you been?"

"Really well, Professor Rematti."

"I'm Raquel." She had the instinctive ability to put people at
ease. Even when she was cross-examining a hostile witness, she
treated the person with apparent rapport until, still engaging him
or her almost deferentially, she shifted quietly into a devastat-
ing series of questions that a confused, suddenly off-balance witness didn't expect. She asked Theresa, "What are you doing these
days?"

"I work in the public defenders' office in Suffolk County."

"Good for you." She was genuinely pleased to hear this. "Almost all your classmates run headlong into corporate law firms,
some of them to pay off student loans, some for the love of money,
some for both reasons. A young public defender learns so much
about human nature. And about injustice. And the vanishing art
of how to try a real case."

"I'm learning, Raquel. But slowly." Theresa found it difficult
to use her former professor's first name. Still tentative and nervous
in the presence of this famous woman, she raced to explain why
she was there even though Raquel hadn't yet asked the question:
"But I haven't learned enough to handle a murder trial for a man
who's being called by every newspaper and television station in the
world the *Blade of the Hamptons* or, as the *New York Post* loves to
put it, *Juan the Knife*."

It was then that Raquel recognized that this was no ordinary
courtesy visit from a former student. Over the last several weeks
she'd read newspaper and magazine articles and watched television
news about the Mexican immigrant charged with the murder of
Brad Richardson, the billionaire hedge fund owner, author, and
philanthropist. The "alien" was again and again called either the
Blade of the Hamptons or *Juan the Knife*. Raquel was struck, as she
had been many times in her career, by the intensity of the hate lev-
eled at some men and women charged with a crime. Even Bernie
Madoff, who had only stolen money from people who were as

greedy as he was, had become a universal pariah. No one believed in the presumption of innocence. *Unless, of course,* she often said, *they were indicted.* It was then that even a right-winger or a Tea Party member whole-heartedly and suddenly embraced civil liberties. Oliver North certainly had.

Theresa told Raquel she was "scared" to defend Juan Suarez. She was intimidated, she said, by the worldwide news coverage the case was receiving. She wasn't certain that she or anyone else in her office had the strength and skill and resources to try the case or to withstand the onslaught from reporters and bloggers. It was painful to Theresa to open the Google entries that now referred to her. Her identity on the Internet had once been only her name and her status on Facebook—in other words, almost complete anonymity. Now there were pages and pages of references to her, not one of them flattering, and most insulting and demeaning. Vicious words: lightweight, sucker, incompetent, not qualified. And the stupid variations on her name. Ms. Boo-hoo, Ms. Boo-boo, Ms. Wowie, Ms. Fooey. There were three anonymous bloggers—or one with different screen names—who were incessantly trashing her. Every word these crazy cyber stalkers wrote instantly became etched forever on Google. She cringed at the thought that her great-grandchildren would someday see the postings.

"Theresa, the amount of contempt that a criminal defendant— not to mention his lawyer—faces used to amaze me. Now it saddens me."

Theresa responded quickly, like a child making a confession. "I can't leave my house without being asked what he's like, what his real name is, when he came to this country—even why he killed the Borzois."

"The what?"

"Two dogs were killed at the same time as Brad Richardson. With a machete, apparently the same one. Sometimes I think he's going to be indicted for animal cruelty. And," she smiled, "I've never tried a case for animal cruelty."

"And let me guess, Theresa, not one of those reporters asks you about the possibility of his innocence. And not one of the bloggers ever mentions the presumption of innocence?"

She shook her head *no*. And then she brought herself to the question that had led her to Raquel Rematti. "Can you take this over from us?"

It had been two or three years since Raquel had represented a client in a highly publicized case. The last one was an assault and gun possession charge against a famous rapper and record producer named 007-Up. The charges were dropped because the three witnesses against him had in fact been in Miami, not in New York, when 007-Up was arrested in East Harlem. Listening to Theresa Bui, Raquel was swept by the rush of adrenaline she always felt when there was the opportunity to represent a notorious client.

"Who knows you're here?" Raquel asked.

"No one. I didn't speak to my bosses. I know that only two of them have handled one or two murder cases. The clients were convicted in an hour."

Raquel said, "That's not unusual, Theresa. There's a pretty reliable statistic that ninety-eight percent of the murder trials in this country end in convictions. If trial lawyers were judged like major league hitters on their batting averages, little kids would throw away the baseball cards with our pictures on them."

Theresa smiled, but only faintly. "I think he could be innocent, Raquel. I don't know, of course, but I think so. I want him to have a chance."

"I'll go to see him, Theresa. It'll be his decision. And I need to get a sense of the man before I take him on."

"Good, thank you."

"Another thing," Raquel said. "I'll need you to work with me. Only wizards work alone. I'm not a wizard."

"You're not?"

They smiled at each other.

Raquel Rematti knew from that moment that she would take on Juan Suarez. It was the attraction of the challenge, the lure of the outcast. She had always found that combination irresistible.

And it was even more irresistible now, as she was seeking to leave behind the cancer that for the last year had, like a stalker, been trying to claim her life.

14.

JOAN RICHARDSON WAS IN a place she'd always loved: the Plaza Athenée hotel, on the Avenue Montaigne, in Paris. Through the slatted wooden shutters, the ceiling-to-floor windows let soothing light from the sunny winter afternoon into the room. The stately windows, the understated furniture of the hotel suite, and the glorious allure of the cold and sunny Paris streets just outside usually calmed her on her visits to the city. But this afternoon she was restless, irritable, and constantly in motion.

She had come to Paris with Hank Rawls, because the producers of a movie based on one of his novels had asked him to take a small role. She also saw Paris as a refuge from the endless daily publicity dominating her life since Brad's killing. While he was alive, they attracted many reporters and photographers, particularly when they donated the money for a new wing at the Met and the reconstruction of the East Hampton library. She had enjoyed the level of attention from society reporters, financial journalists, and photographers. She sometimes treated the photographers with the same care she'd shown to the yard workers, on the first day she met Juan, when she invited them into the East Hampton house because of the rain on that chilly April morning. In the past, she would from time to time send coffee, sandwiches, and fruit to the reporters and photographers who waited on the street for Brad and her to emerge from a dinner party. They rewarded her with attractive pictures on Page Six in the *Post*, on the society page in the Sunday *New York Times,* on the cover of *Town & Country* and *Elle.* She treated the elfin, 80-year-old Bill Cunningham, who had taken society pictures for the *Times* for decades, as a friend. He moved all over Manhattan on his bicycle. He never once failed her: all the photos were flattering.

But now, even months after Brad's killing and more so as the trial approached, it was all different. As she told Hank Rawls, "I've gone from being the cover girl, the Jennifer Aniston sweetheart, to the scheming shrew, Cruella DeVille." The stories about her in newspapers, magazines, and tabloids, and on television and the Internet were relentless. *The billion-dollar babe, the girl who loved to "party down," the lady with her own Senator.* Since Brad's killing, Joan was never alone on the Manhattan streets except when she managed to slip out of her apartment building through the service entrance wearing the clothes of a fortyish cleaning lady and an over-size Yankee baseball cap. She was always conscious that outside the building were people with cameras, tape recorders, and notebooks waiting for her, and that her chances of escaping in disguise were remote.

Hank, who had spent his life in public since the time, at 27, when he first ran for a seat in the Wyoming Congressional district where he was raised, seemed bemused by all the attention. He was long past campaigning for political office. He no longer had any need to worry about the company he kept or the places he went. His publisher and his managers believed that the added exposure he received as Joan Richardson's boyfriend—he had been the boy-friend of many famous women—was one of the many factors that fueled sales of his books and the movies based on his books. It was also true that he had loved Joan Richardson, although her ner-vous distractions and her fears and her impatience (and her jealous possessiveness) were the kinds of traits that had led him away from many women in the past. Hank liked having fun. Joan Richardson had, for the last year, been a lot of fun. Now that Joan was virtually crumbling under the pressures that followed Brad's death, Hank wanted to be patient with her. At 60, he consciously decided to teach himself, if he could, the traits of patience, tolerance, and acceptance. But he knew he had a short attention span.

When Hank emerged naked from the marble bathroom, toweling himself, he saw Joan doing something completely uncharacteristic. She was smoking. It was a Gauloise. The pack was on the table beside the bed, as succulent-looking as a French pastry.

He smiled at her. "Aren't you worried about crows' feet around the eyes?"

"I'm a wreck. I used to smoke at Stanford. When I got my first modeling job, I quit smoking. For years I've wanted to smoke again."

"Doesn't the Surgeon General warn women off because of what smoking does to their eyes? It's right there on the packs: 'Warning from the Surgeon General for all gorgeous women: Smoking causes wrinkles.'" Hank Rawls had attractive, cowboy-like lines around his own eyes, not from smoking but from long spans of time in the sun—in Wyoming, on beaches in Europe and the Caribbean, on boats, on his long foot races.

Joan smiled. "Say that again? When did a woman get to be the Surgeon General?"

Hank laughed. He wore a gold Breguet watch on his left wrist. It was, he liked to say, Winston Churchill's favorite model. He glanced at it on his naked arm. "I better get some clothes on. I need to be on the set in two hours."

He made no effort to hide how much he was looking forward to his three-sentence, one-minute role as the United States Secretary of State, in an expensive thriller (explosions, love affairs, guns, assassinations, cars driving upside down on the ceilings of tunnels, Arabs, FBI agents) based on a novel he'd published two years earlier, *Extraordinary Rendition.*

"How long did you say it took you to memorize your lines?" she asked, trying to lighten her mood.

"Memorize them, baby? I wrote them."

He dropped the towel to the floor. Naked, he walked toward her, moved the hand in which she held her cigarette away, and embraced her, bending her backwards slightly, tango-style. He stiffened, instantly aroused. He whispered into her ear: "I'll take care of you later."

"Get out of here," Joan said, playfully, relieved that her mood had turned quickly. "You don't want to keep Matt Damon and Nicole Kidman waiting."

"Who?"

"Get your cute ass in gear, Mr. Secretary."

Just thirty minutes later, Joan was again impatient, distracted, and nervous in the Bentley, as the uniformed driver cruised slowly by all the classic Paris buildings—the smooth stone facades, the tiled roofs—on the way to the ornate Italian embassy where the filming was taking place. She barely glanced at the Seine, at the Ile de la Cité (that magic island dividing the river), the Louvre, or the low, curving stone bridges over the Seine.

Hank said, "All right, Joan, it's time to talk. You've been down over the last two days. I fell in love with and I still love a beautiful, generous, vital woman. We shook off the reporters on the way to JFK. Didn't that help? Nobody has found you here."

"I'm really, really confused, Hank. Worried."

He looked at her, waiting for more.

She said, "I spoke to Jake yesterday." As much as she hated to use the words, Jake Hecht was her "public relations advisor." A former journalist, he had an uncanny ability to learn about news reports before they were printed, broadcast, or posted on the Internet. Jake Hecht was like a game fixer: through a bribe, a fixer could react impassively as a horse race was underway because he lived in the future, he knew the outcome.

"What did our little wizard learn?"

"That bitch Raquel Rematti has been giving interviews. Jake said she'll be a guest tomorrow night on CNN. She'll say that she's at last persuaded the DA to subpoena *you* to go in front of a Grand Jury."

Hank Rawls's body was instantly suffused with that spasm of anxiety he'd only experienced two or three times in his life, including when, fifteen years earlier, he first saw the long-lens pictures of Cynthia Hall and himself on that remote, sun-drenched beach on Saint Kitts. They were naked. He was married to someone else at the time. As soon as he saw the pictures, he knew that his short campaign for President was over. "Maybe Bill Clinton could survive this," he had told his campaign manager. "I can't."

Deliberately concealing his anxiety, he said, "Don't worry, sweetie. I've told you that was the other shoe. They always look at the husband or wife first, and then at the boyfriend or girlfriend. Don't forget, I'm a lawyer, even though, thank God, I never practiced a day in my life."

Over the last two months, Joan Richardson had sat in front of a Grand Jury on three separate days. Each day was a draining ordeal. The badly dressed young prosecutor, Menachem Oz, never once was pleasant, never treated her with the kindness or sympathy she imagined a widow of a murdered man might deserve, or with the respect she thought one of the most generous philanthropists in the world merited. Menachem Oz—a name she could not forget—had the sour demeanor of an Orthodox Jew from Brooklyn, which he was. He wore a yarmulke. His suits were off-the-rack from Target. He was very smart and very tenacious. She was afraid of him.

And she had lied to him. Menachem Oz knew it and again and again returned to questions about the day Brad was murdered, searching her for inconsistencies. "What time did you wake up?" "Where did you go in Manhattan?" "Who was your housekeeper?" "Was she there that day?" "Did anyone visit you?" "Were there any deliveries?" "How long were you at lunch?" "Did you eat alone?" "How many times in the last year have you had lunch alone?" "What are the names of the doormen who worked at the building that day?"

She had lied in her answers to almost all of these and many other questions. Joan never said that Senator Rawls came to her apartment in the morning of the day Brad was killed and that they didn't leave until seven that evening, both of them dressed in classic evening clothes for the party at the Met. Instead, she said she'd had a lunch alone at a small restaurant on East 77th Street and then strolled uptown on Madison Avenue, stopping at the intimate Crawford-Doyle bookstore between 81st and 82nd Streets.

Menachem Oz knew she hadn't been in the bookstore. "Did you use a credit card to buy books?"

"No, cash."

"What was the book?"

"You mean the name?"

"Right, the name of the book?"

"The *Collected Poems* of Philip Larkin."

She knew the skein of her senseless lying was fast unraveling but felt powerless to stop herself.

As the Bentley approached the rented embassy, she waited for Hank to say more. He leaned forward, looking at the camera trucks, the catering trucks, and the trailers where the lead actors had their private rooms. He was excited, like a boy arriving at a carnival, or like a politician approaching a cheering crowd.

The Bentley slowly made its way toward Helen Whitehouse, one of the assistant directors. Helen opened the door of the car. She was 25. She looked at him as though he were her favorite man in the world. As Hank Rawls rose to his feet, he engaged the woman with his famous smile and said, "Helen, it's just great to see you."

When Joan emerged from the car and was introduced to her, she entered the force field of the tacit, excited connection between her lover and this young woman. She had no doubt that Hank Rawls would in the not-too-distant future be screwing Helen Whitehouse.

Joan Richardson was wrong. That had already happened.

15.

RAQUEL REMATTI WAS ALWAYS struck by how much Riverhead, the town seventy-three miles east of Manhattan where Long Island divided into the North Fork and the South Fork, resembled the decaying factory cities of Rhode Island, southeastern and north-eastern Massachusetts, and southern New Hampshire. Instead of abandoned factories, Riverhead had abandoned gas stations, most of them on lots with grass and weeds growing through the fissures in the broken concrete. There was even a rusty *Esso* sign rising over the lot of a long-closed gas station. *Esso* signs were artifacts of another era, like the big cars with whitewall tires she could remember from her childhood in the late sixties. Most of the storefronts on Main Street in Riverhead were boarded over with plywood. Graffiti was sprayed on the plywood. The only active stores were essentially indoor flea markets. There wasn't even a McDonald's or a Burger King.

The residential streets around Riverhead had the look of small towns in Appalachia; there were hundred-year-old houses that must have looked poor when they were built, pick-up trucks in the driveways, and sofas and stuffed chairs on the porches. Raquel knew the poverty of most of America—the de-crepit housing, the rundown public schools, the bleak shopping malls—the America that the cheery, pervasive television and print advertising for cars and vacations and prescription drugs never depicted.

Several years ago, on a trip driven by a reluctant nostalgia, she had returned to Haverhill, Massachusetts, where her family had lived for three generations. Arriving from Sicily in the 1920s, her grandfather had worked for years in a shoe factory in Haverhill alongside the sulphurous Merrimack River, and her father worked there too until the cold day in 1976 when the immense red brick factory building was shut down without any notice to anyone. Raquel was still in high school then, but already tall, strikingly attractive, and first in her class. She knew she was destined for scholarships at any one of several legendary colleges and that she would leave Haverhill behind. The sight of those old factory buildings, some of them renovated but most abandoned and strewn with black graffiti, still painfully tugged at her when she drove through the familiar streets: as a girl she would meet her handsome, happy, and strong father on the iron pedestrian bridge that spanned the Merrimack, which he crossed every day for forty years on his way to and from the factory. She still longed for him: in 1990 he had died of cancer, the disease that had almost taken her own life over the last year. She could still sense his manly, all-enveloping presence.

The prison was on the outskirts of Riverhead. It was a sprawling single-story cinderblock building constructed in the 1970s and surrounded by fences with barbed wire. It was set in what was once a potato field. Raquel passed through the outside security point and parked her car near the main entrance. Many of the cars in the visitors lot were older Mazdas, Toyotas, and Fords. They were the cars and oversize pick-up trucks of family members visiting prisoners. There were also a few Mercedes and BMWs, the cars of visiting lawyers.

For more than a month, Raquel had regularly stopped on Friday afternoons at the prison to visit Juan, sometimes just for twenty minutes or so, on her drives from the city to her weekend house on the Atlantic coast in Montauk. She had bought the house as a generous gift to herself after the terrifying nine months in which she learned she had breast cancer, underwent debilitating weeks of chemotherapy, and the loss and reconstruction of her left breast. Raquel had always loved life, and she was in utter dread at the thought of losing it during the grim months when the cancer took greater hold before it just halted and was reversed, a miracle she attributed to the cures her doctors delivered and also to the prayers she recited. She was raised as a Catholic and had remained one—a fact that she didn't usually disclose in the world in which she now lived—and believed in the will of God. She was convinced she'd been given a second life, that she'd lived two lives in one. As in the lines in Luke that described the Prodigal Son—*For this thy brother was dead and is alive again.*

Since her first meeting with Juan, she was fascinated by him and the place where his life had brought him. She was also fascinated by the incessant attention focused on him and the murder of an immensely wealthy man. It was as though Juan were accused of killing Mother Teresa. There were endless news reports dwelling on how the mysterious alien had managed to win the affection and confidence of one of the wealthiest and most philanthropic couples in the world, Brad and Joan Richardson. The *New York Post* carried stories about the "rat" who had insidiously worked his way into the Richardsons' storied lives and then betrayed them. The articles mentioned that the Richardsons also cared generously for the rat's "undocumented" wife and children, who had disappeared, probably with cash stolen from the Richardsons' estate, on the same day Juan was arrested "after leading the police on a wild run through the woods as he tried to escape."

When Raquel had announced that she was taking over the defense of Juan Suarez, the publicity ratcheted up yet another notch.

The press conference took place on the sidewalk at 57th Street and Park Avenue, near the lobby of her office building. It was a clear, chilly fall day. The crisp sunlight fell on Raquel's taut, beautifully structured, Sicilian-dark face as she spoke. "As more is revealed in this painful case," she had said, "we'll learn that the arrest of Juan Suarez was not the result of a thorough professional investigation, but a symptom of some of our worst instincts as a nation. Juan Suarez is not a blade. He is not a knife. He is not an alien. And he is not an insidious rat. He is part of an invisible, much-scorned population whose presence we as a society don't want to acknowledge, although we take advantage of it. We treat these people as invisible, but they are our nannies, maids, gardeners. We are demonizing the most vulnerable people among us. Juan Suarez had no motive to commit this crime. He had no reason to commit it. And he did not do it."

Images of Raquel speaking in the clear fall air, with flowers still in bloom behind her on the colorful median dividing Park Avenue's uptown and downtown traffic, were broadcast around the world. On the day after the press conference, the headline in the *Times* read: *Famed Celebrity Lawyer Takes Over Defense in Hamptons Murder.*

Raquel Rematti was tall and imposing, and she was surprised that Juan was four inches taller than she was. When they first met, Juan's size and vitality surprised her, just as Joan Richardson had been surprised months earlier by how vibrant Juan's presence was. Raquel had grown used to seeing the small, cowed men who were steadily appearing on the East End of Long Island. She genuinely wanted to believe she had no race or other prejudices, but the difference between Juan and the other Mexican, Nicaraguan, and Ecuadorian men she saw along the roadsides and in the yards of Southampton, East Hampton, and Montauk was too striking for her to deny. *Where did he really come from?* she wondered. To her, he looked like a Spanish aristocrat, not an immigrant day laborer. She was disappointed with herself that she made these comparisons, but she did.

They always met in a small room with plastic, childlike chairs and desk, all pink. The guards, one of them a very heavy black woman with a tattoo of a flower on her neck, insisted that the door stay open. The guards had pistols. Juan Suarez was an important prisoner, almost certainly the best-known ever held in the Suffolk County Correctional Institution.

Raquel Rematti never took notes. Leaning forward so that they could talk quietly, she sat directly across from Juan at the plastic table. She had learned long ago that the intimacy of a lawyer sitting close to a client, speaking quietly and without the lawyer taking notes, fostered the growth of confidence.

"Juan," she said, "do you remember where we left off last week?"

They had abruptly been stopped when they met a week earlier by the harsh alarm bell that was a signal for a head count. When that alarm sounded, every prisoner had to return to his cell no matter who was visiting him—lawyer, wife, priest, parent—and the visit couldn't resume until the lockdown ended. Raquel left because more than two hours passed without any sign of the end of that lockdown. She had a sense that the guards did this to make visitors and inmates as uncomfortable as possible.

"Yes," Juan said.

"Tell me more, Juan, about everything you remember about the first time you saw Mrs. Richardson with Senator Rawls. You told me it was at a party on the Fourth of July."

It had taken all of Raquel's skill at generating a client's confidence gradually to bring Juan, reticent by nature, to speak about Joan Richardson and Hank Rawls.

"It was a big party," Juan said. "I met everybody at the front door. I see right away that Mr. Rawls and Mrs. Richardson are friends."

"What did you see them do?"

"At first they walk around and talked to people. Like they were giving the party."

"And what else?"

"Later they held hands."

"Did Mr. Richardson see that?"

"Sure, everybody saw that. No one cared."

"Didn't Mr. Richardson care?"

"No. They didn't spend much time together. He goes away a lot. She doesn't."

"Mrs. Richardson and this man Rawls: Can you tell me anything else?"

"That night you mean?"

"Let's start with that night."

"Later. They are at the pool. They did things to each other."

Raquel asked, "What things, Juan?" She knew she was driving forward into new terrain, more and more overcoming Juan's reluctance to say anything negative about Joan Richardson. She had brought Juan around, at least to some extent, by letting him know that it was Joan Richardson who told the police she believed Juan killed Brad, and Juan remembered the stony face of Joan Richardson behind the tinted glass of the police car against which he was thrown when he was arrested.

"He put his mouth down there on her."

"And you saw that?"

"They are outside, near the pool, Raquel. Dark out. But they are not hiding."

"Did anybody else see them?"

"I think only me."

"Where was Brad?"

"Not far off."

"What was he doing?"

Juan remembered that Brad was holding Trevor's hand. "He is with friends. But not far off, Raquel."

She knew that clients lied to her most of the time. Even when some told her what might have been the truth, she could never be certain that it was in fact the truth. There were other clients who never gave her any story at all: those were the most dangerous ones because they assumed that Raquel would fabricate a story for them, and she never did. In her freshman year at Swarthmore a professor in the class on the Victorian novel had spoken of the "willing suspension of disbelief" that a reader should bring to a work of fiction. Long after she had forgotten everything about the plot of *Vanity Fair*, she remembered those words. But for the opposite purpose: she had to bring disbelief to everything she heard.

But with Juan she had a sense, although not a certainty, that he was a truth-teller. He said he had not killed Brad Richardson, so why not believe him? How would she ever know the truth? "Isn't that all we know about truth?" Raquel frequently asked her Columbia students. "That the truth is what happened."

"Did Brad ever say anything to you about how he felt about his wife? Everyone seemed to know, Juan, that Mrs. Richardson and Rawls were special friends."

"Brad was a happy man, nice to everybody. He treats his wife and Mr. Rawls in the same nice way."

Raquel rose from the chair, touched Juan on the shoulder to signal that he should stay seated, and walked to the vending machines. She bought candy bars and sodas for herself, for Juan, and for the three guards. The guards silently accepted the sodas and candy, as did Juan.

Now was the time, she knew, to ask Juan a question she could not have asked before. It was because she intended to ask this question that she had not invited Theresa Bui to join her on this visit. Juan, she sensed, might not answer if Theresa were there, even though he always welcomed her warmly. "Can you tell me anything about you and Mrs. Richardson?"

Juan put down the Diet Coke can from which he had been sipping. He looked directly into Raquel's eyes.

"I was Mrs. Richardson's boyfriend, Raquel."

Of course, Raquel thought, *what woman, or man, wouldn't be this man's lover?* Slightly uneasy with what he said and her own reaction, Raquel glanced down at Juan's hands. They were large and powerful. The veins looked like hard ropes beneath the skin.

"You made love to her?"

Juan appeared slightly confused, as if not believing that Raquel didn't understand the meaning of *boyfriend.* "Sure, we did."

"When was the first time?"

"I don't know."

"Before you saw her with Senator Rawls at the pool?"

"Sure."

"After that as well?"

"Yeah."

"How many times, altogether?"

"You mean me and Mrs. Richardson?"

"Yes, that's what I mean."

"Lots, Raquel, lots."

"The last time?"

"The last time?"

"Yes."

"Two days before Mr. Richardson died."

"Did Brad know about you and Mrs. Richardson?"

He paused. "Why are you asking this?"

"It's simple, Juan. She's going to testify against you at the trial. She will work with them to get you convicted. When I ask her questions I need to make her seem biased against you."

"What is that word?"

"That she has something against you, that she's willing to lie to hurt you."

"Why would she hurt me?"

"I don't know *why* about anything, Juan. All I know is that she will try."

"I never hurt her."

Raquel knew she was in a strange business. It was a world where ordinary human standards—such as *I love you, I wouldn't hurt you*—didn't apply, and where people did incalculable damage to others to protect themselves. "It doesn't matter that you didn't hurt her. Let me tell you this, Juan. Part of my job is to make people suspicious of her. Who is to say that she didn't have someone kill him? Do you understand? My job is to protect you. If I can make it seem that somebody else might have killed him, then I've raised reasonable doubt."

"Doubt?

"We talked about this."

Like many other terms lawyers and judges used, it was elusive to define *reasonable doubt*. The explanation judges gave to jurors was opaque, a classic tautology. Proof beyond a reasonable doubt, judges said, didn't mean the prosecution had to prove guilt beyond all doubt. That wasn't possible. At the other extreme, you couldn't doubt everything. A reasonable doubt was located some place between no doubt and doubt about everything. Reasonable is reasonable. As she often told her students, the definition was absurd. She had often heard jurors ask again as they deliberated for an explanation of reasonable doubt. The judge always repeated the same words, as though repetition would create meaning. "It's a joke, ladies and gentlemen," she told her students. "But in this business, the business of representing criminal defendants, the beauty of it is that the definition of reasonable doubt gives you something to work with, you have the chance to make soap out of stone."

Juan said, "I didn't kill Mr. Richardson, Raquel. You know that, don't you?"

Raquel Rematti was trained to bring doubt to everything. But she said, "Of course I believe you, Juan. I do."

16.

As SOON AS KATHY Schiavoni graduated from East Hampton High School, she fulfilled the two driving ambitions of her teenage life. She had a silver earring pierced through her right eyebrow, and she immediately moved to the Lower East Side. She spent six years in Manhattan. She worked as a waitress, a nanny, and a dog-walker. She had only two boyfriends. Each of them was with her for three months. Both of them were haphazard, lazy cocaine-dealers. They were addicts, and dumb enough to use the money they earned from selling drugs only to buy drugs for themselves. She was afraid of cocaine, but loved each of them. Kathy, slightly overweight, with frizzy reddish hair and a plain face, was devastated when they walked out on her. She imagined that she would never again find another lover.

At twenty-five she returned to East Hampton. She rented a small apartment on the third floor of a building on Main Street near the East Hampton Cinema. Her parents lived in a neat ranch house less than a mile from her apartment, beyond the windmill and the wood-shingled Episcopal Church on the Montauk Highway. She ate dinner with them on Sunday night once every two months. She worked, at the cash register, in one of the few locally owned hardware stores. At nights and on weekends, for five years, she made the long drive "up-island"—in the direction of New

York City—to dreary, over-populated Smithtown, where she took courses in criminology and law enforcement at a community college. Although she had been at sea in her high school courses in biology and basic chemistry—her grades were just above passing, a gift from her teachers—she now gravitated to forensics, to lab work, and to DNA testing.

With pliers on one rainy night, she pulled the silver spike from her eyebrow; she had a festering infection for a few weeks. When the eyebrow healed, it was almost as though it had never been pierced. Only one of the two men who became her lovers in East Hampton ever noticed the almost effaced hole. "I had a spike," she said. It was important to Kathy Schiavoni to tell the truth.

She had worked in the police lab in Smithtown for seven years when she was given the plastic bag tagged with the identification "Richardson sheets." Normally unfazed by any evidence she was handed for testing, she immediately recognized that the Richardson case was what she had heard described at headquarters as a "big, big one, the biggest ever out here." None of the several dozen cases she had testified in as an expert had ever received attention from the newspapers. They were anonymous, unremarkable trials. Kathy was a stolid, careful witness. In every case in which she testified, the defendant had been convicted.

In handling the "Richardson sheets," she didn't want to be distracted by the visibility of the case, but she was even more careful than usual. She was given several strands of hair from Juan Suarez's head. She also had a group of ten of his wiry jet-black pubic hairs. There were at least five distinct areas on the luxuriant sheets from the Richardson bedroom that she recognized even before testing them were stained with vaginal fluids and semen: the stains were flaky and off-white.

Working quietly, knowing that Margaret Harding, the assistant district attorney handling the "billionaire murder" case, was waiting impatiently as usual for the results, Kathy spent several days before she made an appointment at Harding's cluttered office in Riverhead.

When she arrived with her report in a document-sized plastic cover for her appointment at ten, she had to wait for Margaret Harding for a full hour. Harding was a late riser. She was, in Kathy Schiavoni's eyes, a prima donna, more like a manicured Manhattan woman with a house in the Hamptons than a local working girl. Kathy neither liked nor disliked Margaret Harding. The lawyer had a job to do, and Kathy understood that she did it well, although she was difficult.

Margaret Harding was always late. It was her entitlement. Everyone knew that for the last several months she'd been spending late afternoon and early evening hours at her apartment in Quogue with her boss, Richie Lupo, the Suffolk County District Attorney. Although Richie was the boss, he never tried a case and rarely walked into a courtroom. He often called press conferences. He loved being on camera: with the even, regular features of Mitt Romney, he looked more like a WASP than an Italian. Richie Lupo was married. A Republican who ran on law-and-order, family values advertisements, he had been re-elected three times to four-year terms. He was certain he would never lose an election. He called himself "the DA-for-Life."

"Kathleen," Margaret said when she swept into her office at eleven-thirty, knowing that she was the only person in the world who called Kathy anything other than Kathy, "can I get you a cup of coffee?" *The bitch,* Kathy thought, *she isn't even going to apologize for being late.*

"I've had six already, Margaret. Thanks."

"How do you stay so calm with so much coffee?" Margaret sipped her own black coffee from a plastic cup. She grimaced. It was bitter. Even when she grimaced, every fine feature of her face was attractive.

"Beats me," Kathy answered. She always maintained a terse blandness with Margaret because she knew she could never engage her in that level of quick conversation Margaret had mastered.

Margaret's cell phone chimed a refrain from Beethoven's Fifth Symphony. She snapped the small, shiny instrument open, without hesitation, as if Kathy weren't even in the room. Whoever was on the other end of the conversation spoke more than Margaret, who was smiling. Although reserved and private herself, Kathy had become an acute observer of people, and she knew it was Richie Lupo, calling to follow up on the evening before or even on the sex they had that morning.

As soon as Margaret flipped the phone closed, Kathy said, "I've got the Richardson test results. At least as far as I can go on what I've been given." She slipped a copy of her eight page report, labeled *Confidential*, out of her valise.

"God," Margaret said, smiling, "I thought I'd never see this day. Talk to me."

"Why don't you read it," Kathy said. She found it difficult to have a conversation with Margaret Harding, an impatient woman who had a reputation for interrupting the Pope.

"No, talk to me, Kathleen. I can read it later. Give me the skinny."

"Suarez's DNA is all over the place. There was even a pubic hair from him wedged in the stitching of the sheets in the Richardsons' bedroom."

"Really?" Margaret was excited, as if sharing a racy secret with another woman.

"Yes, really." Kathy placed the report on the edge of Margaret's messy desk. How could such a sleek, fastidious woman, Kathy wondered, be such a slob?

"I'll read this later. Go on, girl."

Kathy paused. "There were other secretions."

"Lordy! Quite a busy bed. Maybe Joan Richardson isn't the corn-fed country girl we see in *Town & Country*, or Eleanor Roosevelt, or Malala?"

"One of the other semen stains is a near-perfect match for Brad Richardson."

"My, my, who do you think he was in bed with?"

"It was his bed," Kathy said, laconically. "He had a right to sleep there, too."

"God, is she something else. First the gardener and then the hubby, or the hubby and then the gardener, or could it be both at the same time?" Margaret took another sip of coffee. "It's convenient that way: she wouldn't have to change the sheets, if it all happened together. A conga line."

"Actually, and you may enjoy this even more, there is at least one other semen stain that doesn't match either Brad Richardson or Juan Suarez."

Margaret leaned forward and lifted the report. "God, how I love this job.""So who was the third stain? Sounds like a good movie title: *The Third Man. The Third Stain*."

"I don't know whose semen it is. What I need to complete the report are samples from any other men who may have been in the house for the two or three days before the killing."

"That could be a cast of thousands."

Kathy recognized that Margaret was trying to be chummy, to have a girl-to-girl conversation. Kathy, stolid and persistent, said, "I'd also like to have a sample of Joan Richardson's DNA, preferably a vaginal swab."

"Listen, between us girls, I think Joan is interested in protecting her family jewels from any more exposure."

"We know," Kathy said evenly, "that her friend Senator Rawls was around. I'd like a DNA sample for him, too. There's a mosaic, I think, on these sheets. I want to be thorough."

And then Margaret surprised Kathy Schiavoni. Margaret said, "I also know that Brad Richardson had special friends. This can get naughty, but it could even be, Kathleen, that the stain from the unknown male was dropped there at the same time as the stain from Brad. I don't think Senator Rawls was taking care of the wife and the husband at the same time. At least his publicity people have wanted us to believe for a long time that he plays for one team only. You know, that Clint Eastwood style."

Kathy smiled faintly. "I need to get back to the lab, Margaret. How long do you think it will take to get a subpoena to get some hairs from Rawls so that we can compare them to the other stains?"

Suddenly Margaret looked petulant. She sat back in her chair and touched her cell phone as if preparing to make a call. "Kathleen, that's our job. We do the mosaics. We pull all of the evidence together, not just DNA. Your job is to give me the pieces; mine is to do the mosaic. I'll have to talk to Menachem. And to Richie, of course. And to Halsey. We can't just go out and get a judge to issue a search warrant to cut the pubic hair of a former U.S. Senator and a bereaved billionaire widow. But you don't need to worry about that, Kathleen. We'll deal with it."

"But I do need to worry about a complete report, Margaret. That's my job."

"I'll read your report. Maybe you're short-changing yourself. Maybe it's complete just as it is. I'll let you know."

It was only when Kathy walked through the bright mid-autumn air of the parking lot toward her Mazda that she realized how the odor of perfume—which she had loved as a teenager when she took bottles of inexpensive perfumes from her mother and sprayed herself but now never used—disturbed her. There was an odor, very faint, of perfume that enveloped Margaret Harding and permeated her office. Kathy, who no longer noticed the stench of blood and flesh, had an almost physical revulsion to the scent; it made her throat constrict. But soon the clear snapping air took away all traces of the perfume that had settled on her own clothes while she was in Margaret's office.

17.

AFTER SO MANY YEARS in public life, Hank Rawls couldn't remember when he felt as uncomfortable as he did now. As Menachem Oz pretended to glance at some yellow notepaper, Hank on the witness stand shifted his nervous gaze from this homely man whose yarmulke somehow stayed in place on his bald head to the three rows of people who sat behind Oz. The faces of these twenty-three people, all white, all members of the Grand Jury, most in their fifties and sixties, were focused on the witness. Hank Rawls, himself a performer, knew that this poorly dressed lawyer was simply pausing for effect to let the last series of questions and answers resonate with the intent people behind him. *I'm sweating*, Hank Rawls thought in that long drawn-out pause, *like fucking Richard Milhous Nixon*. No matter how he tried to compose and settle himself, he couldn't make the sweating stop. He could only hope that his weathered blond skin made it undetectable.

There was a nasal intonation in Menachem Oz's voice. "Let me ask you this, Mr. Rawls. You told us you couldn't remember how many times you saw Ms. Richardson in the month before her husband was killed, is that right?"

"I really can't, Mr. Oz. That was two or three months ago, wasn't it?"

Menachim Oz didn't answer questions, he asked them. "And you can't even give us an estimate, correct?"

"I just don't remember, Mr. Oz. I don't want to guess. My new book had just come out. I was traveling a lot. I told you that I can give you copies of my diary for those weeks. They show where I traveled."

"We'll get to those, Mr. Rawls. But what I want now is simply your best recollection."

"Of what?"

"The number of times you saw Joan Richardson during those four or five weeks."

"The weeks before Brad died?"

"Those weeks, Mr. Rawls."

"Three times, four times, maybe six."

"Did she travel with you?"

"During those weeks before her husband died?"

"Those weeks."

"Absolutely not."

"Why absolutely, Mr. Rawls? Didn't she travel with you to Paris just a week ago? You remember that, don't you?"

That riveted Hank Rawls's attention. How the hell would Menachem Oz know that? Hank toyed with the idea of asking for a recess so that he could leave the room and talk to his lawyer, Josephine Hart, in the hallway where she had been waiting just outside the locked Grand Jury room. He knew that Josephine, a black woman in her mid thirties and a former federal prosecutor, would tell him that there was nothing she or he could do and that he had to go back into the room alone and answer anything and everything that Menachem Oz asked him or risk being taken in front of any available judge to be threatened with contempt for refusing to answer a question. "The only way you can refuse to respond to a question," Josephine had said in her languorous

Southern accent, "is if you take the Fifth Amendment. You pro-bably don't want to take the Fifth."

"Look, Mr. Oz, I know I didn't travel with Mrs. Richardson in the four or five weeks before her husband died."

"But you did travel with her before that period, correct?"

"I said that, Mr. Oz, a few minutes ago."

"And after he died, isn't that right?"

"Right."

"To Paris, correct?"

"To Paris."

Suddenly, as if on some cue, a woman in a black sweater and expensive black slacks entered the room. He assumed she was the lawyer whose name Joan had mentioned several times as "that Harding bitch." The jurors obviously knew her: they continued to stare at him, not at Margaret Harding.

Without skipping a beat or glancing at Margaret, Menachem Oz asked, "Now you told us before our break that you were with Joan Richardson on the night Detective Halsey called her, cor-rect?"

Hank shook his head as if to say an exasperated *yes.*

"Remember, Mr. Rawls, you have to answer with words."

"Yes. The answer is yes. I said that already."

"And you were with her during all that day, correct?"

"That's right."

Suddenly there was, Hank Rawls sensed, an even more rapt at-tention among the people in the room; a few of them whispered. And Margaret Harding leaned forward, anticipating something.

Joan Richardson, he now fully realized, had lied to these people about almost everything.

"Were you in her apartment that day?"

Hank took a sip of water from a steadily deteriorating paper cup. "I was."

"From when to when?"

"Late morning to the time we left for a party."

"How many hours?"

"Five, six, seven, I'm not certain."

"Was anyone in the apartment with you?"

"No."

"Did you make any cell phone calls in those hours?"

"No, I don't think so."

"Did she?"

"Not that I saw."

"Did you use a computer?"

"No."

"Did she?"

"I didn't see that happen, Mr. Oz."

"Do you have a BlackBerry or iPhone?"

"Of course. An iPhone. I couldn't communicate with my five-year-old granddaughter unless I had one."

Menachem Oz didn't smile. "Did Mrs. Richardson use your iPhone during the day?"

"Mr. Oz, we weren't there to make calls or send emails or text messages."

"What did you do during those hours?"

"What do you think we did? Use your imagination."

"What did you do during those hours?"

"Had sex. I made lunch for us. Then more sex."

"How often?"

"Come on, Mr. Oz."

"How often?"

"Five or six times. The miracle of Viagra."

Even Menachem Oz smiled as some of the people in the Grand Jury laughed. "Did the two of you talk about Brad Richardson that day?"

"No, we didn't."

"When did you find out that Brad Richardson was dead?"

"That night, at the party in the museum."

"How did you find out?"

"From Mrs. Richardson."

"What did she say?"

"She said he was dead."

"Did she say anything else?"

"That he was murdered."

"Did she say when she found out?"

"No, but I assume while we were at the party. Clearly she didn't know before that."

"What did you do?"

"I didn't do anything, Mr. Oz. I didn't know what to do. It's way beyond the range of my experience in life to have a woman tell me that her husband had just been murdered."

"How did she react?"

Hank Rawls waited. He was genuinely baffled, even annoyed, by the question. "She was upset, Mr. Oz. As you would expect. She loved her husband."

"Did she cry?"

"No, Mr. Oz. Was she supposed to?"

"What happened next?"

"She left. She said she was going to East Hampton."

"Did you go?"

"No."

"Why not?"

"What could I have done, Mr. Oz?"

Standing at the podium on which documents and an open bottle of Evian water were spread, Menachim Oz again flipped through the pad of yellow paper in front of him. The subject shifted as he asked, "How well did you know Brad Richardson?"

"Not well. He was a friendly man, somewhat shy, I thought."

"Did he know you were having an affair with his wife?"

"Come on, Mr. Oz, how would I know that?"

"Did he know it?"

"I didn't tell him."

"Did Mrs. Richardson tell him?"

"Ask her."

"It's you I'm asking, Mr. Rawls."

"I didn't hear her tell him, if she did. What did she tell you?"

"Did she ever talk about divorcing Mr. Richardson?"

"Not to me. Did she, Mr. Oz?"

Like other men who had no sense of humor, Menachem Oz made it obvious when he took a stab at it. His voice was a shade higher as he said, "Remember, I get to ask the questions, Mr. Rawls."

No one laughed.

But several people did laugh when Hank Rawls said, "So, is that what's been going on here?"

"Mr. Rawls, do you know if Mr. Richardson had any affairs?"

"To be honest, I didn't know Mr. Richardson well, but it seemed to me he didn't take an interest in other people that way. So I don't know the answer to your question. I never saw him in bed with anyone."

After another interlude in which he shuffled the papers on the podium in front of him, Menachem Oz moved on to new territory. "What did you know about Juan Suarez?"

"He worked for Brad and Joan."

"What kind of work?"

"All that I saw him do was greet people at parties."

"Did Mrs. Richardson ever say anything about him?"

"Yes."

"What?"

"That he was an attractive man who was also very sweet and smart. And that he took good care of his family."

"Did she say anything else?"

"Mr. Oz, I know it's not politically correct to say this. But he was a servant, plainly an illegal immigrant, he wasn't someone she mentioned often, and I never asked about him. I had no reason to."

"Has she said anything about Juan Suarez since her husband died?"

"That she wishes she'd never seen him. She feels responsible for bringing him into their lives."

"Did she tell you what his real name is?"

"Real name? Juan Suarez."

"Did she ever use another name for him?"

"No."

Menachem Oz spent at least a quiet minute at the podium, using a pencil to check off subjects he had covered. Hank hoped this was a signal that Oz was winding down.

"Mr. Rawls, did you ever have sex with Mrs. Richardson in a public place?"

"Repeat that, Mr. Oz. I can't have heard that correctly."

Oz was looking down at his notepad. "Did you ever have sex with Mrs. Richardson in a place where other people could see you?"

"Enough, Mr. Oz. That's it. I'm not going to answer that."

"You have to."

"No."

"Is that no, I didn't?" Oz asked.

"No, as in *no* I won't answer."

"A judge will order you to do that or hold you in contempt."

"Listen to me, sir. Let me keep it simple for you. I will not answer that."

"We'll see," Oz said. He looked up from his notes. "Do you know a man named Trevor?"

"You mean any Trevor in the span of my entire life?"

"Since you met the Richardson?"

"I'm a well-known man, Mr. Oz. I'm not a private person. I meet many people every day. Some of them, maybe many of them, are named Trevor."

"Did you ever see a man named Trevor with Mr. Richardson?"

Hank did remember a flamboyant man, undeniably gay, who had spent most of the last Fourth of July party with Brad. "I did, I think. If it's the man I think it was, he was with Brad at the party."

"The same Fourth of July party you attended with Mrs. Richardson?"

"Please, Mr. Oz. We've been over that party again and again and again. Nobody gave me a roster of who was there."

"What is Trevor's last name?"

"I don't know. I wasn't introduced to him, Mr. Oz."

There was less than a five-second lapse before Menachem Oz veered to yet another subject. "What plans do you and Mrs. Richardson have?"

Hank felt a sudden and vivid anger: he was tired, he was annoyed. "I don't understand the question."

"What plans do you and Mrs. Richardson have?"

"We talked about having dinner tonight."

"How often have you talked about marriage?"

"You know, the only thing I remember from law school is that you need a foundation for a question." He took a sip of water. "You're assuming we discussed getting married. We didn't."

"How much money does Mrs. Richardson have?"

"More than God, I assume. At least that's what the newspapers say. She doesn't give me any of it. Hell, I pick up the check at dinner."

"Did she ever tell you how much she inherited from Brad Richardson?"

"Let's stop this game, Mr. Oz. I'm not stupid, sir. And the folks behind you aren't either. So let me be clear—I didn't conspire with Joan Richardson to kill her husband. We didn't hire a hit man to kill her husband. I have no plans to marry Joan Richardson. And I never got a dime from Joan Richardson."

"Are you finished, Mr. Rawls?"

Hank leaned forward in the witness chair. He sat back. He looked at Menachem Oz with his stony, cowboy gaze. "Are you, Mr. Oz?"

Menachem Oz said, "For today. We'll let your lawyer know when you're coming back."

It was a drizzly afternoon when he left the grim, utilitarian Riverhead courthouse. The landscape was dreary and sad: bare wet trees, ramshackle houses, and rusted Toyotas and pick-up trucks parked on the streets. A wet, heavy snow had fallen two days earlier, quickly melted, and now made dirty streaks on the ground.

In that barren landscape, the only new object was the black Mercedes that Hank Rawls had summoned from his cell phone as soon as he walked out of the Grand Jury room. Just as he was about to slide into the car, he was suddenly surrounded by a group of reporters. He was blindsided by this. He had assumed that his appearance was a secret and that no one outside the DA's office would know the date or place of the appearance of the legendary Hank Rawls before a Grand Jury.

Instinctively beaming that engaging smile that had made his life so easy from boyhood, he slipped into the back seat without saying a word. He was furious. He recognized the subtle hand of Raquel Rematti in the unexpected appearance of reporters, and he wanted to find a way to punish her. Joan Richardson, he now realized, had been right to hire private investigators to find something to discredit her, to intimidate her, even to drive her away from the case. *Let's find a way to make the bitch suffer*, Joan had said. *Yes, let's*, Hank now thought as he told Davey, "Don't run anybody over, but get the fuck out of here."

18.

JUAN SUAREZ HAD FACED so many changes in his life—the impoverished village where he was raised, the arid border between Mexico and Texas, the unbearable passage in the airless trailer (no water, no toilets) across half of America to the gigantic, strange streets of Manhattan—that, after the first weeks in solitary confinement, he managed to find a tense regularity in his new life. He was up at five each morning, well before the siren wailed, a sound that could wake the dead. He washed his face in the small basin in his cell, shaved, and dressed in the jumpsuit he kept as neat and smooth as he could. At first, food was passed to him through a slot. Eventually, as he was awarded small liberties, he was allowed to eat breakfast at a table with black and Hispanic men. Ordered not to speak with anyone, he swept and mopped floors until lunch. He spent the afternoons resting quietly in his cell. One of the guards gave him books in Spanish. Educated by Catholic nuns until the seventh grade, he was a slow but competent reader. One of the books was *Don Quixote*. As early as the third page, he was laughing out loud in his cell. He had never known books could be funny. By the end of each tedious day, he was usually asleep before the lights went out.

And there were the two hours every Tuesday and Thursday when he was let into the exercise yard along with dozens of other men. He learned to play basketball: the pleasure of the fast runs, the crafty passes, the graceful leaps. He had always been an instinctive, natural athlete. His basketball games were always with the black and Latino men.

And there were also the Friday visits from Raquel Rematti. Even at the first meeting Juan was at ease with her. They exchanged warm handshakes. Raquel wore tasteful suits, and Juan found that respectful. They often looked directly, calmly into each other's eyes. After the first two visits, she had even started to kiss him quickly on the cheek when she left. He was looking forward to the day when he could give her a quick embrace. She was a shapely woman.

Juan eventually heard rumors—for there were always rumors at mealtimes, in the yard, in the communal weekly showers in the vast shower rooms—that Raquel was a "big, big" lawyer. He was sometimes asked how he had been linked up with a lawyer who, as one of the other prisoners said, was *siempre* on television and in the news. Once one of the prisoners had excitedly told him he had seen Raquel on television the day before. Juan was one of the few prisoners not allowed to spend any time in the recreation room where there was a television. The two other prisoners awaiting trial for murder—both white men, named Lombardo and Gianelli, who always had other men surrounding them in the yard because they were *consiglieres* in the Gambino family—weren't allowed in the television room either.

Juan even felt safe in the prison. None of the guards ever screamed at him. They never pushed him. When they brought him to the cafeteria to meet each Friday with Raquel, who sometimes came with the kind Theresa Bui, the guards were in fact friendly. Juan was easy to get along with, a good inmate.

The sky above the concrete yard was clear. Voices in Spanish and English rang out through the cool, crystalline air. Some of the guards lifted their faces to the sun, their eyes closed, sunning themselves.

Juan didn't notice the compact, muscular white man who hit him with a piece of a broken basketball hoop. Juan was stunned by the sudden impact, by the unexpectedness of the attack itself, the shattering of his sense of safety. He staggered a few feet, his hands at his back. He knew the sticky fluid he felt was his own blood. For a second he was so dazed by surprise and pain that he didn't focus on the fact that he'd been hit with a piece of steel. He thought something must have fallen out of the sky.

Crouching, concentrated, furious, Juan spun around. The man, stalking toward him, screaming in Spanish, *You fucker*, and handling the curved piece of the basketball hoop as if it were a sword, lunged forward like a football tackler. Juan skipped to his left, athletically. The point of the rod, flashing in the sunlight, just missed him.

The squat, muscular man stumbled slightly, thrown off balance by the force of his own momentum in swinging the broken hoop. At that instant, Juan—who was at least five inches taller and almost as muscular—bent and bolted forward. Juan's powerful, hurtling shoulders drove into the left side of the slightly off-balance man. Juan's upraised hand clawed his face, peeling skin off his cheek and groping for his eyes. Juan had been a skillful fighter all his life. His only instinct was to kill this man.

When they fell to the yard's concrete, Juan pressed his knee into the man's chest and pushed his forearm into his throat. The strong man under Juan, who had the moves of a boxer, freed one arm and struck Juan on the ridge of his left eye with power and accuracy. Juan's head flicked to the side, but that powerful fury that had protected him so well in the cocaine market that was his hometown, in the truck during the four-day drive to New York, and in the territory that Oscar Caliente ruled in Manhattan, overcame the pain in his face. The pain didn't matter: Juan had work to do, and it was to kill this man.

Juan was still pressing his forearm into the now-frightened man's throat—was the cartilage starting to give?—when a guard tackled him and another guard struck him over his shoulder with a black club. Juan immediately went still, releasing the pressure on the other man's throat. As he lay on his back he was face to face with the frightened guard who had tackled him. Juan heard his attacker gasping for breath, gagging, sounding like a drowning man.

And then Juan thought about Oscar Caliente. *The only thing I want from people who work for me is you keep your fucking mouth shut. You never heard about Oscar Caliente. Don't ever forget it.*

Motionless, Juan looked up into the completely blue sky. As he waited to be handcuffed, he knew that Oscar Caliente had somehow sent the now stricken, gasping man to remind Juan that he had never known Oscar Caliente.

Juan never felt safe again.

19.

JOAN RICHARDSON USED HER supple, slender body so intensely and passionately that Hank Rawls shouted at the moment he deliriously came deep inside her. For a few exquisite moments she remained on her knees, still moving back and forth against him. Panting, bracing himself, he slipped out of her, gently falling. He felt her shudder. Her hands were still clenching the pillow under her face. She had strong hands. They seemed to be tearing the fabric apart.

His breath came in short, rapid bursts when he said, almost laughing, "This is God's greatest fucking invention."

Sweaty, exhausted, he stretched alongside her on the damp sheets. He was naked. She was under the sheets. She turned, her gorgeous face smiling at him. "I love you," she said.

They embraced. He still had a hard-on. She felt it against her taut stomach, and she pressed into him. "Love you, too," he said.

They slept for two hours during the cool afternoon. Hank, thoroughly rested, feeling absolutely calm, stared at the ceiling of the bedroom before she woke up. It was early winter. The curtains on the windows were pulled to the side. Wintry light filled the room. There was an unobstructed view of the heights of the trees in Central Park. Since the sun was beginning to set, its light passed through the trees' bare upper branches. On the bedroom ceiling traces of light and shadows moved over the white surface.

Joan was still asleep as Hank Rawls gently lifted her right hand off his chest. He went into the bathroom, also flooded with late afternoon light from a translucent window, and urinated. He washed his face and hands and his tumid penis. Gradually he remembered that when he had arrived late in the morning he was as angry as he had been the day before, and that he was angry with her now. It was the day after he had been torn down by dour Menachem Oz in the presence of the rapt jurors and the black-suited Margaret Harding. Margaret's defiant and attractive face bore a sardonic smile when Rawls said that he'd spent at least five or six hours with Joan Richardson—from late morning to late afternoon—on the day her husband was killed. The memory of her disdain was etched in his mind.

When Joan finally stirred in the quiet bedroom, he said, "Sweetheart, let's go around the corner to the diner. Dress down." It was time to talk to her. He needed to know what lies she had told Menachem Oz. Once he heard them, he would have a perfect excuse to tell her that their affair was over: he could display his anger to her, he would have a reason for leaving.

As he sat on a chair in the bedroom, he watched her through the open bathroom door. They were so familiar with each other that she made no effort to hide what she was doing. Naked, she sat on the toilet. She peed so intensely that from twenty feet away he heard the hiss from the toilet. Then she combed her hair and swept it up to the back of her head; strands fell to the nape of her neck. Just the sight of her luxurious hair alone, Rawls thought, could give him another hard-on. Did he really want to dump her?

At only four in the afternoon, the big Greek diner at 73rd Street and Madison Avenue, five blocks from Joan's apartment, was empty except for the hairy, Greek-speaking waiters and two other customers—a blue-haired ancient woman in a wheelchair and the Jamaican-accented black woman who took care of her. Two reporters—one from the *Times* and another from the *New York Observer*—followed them into the diner and sat at the counter. Joan and Hank recognized and ignored them.

They sat in a booth with vinyl seats, the worn Formica table gleaming between them. "Joan," he said after they ordered a Greek salad for her and a spinach omelet for him, "I had a bad day yesterday. A really, really bad day."

She'd expected him to say this. She girded herself: she loved him and for that simple reason didn't want to lose him.

"He's an awful little man," she said.

"Listen, Joan. I don't want to talk about how ugly Menachem Oz is. Or how bad his suits are. Or what a cheap bitch Margaret Harding is. This is what's important: Oz asked where I spent the day Brad was killed. I told him I was with you, here, in the city, at your apartment. Harding had come into the room at that point, as if on cue, eager to hear what I said. They obviously knew, I realized, that one of us is lying. What did you tell them?"

Hank waited as Joan's blue eyes gazed at him. "I lied. I started lying on the night I drove out there. I have no idea why I did it. Probably to protect you."

"To protect me?"

"I think so. I thought it would make a mess for you if they knew you were with me all day."

"I didn't need protection."

She nodded. "I know that now, I probably knew that then."

"You're the one who needs protection, Joan. It's serious business to lie to these people and more serious, of course, to get caught. I think you have to talk to your lawyer, admit to the lie, and beg forgiveness."

She glanced at the reporters drinking coffee and talking to each other at the counter, acting as though they were casual customers who happened to meet in a diner. Joan, who had once welcomed reporters, now detested them. Lowering her voice, she said, "Yes, I need to do that. And I first need to tell you the truth."

"Confession is good for the soul, Joan. What else did you tell Oz that you think I should know about?"

"He asked lots of questions, Hank. Too many. I'm smart. But even I got confused. And afraid."

They didn't speak during the time the Greek waiter with the big gold chain around his neck placed their food in front of them and asked, "Need anything else now?" He was gruff and unpleasant: there was that sibilance in his Greek accent that male waiters in Greek diners all seemed to have.

With a friendly gesture and his engaging smile—that demeanor that had led him to win every election campaign he'd ever run except the last one—Hank Rawls said, "No, thanks." And, as soon as the waiter left, he said to Joan Richardson, "And what did you tell them about us?"

"That we have been lovers for months, long before Brad died."

"I told them the same thing. They also asked the next obvious question because Menachem doesn't start down a path until he gets to the end: Did Brad know about us?"

"What did you say?"

"That we were in plain view. That I had a history of appearing with women in plain view, particularly on beaches. I'm not sure Menachem knew what I was talking about."

"Did anybody in the room know what you were talking about?"

"I'm sure some did. Most of them were certainly old enough to remember those pictures on the beach. But everybody was hard to read. It was, as the comedians say, a tough audience." He smiled at her, a smile that always disarmed her. "And he asked me questions about you and Brad."

"What questions?"

"For example, whether I knew Brad was gay."

"And you said?"

"I said I didn't know, but I'd been told he was, and I asked why it mattered. And, as I should've known, Menachem didn't answer me. They live in a perfect world, Joan: they get to ask all the questions."

She moved her fork over the surface of her salad, not touching it. "Did they ask you how you knew Brad was gay?"

"Simple, Joan: I said you told me, that this was one of those cases where the wife might have been the first, not the last, to know." Hank sipped his Diet Coke. "And what did you tell them?"

"That it took two years into the marriage for me to find out that Brad had boyfriends, not girlfriends. That I had suspected it for a long time, because of Brad's mannerisms, his glances at some of our male friends. I said that when I asked Brad years ago, point blank, he didn't deny it."

"Did they ask you about Trevor? That guy from last summer? The songwriter? The interior decorator? Whatever the hell he is?"

Joan glanced at the diner's wallpaper: a beige scene of a hillside above a Greek village. Every Greek diner in the city appeared to have wallpaper that memorialized the Icarus myth. In the pastel air there was an image of a boy falling gracefully, wings extended, toward his death in the Aegean Sea. *Icarus*. She said, "Trevor had already talked to the Grand Jury. Thank God I volunteered his name before they asked too many questions, or they would have caught me lying again, denying I knew him."

"How do you know Trevor was there?"

"He's one of those gay nellies who loves to gossip. He calls everybody girl. 'Girl, did you hear about this one?' He despises anyone's privacy. Brad was involved with him, and I was so used to this that I even had dinner with just the three of us, usually at Bobby Van's in Bridgehampton, usually in the middle of the week. The world was there to see us. Brad liked having him around so much that I just gave in at a certain point and didn't resist. I can't stand the little pest."

Hank Rawls, too, looked at the pastel wallpaper. That single scene of Icarus falling was repeated again and again through the diner's interior between every seam in the wallpaper. "And they asked me about Juan Suarez and you."

She pushed her food aside and reached for his hand. His fingers were closed and didn't respond to her touch. She asked, "Did they ask what you knew about why Juan killed Brad?"

"No, Joan, they never asked that. They asked about what kind of relationship you had with Juan."

"God, what's going on?" she said. "This is too much. He worked for us. We paid him. We paid his wife, too, and sometimes we had his little kids over to play at the pool. What did you say?"

Hank spoke quietly, "I told them the truth, Joan. I told them I didn't know anything more than the fact that he worked for you. And Oz asked me what kind of work, and I said that all I had ever seen was that he worked at the parties. I never saw anything else."

Still whispering, Joan said, "What else did he ask? Was there anything else?"

"He asked me if I knew that you were having sex with Juan Suarez."

"My God," she said. "Where does this end?"

"Did you?" Hank asked.

"No, Jesus Christ, no."

He glanced at her, and then looked away. To Joan, he now looked impatient, or weary, or skeptical. His sweet, exhausted groans that afternoon as he collapsed at her side seemed to have happened in another world and long ago. "He also asked if you knew Juan's real name."

"Wasn't Juan his real name?"

"Was it?"

"Of course, at least that's the only name he gave me."

"Menachem seemed to think his real name was Anibal, Anibal Vaz. Did you ever hear that name?"

"When he asked that question I said no."

"And that was a lie, wasn't it, Joan? Why are you lying to me now?"

Sliding to the side the plate with the food she hadn't touched, she put her hand over his clenched hand. "I'm not," she said. "Not about Juan Suarez. He was a handyman. He worked for us for months. Brad was attached to him. But the truth is Brad had reached the point where it was hard for him not to court another man. Court is the right word—Brad had the manners of a Southern gentleman. Something may have happened between him and Juan. And Juan killed him."

This is insane, Hank thought. *She has no idea what the truth is.* As he'd been doing for the last twenty-four hours, Hank was calculating the losses he might soon suffer by having been her lover before her husband died and by continuing as her lover—as what the newspapers called the "lady billionaire's boyfriend"—after her husband's death. When he searched his name in Google, Bing, or Yahoo the first five pages were sensational entries about his relationship with Joan Richardson, as if that were all he had ever done in life. It was only deep into his Google pages when a reader looking for information about Hank Rawls would see that he had been a United States Senator, had briefly run for President, and was a best-selling novelist, and an actor. Fifty years from now, when people looked at the Internet to learn about him they would come away with the impression that all he had done in life was to be the boyfriend of a very rich woman whose husband had been murdered in the Hamptons. He said, "And they asked me how much money you inherited from Brad."

"How could you know, Hank?"

"They were fishing. Hell, maybe Mr. Oz has it in his mind that a gorgeous woman has to buy my love." For the first time in the conversation he gave her one of his engaging smiles: he had the gift of lighting up any space he inhabited. "But Hank Rawls can't be bribed."

She smiled, briefly. "This is really painful, Hank. I loved Brad for a very long time. I had my difficulties with him. He had his with me. But, God, don't these people realize that it was my husband who was killed? Don't they know what I saw when I walked into that house? I could smell the blood in that room. His and the dogs' blood." She closed her eyes. "I know they think I had him killed, and that I hired Juan Suarez—my lover—to do it."

"Both of us have to live in the real world, Joan. And the real world for us today is that Mr. Oz and his bosses want to get more than the conviction of a Mexican gardener. And they have a license to roam anywhere they want, and they are looking at you, at me, at Ozzie and Harriet, at al-Qaeda. But we are the most obvious."

She leaned across the Formica table, whispering. "I'm scared, Hank."

"And there's something else, Joan. You lied to them. That makes them very angry. You hurt their case against Juan. Before they can use you as a witness, they are going to have to tell Rematti you lied to them and to the Grand Jury."

She waited for more. When he didn't say anything, Joan asked, "Do you want to leave me?"

How many times, he wondered, had he heard this question? Twelve? Fifty? He'd never spent more than two years with any one woman, and, as a beautiful, golden-haired boy, he had started a lifetime with women when he was fifteen. When he had to abandon his short campaign for President after the pictures on the beach first appeared in the *National Enquirer,* he briefly saw a psychiatrist. She was a woman who had treated at least seven other Senators. She probed him about why there had been so many women in his life. She said there had to be complex answers.

For him, the real answer was simple and obvious. He was attracted to women, and there were many women in the world, and many of them were as restless, fun-loving, and adventurous as he was. *Why not?* was the real question, and *Why not?* was the real answer.

And, besides, there was this: the most intense pleasure in his life—more intense than winning elections, giving speeches on the Senate floor, appearing at parties for his books and now for the movies in which he had roles—was that moment when he first entered a new woman, that moment when her vagina embraced him, the newness of it, the pleasure, the closeness, the movements, the words, the odors.

Hank Rawls was not about to abandon that for Joan Richardson, as gorgeous as she was, and until now as vital and fun-loving as she had been. He had arrived at her apartment earlier to tell her he was leaving because she was a liar. But now he decided he could postpone that, at least for another day or week or more.

Hank Rawls raised her hand. He kissed her fingers. He said, "Let's go back to the apartment."

20.

KATHY SCHIAVONI ENTERED HER seven-digit code on the keypad next to the door that led to the windowless, musty locker room in which current case evidence was stored. Once inside the room, her first task was to write in an old-fashioned ledger her name, her time of arrival, and the purpose of her visit. She wrote: "Examination of the Richardson sheets."

There was always a metallic chill in the room; there was also always the smell of chemicals and compounds—formaldehyde, ammonia, and cordite and gun grease from the confiscated bullets, pistols, and weapons that were stored there.

She walked directly to box 6773, one of the more than two thousand lockers in the warehouse-size building. She knew the combination to the lock and opened it.

The box was empty.

Kathy Schiavoni walked to the computer near the entrance to the icy room. The computer contained information disclosing who had access to lock box 6773. Only her name appeared on the screen, with seven different dates of removal and return. No one else had signed in to remove the sheets and no one had signed them out.

Kathy was methodical and deliberate, so different from her earlier self when she was rootless and confused in her six fugitive years in Manhattan. As soon as she left the building, she scrolled on her cell phone to Bo Halsey's number. He was the only man in the world she believed she could trust.

After leaving the Army in 1987, Bo became a friend of her difficult father, a Vietnam veteran. Bo joined the VFW club in Sag Harbor, the youngest member of the group, because her father had asked him to do that. Years later, she and Detective Halsey, now approaching early retirement age, had worked on three cases together. Her contacts were usually with the haughty lawyers in the District Attorney's office, who treated forensic technicians like servants. Whenever she needed to speak to a field person—a cop with "boots on the ground" as they liked to describe themselves ever since Bush invaded Afghanistan and Iraq—she turned to Bo Halsey. Without ever expressing it, he felt an obligation to give special treatment to Kathy Schiavoni; she had been a lost, unhappy teenager when he first knew her but had evolved into a dedicated professional. He admired her. Transforming yourself was tough. He knew that to move from lost to found, from dead to alive, to be the prodigal child returning home, was a kind of miracle.

He recognized her number on his own cell phone when it vibrated and lit up. He was fishing in the channel of salt water that flowed under the stone bridge linking Sag Harbor to North Haven. Bo Halsey spent hundreds of isolated hours fishing there every season of the year, even in the winter on the days when the weather was mild. He had found as he grew older that he preferred the slowness of fishing for salt-water bass in this channel to deep-sea fishing or fishing from the beaches along the Atlantic coastline in Southampton, East Hampton, and Montauk. And he preferred the winter months, when he was almost always the only fisherman.

"I'm in Riverhead," she said. "I'd like to see you. It'll take me forty-five minutes, maybe thirty, to get there."

"Take your time," he said, "I'll be here all day."

Almost an hour later, Kathy parked on Long Wharf in Sag Harbor and walked to the bridge. The marinas, which in the summer were crowded with colorful boats and yachts, stretched around her, entirely empty. The American flag snapped at the top of the flagpole at the entrance to the marina: the metal fastenings on the ropes struck the hollow pole, resonating. Below the bridge Bo Halsey stood on the stony shore. He was alone. His hands were on the filament-line of his fishing rod. The water that raced through the channel was shallow, passing over rocks and sand rivulets, like rapids in swift water in the mountains.

A somewhat overweight, ungainly woman, Kathy walked unsteadily down the slope to the shore. She held her left hand above her eyes to shield them from the bright winter sunlight that glittered over the water. Bo Halsey was gazing at the place in the icy, fast-moving water where his lead had landed.

He said, "To what, as they say, do I owe this honor?"

They didn't need any small talk or pleasantries to start a conversation. They knew each other that well.

"Something's really pissed me off."

"What can bother anybody on a great day like this?" He moved his fishing pole like a wand: the sinuous line again arced above the fast-flowing water and then came down thirty yards from the shore. Bo hadn't once looked at her. Never married, he was essentially shy with women, even with her.

"I was testing the sheets from the Richardson bedroom for the Suarez case. I looked in the evidence box an hour ago. The sheets have gone missing."

He now turned toward her, smiling. "Funny how evidence can just get up and take a walk around the building." When he met her at her parents' house while she was still in high school, her father wanted them to feel as though they were older brother and younger sister, despite the age gap between them. Brothers tease little sisters, Halsey thought.

"Bo, cut out the shit please. I'm totally aggravated. I told Harding that Suarez's DNA was on the sheets, that Brad Richardson's DNA was there. And that Joan Richardson's vaginal stains were there as well."

"You should wash your mouth out with soap." He laughed and wanted her to laugh as well. "You ladies in the lab talk pure filth."

"Nice going, Bo. But I need you to listen. There was another person's DNA. From sperm, on the sheets."

"It's always a good idea to wash your sheets after a murder."

"I asked Harding to get a search warrant for a sample of Hank Rawls's hair."

Turning again toward the water, Bo Halsey steadily reeled in the line. He cast again. The tip of the rod, propelled by the deft motions of his left hand, swept back and forth, a blur except for the edges of the arc where each sweeping motion seemed to stop momentarily as though in a freeze frame before becoming a blur again.

"And you want hairs from the head and crotch of a once-upon-a-time Presidential candidate? Right?"

Kathy Schiavoni knew that every conversation with Bo Halsey was a process of excavating through his cynical demeanor, bred by four years in the Army, and more than twenty years as a cop in New York City, to a level where he was somewhat softer, somewhat more open, and thoughtful. It was difficult to get there. She said, "I think Suarez is entitled to know who put the extra semen stain on Joan Richardson's bed. The jury's entitled to hear that."

A crystalline breeze blew inland from the wide harbor, chilling both of them and rattling the branches of the desiccated nearby reeds and brush. "Hey, baby, I think it's up to the dark princess and her frog prince Lupo to decide who gets hit with the pleasure of a search warrant. Five cops crashing into your house with a search warrant for your crotch hair is a pretty big deal."

"Bo, listen to me, there was obviously another man in the house sometime just before or during the day Richardson was killed. Suarez's lawyer has a right to know that and to know who it was."

"Rematti has no reason to have any idea that you're testing the bed sheets, Kathy. Forget it. It is all, as they say, irrelevant and immaterial. That was not the room where Richardson lost his head. What happens in people's bedrooms stays in the bedroom."

"Isn't that where the money was stolen?"

"Do you think people were having sex with Mrs. Richardson between the time her husband and the dogs had their heads taken off and when the money was lifted? Come on."

"Come on, Bo, this is important to me. You're the senior guy in the office. You might not even need a search warrant. Just contact Rawls and see if he'll come in voluntarily to give it to you."

Bo genuinely liked Kathy Schiavoni. He had once even thought about asking her out to dinner, but his innate, crippling shyness about women prevented him. "When I was in the Army, Kathy, a spade from Detroit was taking a shortcut in front of the company headquarters. It was a dirt yard. But it had signs on it saying 'Keep Off the Grass.' There was no grass, it was as bald as my head. A lieutenant from some fucking place like Louisiana, a classic redneck, Gomer Pyle-type of guy, walks by and yells, 'Soldier, you're walking on my grass. Say sorry to my grass,' The black guy looks at the dirt, then says to the lieutenant, 'Never gonna happen, sir,' and walks away." Bo paused. "Never gonna happen, Kathy. I'm a year away from retiring early. I could give a rat's ass about some guy's pubic hair, Juan Suarez, Margaret Harding, Richie Lupo, Brad Richardson, Raquel whatever the fuck her name is."

He saw that Kathy was angry and struggling with what to say. "I'll handle this myself, then, Bo."

Staring at her, remembering her as a teenager, Bo said, "Be careful, Kathy. I want you to be safe."

Just as Kathy Schiavoni turned to walk up the slope, the silvery line of Bo Halsey's fishing rod rose, snake-like, iridescent in the bright air.

21.

RICHIE LUPO'S OFFICE WAS sprawling. Located in a drab two-story municipal building constructed almost entirely of brown cinderblocks in the outskirts of Riverhead, it overlooked a high school football field with deep ruts in the brown grass. In contrast to the drabness of the other offices in the building, the office of the District Attorney of Suffolk County had wood-paneled walls, bookcases, a credenza filled with law books, and Richie's many trophies and memorabilia on every available surface except his desk, which was completely clear.

Raquel Rematti, who always tried to meet the head of every prosecuting office she dealt with, recognized from the first handshake that Richie didn't like her. He did little to conceal the contempt he wanted to convey for a lawyer who had a storied career. In Richie's domain in Suffolk County he barely tolerated outsiders who came in to represent clients, and Raquel Rematti was a special outsider. Raquel, for her part, wasn't going to let the hostility bother her. This visit was not about her; she had a reason to be there.

"Thanks for letting me see you, Mr. Lupo. And Margaret, it's good to see you again, outside of the courtroom."

Glancing first at Margaret Harding and then at Raquel, Lupo said, "Ms. Rematti, what can we do for you?"

"You can help me save a man's life."

Riche Lupo glanced again at Margaret Harding, as though looking for guidance in how to deal with this woman. "Help me understand," he said to Raquel. "You've lost me already."

"I went to visit my client last Friday."

"Which client is that?"

"I only have one client out here at the moment, Mr. Lupo. That's Mr. Suarez."

"What do you want to tell me about Mr. Suarez?"

"When I saw him last Friday his face was bruised and he had a stab wound in his back."

"He's gotten proper medical care, hasn't he?"

Raquel wasn't surprised that Riche Lupo already knew about the attack. She said, "His medical care is not my major concern. He's young and strong. He'll survive the bruises and wounds. But obviously his life is in jeopardy."

"How so? Did he tell you that?"

"Not at all. Mr. Suarez is a stoic. He said very little, but it's clear, isn't it, that he didn't slip and fall in the shower."

"You know, Ms. Rematti, I got an incident report from the prison." He touched a piece of paper on his desk and glanced at it as though checking a sentence. Richie Lupo said, "He seems to have attacked another prisoner, unprovoked, and that prisoner was severely injured."

With an unexpected edge of anger in her voice, she said, "It didn't happen that way. People with stab wounds in their backs generally aren't the attackers."

"Is that right? I should believe one Juan Suarez, if that's his name, and not three prison guards who filed the incident report? Now why in God's name should I do that?"

"What you should do, Mr. Lupo, is take whatever steps you need to take to protect my client's life."

"Take steps? I don't know what happens in other parts of the country, Ms. Rematti, but in this part of the world the DA's office has absolutely no control over prison security. That's all up to the prison. I'm sure you know that. Pigs will fly before the prison listens to me."

"Look, I want to avoid taking this to the judge. You know as well as I do that all you have to do is pick up the phone and the prison will do much more to protect him. The judge doesn't want a dead defendant on her hands."

"Go to the judge, Ms. Rematti, be my guest, and she'll give you exactly the same answer I'm giving you—the prisons make their own rules and do what they feel they need to do to create a secure environment. Secure, that is, for the guards, the other inmates and, last on the scale of priorities, your client."

"I don't think she has that narrow a view of the scope of her powers."

"You know what, Ms. Rematti? I think I know the judge far better than you do. She and I went to law school together at Hofstra. I can't stop you from asking her to get what you think your client deserves. In fact, your client should have thanked his lucky stars that he was able to get around the prison for work and exercise and meals. They've been pretty lenient toward him. If I had anything to say about it, he'd be in lockdown twenty-four hours a day, seven days a week. Which is where he is now, and he may stay there for good. That should protect him."

"Somebody tried to kill him, sir. I see jails that are more humane in Alabama."

Richie Lupo was staring at Margaret Harding as though looking for her to express admiration for him, for his bravery in challenging the legendary Raquel Rematti. "I don't know anything, Ms. Rematti, about jails in Alabama. This isn't Alabama. It's Suffolk County."

The words that formed in Raquel's mind were distinct—*You're an asshole, Richie Lupo*—but years of self-discipline suppressed the words. Finally she said, "Mr. Lupo, I can have the *New York Times* and CNN here in ten seconds to hear about the attempt to kill my client and the fact that the guards, after turning their backs on the assault, then filed a false report. They intervened only after Mr. Suarez got the upper hand."

Richie Lupo was now angry. He leaned toward her. "Bring them out, Ms. Rematti. You know what? I don't give a flying fuck what they say. As I said, this is Suffolk County. I like it fine here. I'm not going anywhere, and I don't want to go anywhere. Anderson Cooper can piss all over me. I win elections, he doesn't."

Raquel too was angry. She was almost startled by Richie Lupo's rant. In her career she'd had many tense and acrimonious encounters with prosecutors—after all, this business was not for the faint at heart—but there was something outside the pale, off-the-reservation, about Richie Lupo, who resembled Mitt Romney but spoke like Rush Limbaugh. Was he, she wondered, putting on an act for the very attractive Margaret Harding? Was he crazy? "I get the complete picture now, Mr. Lupo." She stood up. "I'm going back to planet earth."

As Raquel left the room, she heard Richie Lupo and Margaret Harding laugh. It was loud and derisive laughter.

22.

THE VIDEOTAPE WAS GRAINY. Bo Halsey had spent hundreds of hours in his career staring at blurred photographs and then, with the advent of surveillance cameras everywhere, the faint images of people on tape. After five repetitions of the three-minute tape, he recognized the men depicted on it. They were Cerullo and Cohen. They were hastily moving cash from the Richardsons' stately bedroom to the bathroom. While there was no surveillance tape of the bathroom, Cerullo and Cohen weren't carrying it out of the house then. Bo Halsey knew they were hiding it.

"When did you see this tape?" Halsey asked Ang Tien, the youthful Asian technician who, two days earlier, had asked for an appointment with him.

"Last week."

"Why were you looking at tape from the bedroom? He was killed in his office on the first floor."

"Someone from the security company must have been like curious. She would have known the locations in the house where the security systems were. It's a subtle system, kind of beyond the state of the art technologically, you know. Like very advanced. It doesn't rely on cameras. It relies on sensors that aren't like visible to anyone looking for them. So she probably thought it would be like interesting to review footage from a house where, you know, a murder happened."

"And she knew to look in the bedroom?"

"Apparently."

"Why would anyone in his right mind have a surveillance camera in his bedroom?"

Ang Tien was young, geeky. Halsey knew that Ang spent hundreds, possibly thousands of hours every month gazing into computers. He had no friends or girlfriends; his computer life was the only life he wanted to lead. Bo Halsey was once impatient with the young generations of police officers who worked for him and who used *like* and *you know* in every sentence. But, despite that annoying tic, many of them were smart and hard-working. Ang Tien, the grandson of a Vietnamese soldier who had fled Saigon in a helicopter in 1975 as the North Vietnamese army rolled to victory, was very smart: he had helped Bo in other cases, and his information and results were always reliable.

"Have you shown this to anybody else?"

"No. You're in charge of the investigation. I thought, you know, I should go directly to you."

"Do you recognize the men in the tape?"

"No."

"Do you see what they're doing?"

Ang Tien was struck by the question because it was so unnecessary. He wondered for a moment whether Bo Halsey was taunting him. It was obvious what the men were carrying.

At last Ang said, "They're like carrying cash."

"Is there any other footage of them later that night?"

"No, just as there's no footage of them before this scene. The sensors in Richardson's office were turned off like about five minutes before he was killed. But not in the bedroom, like whoever turned it off in the office didn't, you know, do it in the bedroom. The surveillance system is in zones, and the service can be turned off with a password in a keypad, but there were like different keypads in that house."

Halsey had Ang replay the scene. At the start of the sequence, Cohen and Cerullo were repeatedly glancing toward the ceilings, searching for telltale camera eyes. Bo Halsey was disturbed by the scene, but not surprised. Years earlier, when he was a narcotics detective in Manhattan, Cerullo and Cohen had risen quickly through the ranks and become detectives. Neither of them worked for or directly with Halsey, but the word on the job was that they were rogues, executing search warrants for drugs and cash in targeted apartments and entering on the inventories only half the cash and drugs. They kept the rest. Halsey was already working for the Suffolk County Police when first Cerullo and then, a year later, Cohen joined the department. They came from politically connected families in Suffolk County. They now reported directly to Bo Halsey, and the three of them were the ranking homicide detectives in the county. They annoyed him, he thought they were jerks, and he no longer tried to conceal his contempt for them.

Ang Tien asked, "Who are they?"

"How the fuck do I know?" Halsey asked. "Sit on this until I tell you what to do."

Ang Tien was very obedient. "Sure, Detective. It's easy to save. I'll give it to you when you need it."

23.

MARGARET HARDING, IN A soft voice, said, "Can we talk, Raquel?"

They had just finished a brief, routine appearance in court. Raquel was surprised by the question. Since the last meeting with Harding and Richie Lupo, Raquel experienced something she hadn't allowed herself to feel in years: she was angry with them, and she took their attitude personally, as an affront to her. It was Raquel's style not to engage in angry exchanges, not to try to intimidate other lawyers by screaming at them, and not to conduct herself as anything other than a calm, determined, dignified lawyer. It was a rare approach for a lawyer anywhere, and particularly rare in New York. She found she was more effective when she didn't allow herself to be antagonized or insulted. Her crafty mother, born in Italy, had told her, "You can kill with kindness, Raquel, and if you stay calm you'll live longer." So her lingering anger and resentment had unsettled her for several days; the disquieting feelings had just started to lift when Harding spoke to her.

"Margaret, certainly, let's talk," Raquel said, almost brightly, as if they were agreeing to have coffee together. "Theresa will join us."

Standing attentively nearby, Theresa Bui looked surprised but pleased. Over the last several weeks Raquel had recruited her into the work of defending Juan Suarez. Theresa was diligent and orderly; she was also a gifted writer who crafted skillful and effective letters, affidavits, and briefs. This skill was important in any case, and especially so in a case such as this one: CBS had already done a half hour broadcast, *Murder in the Hamptons*, about the case. Everything Raquel did was scrutinized. All the court filings were lodged electronically with the court. And as soon as they were filed the Internet lit up with the news. The reactions for "comments" routinely vilified her.

Raquel always told her students that, even for a dynamic trial lawyer, writing was ninety-five percent of the work a lawyer did. The time a trial lawyer spent in a courtroom was a fraction of her time devoted to writing in the office. "Five percent inspiration," Raquel told her Columbia students, "ninety-five percent perspiration." For Raquel, having Theresa working with her lessened some of the burden, and in any event Raquel had mentored other women lawyers over the years.

And Raquel recruited Theresa because she liked her. Although Theresa had initially acted as if she were in awe of Raquel—and she was—she soon let her guard down. Theresa moved in a world of people under thirty-five, a world Raquel didn't really know but wanted to know because it seemed to be fun. Theresa lived on the lower East Side, she was attractive, she had many casual and serious friends, she went to clubs, she knew everything there was to know about social media. And she saw that Raquel Rematti, although famous, had few friends and needed them since, as Theresa knew, she was in the early stages, of recovery from a dreadful disease, no matter how robust she seemed.

With the heels of her stylish high-heeled shoes clicking on the floor, Margaret Harding led them to a door with a sign reading *Jury Deliberating*. The room was empty, as it almost always was. She sat down at the head of a long table. Raquel and Theresa sat to her right.

"Thanks for coming in," Margaret said.

"Thanks for asking us." Raquel smiled at her. "What can we do for you?"

Margaret placed a thin valise on the table. She slid out of it three large glossy pictures that resembled the promotional head-shots actors once used before the Internet. "My guess is," she said, "that you can't know much about Juan Suarez except for what he tells you. He seems to have come out of nowhere and to be no one in particular. His wife, or whoever she was, is gone. The kids are gone. Not one of the immigrants who seem to have known him will talk to us. No one even knows his real name. He might, I suppose, have told you all those things. But I doubt it. He's a liar."

Raquel, who was never going to tell anyone what she discussed with Juan Suarez or any other client, smiled at Margaret, not reacting to the word *liar*.

"We think we know a little bit more about him now. We have an experienced and effective lead detective on this case, Bo Halsey. He's been very curious and he's drilled down. Halsey knows how to do that—MP in the Army, detective in New York City before he came out here. He called on contacts he developed with the DEA."

Raquel was now really interested. The world was awash in drugs, but the DEA only had the resources to follow credible leads. If the DEA had information on Juan Suarez, it could be interesting. She said, "I'm going to ask Theresa to take notes. Is that okay with you?"

"Sure," Margaret answered. "It's probably a good idea. The DEA contacts were productive. A few days ago Halsey received a report and pictures. Let me tell you, Raquel, the pictures bear an uncanny resemblance to Mr. Suarez. But they were taken of a man known to the DEA as Anibal Vaz. Not so long ago he was followed to and through those after-hours clubs in downtown

Manhattan. Anibal Vaz was a very well-dressed, well-placed drug dealer, says the DEA. They were on the brink of picking him up in the city, but he just vanished. They think he was working for a guy named Oscar and that Oscar somehow, through some turncoat law enforcement agents, found out that Anibal Vaz was about to be picked up, and made Anibal Vaz vanish before he could talk."

Raquel continued to wait. Theresa was writing on her notepad.

"I wanted to share these pictures with you," Margaret said, fanning the photographs out in front of Raquel and Theresa.

Raquel looked at the three pictures. The first depicted a serious-looking man in the midst of wildly dancing people. It was taken at that instant when a revolving strobe light illuminated him and the men and women around him. He was Hispanic and handsome, but could have been virtually any handsome Hispanic man, not necessarily Juan Suarez. The second showed the same man, in profile, about to walk into a unisex bathroom from which men and women were entering and leaving. The man was closer to the lens than in the first picture, but still at least twenty feet away. It was obvious as he stood near other people that the man was tall, as was Juan Suarez.

The third picture was certainly of Juan—full face, close, as if he were posing for it—but with no context. It was impossible to know where it was taken: nobody was around him and there was no recognizable background. He did appear to be wearing the same expensive black shirt as the man in the other pictures.

As she slid the three photographs back to Margaret Harding, Raquel said, "Pictures can be deceiving. I can't tell who the gay blade at the party is in the first two pictures. The third is a nice headshot of Juan Suarez."

"Obviously the DEA and now we know more about the context of those pictures. They may not be the only ones we have."

"I don't suppose you'll tell me who took these pictures and when. Or give me the other pictures you have."

"Not today."

After a pause, Theresa asked, "So what do you want from us?"

Margaret Harding was surprised that it was Theresa Bui who spoke. But the question itself didn't surprise her. "Obviously," Margaret said, "we want cooperation from him. The DEA would like to know who he knows and who he worked for. They are in the business of rolling up drug distribution rings. If Mr. Vaz, or Mr. Suarez, knows who a man named Oscar is and where Oscar is, then the DEA may want to urge us to do something for Mr. Suarez."

Raquel said, "Let's assume Juan knows this Oscar . . ."

"We don't have to assume. There's a surveillance tape from a Starbucks on Montauk Highway that shows Oscar and Juan talking."

Raquel never allowed herself to be deflected from a question and was too experienced to reveal any surprise. "So let's assume Juan can help the DEA, what does that do for you? You and Richie are not in the business of rolling up drug rings. You're in the business of getting a conviction for murder. And, although I shouldn't say it this way, you have the most sensational murder of the century so far and an accused man who says he's innocent. Let's assume he pleads guilty to a lesser murder charge and helps to bring down a drug ring. What plea deal involving murder or manslaughter can lighten up his sentence in exchange for exposing a drug ring?" Raquel paused, staring at Margaret Harding. "Where's my incentive to give you any cooperation at all if I can't expect anything important in return?"

Both of them loved engaging in this game. It was a world of suggestions, of tentative concepts and of negotiating options that might not exist. "You're right," Margaret said, "I could care less about drugs. You put it exactly as it is, Raquel. My office is in the business of getting murder convictions. But even when there's only one murder, and we have only one dead man, and only one defendant, we want to get multiple convictions when we can."

"Margaret, I don't think you will even get one. At least not Juan Suarez."

Margaret laughed lightly. "This is what I love about our business. I see black and you see white. And at the end of the day, unlike most situations in life, we get to learn whether it's black or white. Who wins and who doesn't. We have no doubt that we will nail Anibal Vaz."

"Thank God," Raquel answered, almost smiling, "Juan Suarez wins. It's too bad about Anibal Vaz."

"We think your client was not alone. He had accomplices, there were people, such as Oscar, who we think had an interest in Brad Richardson. Those people didn't want to do the dirty, dirty work of getting up close and personal with Brad. Blood is messy, so is brain splatter. Your client knew Brad, knew the house, knew his schedule, knew the security system. And knew the Borzois. Not to mention, and most important of all, he knew where to find hundreds of thousands of dollars in cash in the house. And knew that the Borzois would never bark at him or bite him. This case would have been just a bit easier if your client had bite marks on his ankles."

When Margaret Harding stopped, Raquel smiled at her, trying to lure her into saying more.

"There is one other thing. Six or seven months ago there was a knifing of three men at 101st Street and First Avenue, in East Harlem. It happened just after midnight. Two of the men were seriously injured, the other only slightly. He said the attacker handled a long knife as though he was one of those ninja characters in the movies, or Zorro. The blade flashed around like a sword, this guy said."

"Aren't there twenty knifings in the city every night of the week?" Theresa asked. "I live there."

"Sure, but it was an unlucky coincidence for the knifer. One of the injured men was the son of a cop, a captain. You know what cops are like: you hurt one of their kids and you get tracked down as if you hurt one of the Obama girls. It gets real priority."

Raquel said, "It's a nepotistic tribe. They never heard of equal justice for all."

Margaret shrugged. "They hunted for the guy. They didn't find him. But they did find the knife."

Raquel raised a hand. "And you're going to tell me Juan Suarez's fingerprints and DNA are on the knife?"

"That's right, Raquel," Margaret said. She gathered up the glossy pictures and slowly slid them back into the valise. "I hope we've given you enough to work with."

"Is there anything else?" Theresa asked.

"Not today," Margaret said, smiling again. "Maybe later. Let's see what you come back with. I've put enough food on your plate for now. You need to feed me something now. It's only fair, don't you think?"

24.

ALWAYS QUIETLY WATCHFUL, JUAN sensed that Raquel Rematti was uneasy. Usually she was a woman who looked steadily into people's eyes. Instead, when Juan sat at the plastic table across from her and Theresa Bui, Raquel was staring at a sheet of paper in front of her.

"Raquel," he said, "is something wrong?" He glanced at Theresa. Over the last few weeks he had become comfortable with her presence at these meetings. He was an instinctively smart man: he knew Raquel could not defend him all by herself and recognized that Theresa brought skills that could help Raquel and him. But Theresa's face, usually conveying compassion and sympathy, was at this moment blank, her eyes unblinking.

"I've always said, Juan, that you need to tell me the truth. I have to know what the truth is to help you."

Juan gazed steadily at her, nothing evasive in his expression. "I have, Raquel."

"I'm not sure, Juan. A knife was found in New York City. The fingerprints and DNA on it match your fingerprints and DNA."

"I washed dishes in a restaurant in New York before I come out here."

"You told me that, I know that already. But listen to me: a large knife, almost the size of a sword, was used in an attack in the city. It has your fingerprints. And it has your DNA. The victim's injuries were like those Brad Richardson sustained, although the man didn't die."

"Raquel, one night a waiter who didn't like me told me he was going to get me after my shift. Why does he say this? I don't know. I didn't do anything to him. He said, 'I'll get you outside.' I was afraid he had friends, because he say he did. I don't have any friends, no one to help me. So I took a knife with me. The place is uptown, it was dark. I was on the sidewalk. I had to go to the subway, long walk. The man was across the street. Two guys with him. They run at me, and I run away. Then they all around me. They have knives. I take out my knife. That's how it happened."

"What happened, Juan?"

"I hurt them, Raquel. And then, I don't know, I ran away."

"What did you do with the knife?"

"The guy cut my hand. I couldn't hold onto it." He held up his right hand. On the web between the index finger and the thumb was a white scar. Raquel hadn't noticed it before.

"What happened then?"

"I didn't go back to the restaurant ever again. The cops were all over the place. I was afraid."

"How did you get out here?"

"In a car. There are men who drive us from the city out here. I asked, I paid them money, and they took me."

"Did you know the police were looking for you?"

"I know they were looking for me, Raquel. People tell me the cops know who I was. But all I do is protect myself."

"Juan, they kept the knife and then, when you were arrested out here, your fingerprints and DNA matched the ones on the knife."

"I understand. Those men, Raquel, they were trying to hurt me. I didn't do anything wrong."

"The man who was stabbed with the knife wasn't someone who worked in a restaurant. He was a police captain's son out for the night for fun with friends."

Juan said, "The guy who came after me was called Chico. He worked in the restaurant."

"Are you sure? Really sure? None of the three guys worked in the restaurant. They were all brats who were looking for a good time, for a thrill."

"I don't know, Raquel. It was dark. I thought it was Chico, the waiter."

"The cop's son spent four weeks in the hospital, Juan. He'll never be able to move his arm again. All the nerves and muscles and tendons are cut. When a cop's kid is hurt, they never stop looking for the guy who did it."

"They were trying to hurt me, Raquel. They wanted to kill me."

"That doesn't matter. The police and now the prosecutors out here have a knife you used in New York in the way someone out here used a knife on Brad Richardson and the Borzois."

"I didn't hurt Mr. Richardson. I hurt those people, not Mr. Richardson."

There was a pause in the room. "Why didn't you ever mention this before?" Theresa asked.

Without any hostility, Juan looked from Theresa to Raquel. "I wanted you to like me. Both of you. So I didn't tell you that."

"And there's something else, Juan," Raquel said.

"What?"

"I need to know your name."

"Juan Suarez."

"Are you sure?"

"Juan Suarez, Raquel."

"Is that your name?"

"Juan Suarez."

"Is your name Anibal Vaz?"

"No, Raquel."

"Didn't you once tell Joan Richardson that your name was Anibal?"

"Did she tell you that?"

Theresa repeated Raquel's question: "Did you tell Joan Richardson that your name is Anibal Vaz?"

He was still calm. "No."

Raquel was totally focused on him. "Did you ever sell drugs?"

"I did, a little."

"Where?"

"In New York."

"Only there?"

"No, Raquel, a little out here, too."

How disarming he is, Raquel thought, how much like one of those men whose simplicity and attractiveness and sincerity were so compelling—men like the engaging Ted Bundy who was so successful in persuading so many women to go to private places with him before he killed them. A deadly charmer.

Normally skeptical about the stories most of her clients told her, Raquel wanted to believe him. "When did you do that?" she asked.

"Why are you asking me these things, Raquel?"

"Because one of the things I have to do to protect you is to see whether there is information you can give to the prosecutors about other people. I do that because if you have information about other people that's valuable to Harding then she might give you some kind of break."

"What kind of break?"

"We're not there yet. She and I haven't talked about that yet. I can't get there unless you have information about crimes other people did. They won't give you any kind of break, whatever it might be, until I tell them what you might know about what other people have done. It's a step at a time. We go first." She paused. "Do you understand?"

"I do."

"So talk to me."

He held her gaze. "Tom Golden, the guy I used to work for before the Richardsons ask me to work, paid me in cash. I don't think he's supposed to do that. So did the Richardsons."

"That kind of thing is not important, Juan. Not at all. What you need to know is something, anything, far more important."

"I'm not sure, Raquel."

"Let me try this, Juan. Who gave you the drugs to sell?"

"Some guy named Jocko."

"Jocko," she repeated. "How about some guy named Oscar?"

"Oscar?"

"Was there a man named Oscar?"

Juan leaned backward in the small, cafeteria-style plastic chair. "Oscar?" he said.

"They know about someone named Oscar. Oscar runs a big drug gang, in the city and here. They think you know Oscar."

"I don't."

"You don't? They have a tape of you and this Oscar they're interested in at the Starbucks on the Montauk Highway."

"I do know that Oscar, Raquel."

"How much do you know about him?"

"Raquel, please listen to me. What I know about Oscar is that he had his men try to kill me here and that he'll do it again if he thinks I talk about him. I don't want to die here."

25.

RAQUEL SPENT THE NEXT four days with Theresa Bui at her seaside, slightly rundown and cozy house in Montauk. To Raquel, it was the best season of the year—quiet, cold, isolated. The weekend visitors from the city ordinarily didn't travel farther than East Hampton. Montauk Point, at the far eastern end of Long Island, was another forty-five minute drive beyond East Hampton, too remote for a weekend. The only other people Raquel and Theresa saw were in the local IGA market when they drove to the village for milk, eggs, steak, bread, and three bottles of red wine. It was exactly the kind of weather Raquel loved—fog on the ocean and over the narrow peninsula, even denser fog embracing the deck of Raquel's house, and chilly fog at night when the horns on the distant buoys sounded at sea.

They didn't discuss Juan Suarez when they arrived at the house on Friday evening, two hours after the unannounced headcount at the prison abruptly brought their meeting with him to an end. And they didn't mention him all day Saturday as they did the simple things that made Raquel's weekends here so restful: the morning drive to the village for food; the visit to the old hardware store with its scent of wood, paint, and the varnish on the floor boards that Raquel recalled so vividly from her childhood at the hardware store in Haverhill where her father took her to buy nails and car wash; and the afternoon of reading and sweet, brief naps.

It was when they finished on Saturday night their meal of lobster and squash and a bottle of red wine that Raquel finally asked, "What do you think?"

"About Juan?"

"Yes, Juan."

"I think his name is Anibal Vaz."

"I'm not sure. In one sense it doesn't matter."

"It's troubling, Raquel. Lying troubles me."

Theresa, Raquel thought, was still young. Lying would mean something off-center to her. It still concerned Raquel when a client lied to her, but lying was the coin of the realm, not just in the work she did but in the world in which she lived. Even outside of that world, in life in general, people lied about big things and small things; they lied when there was no need to lie, as when someone who has driven twenty miles says she drove thirty, and they lied about issues that matter—a wife claiming she was away on a business trip when in fact she spent those days with a lover. And people lied about guilt and innocence.

"Lying troubles me, too, but I can't just accept that what Margaret Harding and the DEA claim is the truth is in fact the truth. Isn't there a line in the New Testament where a lawyer asks Jesus, *What is the truth?* And Jesus, as I recall it, doesn't have an answer to that question. He has a parable." Sipping her wine and smiling, she said, "Jesus didn't like lawyers."

"Does anyone?"

More and more enveloped in the sleepy aura that three glasses of wine brought to her, Raquel looked out through the sliding doors that opened to the deck over the dunes, the beach and the Atlantic. The doors were partially open. She could hear the hiss of the waves.

"Anibal Vaz, Juan Suarez," Raquel said. "There are millions and millions of people out there who have no reason to carry through life the names they were born with. My grandfather was born Giacomo in Italy. At 17 he became Joe and died Joe at 85. That's the name on his headstone. He was never Giacomo again. There always were people, and there are many more now, who have no reason to have permanent names or addresses, birth certificates, driver licenses, marriage licenses. In fact, there are so many people out there who have every reason not to have real names, Social Security numbers, documents. Under the radar screen, off-the-reservation, disappearing, showing up, reincarnating in place after place. And the longer they live the more unmoored and elusive they become."

Theresa turned in her chair to look out at the deck, the dunes, and the sea. "The problem is this, I think. You know those instructions we give to juries at the end of a trial. *If you believe a witness has lied on one issue, you are entitled to believe, if you wish, that he has lied about everything.*"

"I never believed that instruction. No one lies all the time about everything, no one tells the truth all the time. We're all vulnerable, superstitious, fearful, weak. And we are also brave, determined, optimistic against all odds."

Theresa said, "I'd prefer to believe he wasn't lying. And even if he is lying about many things he could still be innocent."

"And isn't it Hemingway who ended *The Sun Also Rises* with Jake Barnes or Lady Brett Ashley saying, *Yes, wouldn't it be nice to think so?*"

At least a mile out on the Atlantic a freighter blew a very long, hoarse whistle. The freighter would soon let go of the last sight of America—the scattered lights lining the ocean beach until they abruptly ended at the old Montauk Lighthouse—and make its long voyage out into the world.

Three days later, as she sat in her office on Park Avenue with Theresa Bui, Raquel stared out at the black steel-and-glass Seagram Building—the prototype of many other office buildings in Manhattan since it was built in the 1950s but still classic and uniquely attractive—while waiting for the conference call with Margaret Harding to begin. Her secretary came on the line several times to say, "Ms. Harding is about to join the call." Outside of the window the sunlight shining along Park Avenue was intense; there were days in New York when the winter sun filling the long avenue was as bright and pure as it was anywhere in the world.

Finally Margaret Harding's voice rang out. "I'm here."

"So am I. Theresa is with me. Who's with you?"

"Dimitri Brown, a new lawyer in my office who will be working on the case."

Raquel said, "Welcome, Dimitri."

"Hello, Ms. Rematti." Dimitri was a woman.

"Anyone else?" Raquel asked.

"Detective Halsey. I mentioned his name to you, remember?"

"Certainly, I met him in the courtroom. How are you, Detective?"

There was a mumbled, indistinct sound, a man's grunt.

"Anyone else?" Raquel asked.

"Two other detectives working on the case, Dick Cerullo and Dave Cohen."

"Good afternoon, gentlemen." Again there was no response.

Her voice resonating over the speakerphone, Margaret Harding said, "I assume this is a follow-up to the talk we had the other day."

Raquel said, "One other question: are you recording this?"

There was a pause during which, Raquel sensed, Margaret was glancing around her room. "No," she said. "What about you?"

"No."

"So go ahead, Raquel, you asked for this conference."

"I spoke to my client. He does know a man named Oscar."

Margaret Harding was, as Raquel had come to recognize, a very experienced lawyer. She said after a pause, "There's no surprise there. It's a pretty common name. Give me more."

"This is only a proffer, of course, as I'm sure the agents understand. It's just me speaking about something that may or may not have been said, that may or may not be known, that may or may not have happened. I'm not the witness."

"We all get that."

"Your instinct about Oscar may be right, and my client may know who he is."

"That's really no surprise either, Raquel. We have the Starbucks tape, after all. More important, we have informants who know both of them. We need to know how often he has seen Oscar, what Oscar has done, who Oscar knows, where Oscar operates, who works for him, what happened at the Richardson home and in the run-up to the murder. It might be that your client knows only a little, in which case we don't need him and he can go away for life. Fuck him. It may be that he knows enough, in which case maybe something can be worked out. I don't know what that might be, but it might be better than life plus 200 years."

Raquel recognized that Margaret Harding was putting on a little show for the boys in the room. But Margaret was also carefully playing out the script for these kinds of negotiations. "Before we go there, Mr. Suarez needs protection."

"Protection? We've been all over this, haven't we? With Richie Lupo? Your client's in solitary confinement."

"That didn't stop some of Oscar's helpers from getting to him. We need another prison. We need anonymity. We need guards who will genuinely protect him."

"And, Raquel, before we go any further we need more information than you're giving us. I don't think your client really understands. Oscar, we are told, is no mere mid-level drug dealer operating with a few mules. He's developing the Sinaloa cartel in the city and now, the DEA believes, out here in the Hamptons, too."

"They can't really believe, Margaret, that lowly Juan Suarez knows what Oscar's plans are for the Sinaloa cartel. How can a guy like Juan Suarez know anything about the strategic planning of the Sinaloa cartel? They are the most dangerous people in Mexico."

"Did you ever ask your client what he did for a living in Mexico?"

"What did he do there?"

"You know how this works, Raquel. You have to tell me."

Raquel leaned toward Theresa and touched the mute key on her telephone. She could hear but not be heard. She said to Theresa, "Do you have any ideas? I think we've gone as far as we can go."

Theresa shook her head.

After she released the mute key and reconnected, Raquel said, "Let's keep the door open, Margaret. We may be able over time to get closer to where you want to be."

"I know you won't be offended, Raquel, to hear this, but the door is closing soon. Our trial starts in three weeks. Once the trial starts I won't be interested in talking. Or as I used to hear older lawyers say when I started working here, 'The boat is leaving the dock.'"

"Ah," Raquel said. "That old dock somehow always manages to stop moving, or the boat gets delayed."

"Don't count on that."

At midnight, Cerullo and Cohen were inside an unmarked police car at a dreary mall in Smithtown, thirty miles west of Southampton. A cold mist created white halos around the mall's lights. The interior of the car was steamy. The heater was blowing dry, irritating air. Soon after they parked, a black Audi sedan slowly pulled to the side of their car, and Oscar Caliente, swift as a phantom, left the Audi and slipped into the seat behind them.

"So," Oscar Caliente said, "what's going on? I don't necessarily enjoy driving out from Manhattan to see you gentlemen in the middle of the night." His English was far more polished than Cohen's and Cerullo's.

"Suarez is talking," Dave Cohen said.

"What is he saying?"

"Not much so far. But there is a chance that pretty soon he'll talk more. His own lawyer keeps on lifting her skirt and then dropping it, suggesting she has information and then going quiet, teasing us. This is how these fucking lawyers make a deal. 'Show me what you've got and I'll show you what I've got.' It's a bullshit game."

"And how do you know that? What's the source?"

"His own lawyer, that Raquel lady," Cohen said. "The only other Raquel I ever heard of was Raquel Welch. And this Raquel, in her day, must have been almost as good-looking."

Oscar stared at Cohen in the same rearview mirror through which Cohen could see Oscar. "I'm not interested in football-and-beer bullshit," Oscar said. "Don't waste my time."

His words did what he intended them to do: they dropped Cerullo and Cohen into an icy bath of fear. It was Cerullo who spoke next, taking over from the rattled Cohen: "We were at what they call a proffer session. His lawyer was on the phone, the DA was in the room with us."

"Go ahead," Oscar said, "I know what a proffer session is. What did she say?"

"That Suarez knows you, and that he might know what you do, who works for you, who you work for. The lawyer wants us to think Suarez knows a lot."

"The problem you have," Oscar Caliente said, "is that Suarez's lawyer knows too much, or she may. I don't like that. That does not work for me."

Cerullo was facing forward as he spoke. He knew that Caliente was glaring at the back of his head. Cohen, still distracted by the fact that he had annoyed Caliente, was staring out the rain-streaked window.

"And she's not the only one," Cerullo said. "There is a Chinese lady who's working with her. She's been in the room with Suarez when Rematti is with Suarez. They know the same things."

Abruptly, Oscar Caliente opened the rear door. As he was leaving, he said, "So that gives you guys two problems. Fix them."

26.

ALL HER YEARS OF experience had given Raquel Rematti an almost unerring sense of the course a trial was taking, just as a ship's pilot has a sense of where the dangers in a channel are. By the second day of trial, Raquel had the unsettling sense that things were going very badly for Juan Suarez and for her. A television reporter had remarked on air after the first day of the trial that the legendary Raquel Rematti had been "flat" in her opening to the jury. And, late at night, when Raquel had replayed her opening on her iPad, she agreed. Her performance bothered her and her memory of it caused a pang of embarrassment. She had the tense sense that she herself was on trial. This was her first trial since the year-long struggle with cancer, the chemotherapy, and the surgery.

In the difficult week before the trial started, as she and Theresa worked twelve-hour days, Raquel was completely unsettled by the sudden lassitude, the all-pervasive weakness, that seemed to infuse the flow of her blood throughout her body. She knew it might be possible that her anxiety made her feel that way and that it was not the first dreadful signal of a recurrence, a resurgence, of the disease. *Please, God, don't let this happen again.*

Although Raquel kept the sensation of weakness and fear to herself, Theresa, who was young, vibrant, and indefatigable, asked three days before the trial, "Raquel, are you all right?"

"I'm fine," she had answered. "Just tired."

Raquel was also worried about her trial instincts. She had not expected Joan Richardson to be the first prosecution witness. The more conventional approach, and the approach she had expected, was that Margaret Harding would start with the detectives. It took Raquel by surprise when Margaret Harding responded to Judge Conley's instruction "Call your first witness" by announcing, "The People call Mrs. Joan Richardson."

From the very beginning, Margaret Harding wasted no time: her first question, after Joan Richardson had spelled her name for the court reporter, was, "Mrs. Richardson, were you married to Brad Richardson?"

"I was."

"What happened to your husband?"

"He was murdered." Joan's voice was clear and forceful.

"When?"

"In October of last year."

"How do you know that?"

"I saw it."

"Did you see his body?"

"I did."

"Where?"

"In our home."

"Where is that?"

"On Egypt Beach, in East Hampton."

The testimony was already riveting, it had the jury's full attention, and Raquel Rematti was startled by the speed of this. It was like opening a movie about an assassination plot with the assassination itself, in vivid detail.

"And what did you see?"

"My husband, his body, blood on the floor."

"Were you with other people?"

"There were detectives and police."

"What else did you see at the time you saw your husband's body?"

"We had two dogs. They were not far from my husband's body. Their heads had been cut off."

"How do you know that?"

Raquel Rematti knew she had to interrupt this flow of questions and answers. As she stood, she said, "Objection. This is not relevant. This is a trial about the murder of a person, not dogs."

Bland-looking as always, Judge Conley spoke distinctly into her microphone. She sounded commanding, as if her ego was enlarged by the television cameras broadcasting the trial to the world. "Ms. Rematti, I instructed both sides not to explain their objections. Just say 'Objection.' I don't need an explanation for this. Objection overruled."

"Let me ask you the question again, Mrs. Richardson. How do you know what happened to the dogs?"

"I saw their heads in one place and their bodies in another."

When Margaret Harding gave a hand signal to a technician, the lighting in the courtroom dimmed. A police video of the room in which Brad was killed appeared on a white screen facing the jurors. Partially covered in a blood-stained sheet, Brad's body was plainly visible.

"Does this film," Margaret asked, "depict what you saw?"

"I don't understand."

And then Margaret Harding made the question simpler. "Is that your husband's body?"

"It is."

Using a laser beam from a wand no larger than a pen, Margaret moved the beam to the area where the dogs lay.

"And those are the dogs, correct?"

"Yes, they are."

The scene faded and then ended. The courtroom lights were restored. "When did you see this carnage?"

"Objection," Raquel Rematti, standing, said.

Judge Conley touched the black frame of her unstylish glasses. "Rephrase the question, Ms. Harding."

"When did you see this?"

"When it happened." Her voice wavered. "I mean, it was what I saw when the police showed me the room where Brad was and where the dogs were."

"Mrs. Richardson," Margaret Harding asked, "what time did you get to your house?"

"It was late, probably the next day, the very early morning of the next day."

"What did you do?"

"I didn't really do anything. I was stunned. When I got out of the car I stood there for a second, or maybe more than a second, and then I saw Detective Halsey.

"Who is Detective Halsey?"

"He was the man who told me my husband was dead."

"What happened next?"

"We walked to the house. I had no idea what was happening, Ms. Harding. I knew he was dead. That my husband was dead. It was like a moonwalk."

As Raquel recognized, Margaret Harding was a very smart trial lawyer. Margaret had carefully prepared Joan Richardson for her testimony and wasn't going to let her wander off the script. She was beginning to wander.

"Listen to me, Mrs. Richardson: what happened next?"

Joan Richardson, her blonde hair tautly drawn to the back of her head, looked at the jurors for the first time, as if understanding that Margaret Harding was trying to give her direction. "I went into the house."

"What happened then?"

"I asked Detective Halsey where Brad was."

"You were still with the Detective, is that right?"

"Yes.

"And then?"

"He took me to Brad's office."

"What happened there?"

"Nothing happened there, Ms. Harding. My husband's body was in that room, under a sheet. And the dogs were there, too. Dead, too."

"Were those dogs that you and Mr. Richardson owned?"

"They were our dogs. They were wonderful Borzois."

Margaret Harding paused, trying to convey a signal to Joan that she was not to refer to the dogs' rare breed. The jurors were middle-aged men and women who had probably never heard of Borzois or, if they had, associated them with aristocratic European owners. "Mrs. Richardson, who was the person who spent the most time caring for the dogs in the six months before your husband was killed?"

"Juan Suarez."

"Do you see Juan Suarez in the courtroom today?"

Without looking directly at Juan, Joan Richardson said, "He's at that table, with Ms. Rematti."

"Why was it that Suarez had contact with the dogs?"

"It was part of his job."

"He was paid to do that, is that right?"

"He was."

Raquel Rematti, who rarely took notes when a witness she had to cross-examine was on the stand, made a mental note that she had to ask Joan Richardson: "Isn't it true that Juan took care of the dogs because he loved them?" If she answered, as she certainly would, that she had no idea whether Juan loved the dogs,

Raquel could then ask whether she had ever seen Juan play with the animals, feed them, wash them, walk them. Why would Juan, Raquel planned to ask the jury during her summation, kill these beloved dogs?

"Did you tell the police that taking care of the dogs was part of Suarez's job?"

"I did. Detective Halsey seemed to want to know about the dogs."

"Listen to me again: Was that the first time you mentioned Juan Suarez's name?"

"I didn't mention any name just then. I said our handyman took care of the dogs."

"And then you were asked his name, isn't that right?"

"I was."

"And you said Juan Suarez, correct?"

"Yes."

"Were you asked anything else about Juan Suarez?"

"That night? I don't remember very much about that night, I'm sorry."

"Stay with me, Mrs. Richardson, I know this is difficult."

"Objection." Raquel knew she had to break up Harding's gambit of trying to establish some sort of sympathy for Joan Richardson as the bereaved widow, the victim, the lady in distress. Raquel saw her more as the dragon lady, as Imelda Marcos or Leona Helmsley, than the grieving Coretta Scott King.

"Overruled."

"Let me ask you again: Did you give the police the name of Juan Suarez?"

"I did."

"What did you say?"

"They asked who had access to the house."

"And you told them?"

"Yes, I mentioned Juan Suarez, the handyman."

"Did the police ask how much access Juan Suarez had to the house?"

"Yes. He had the run of the house."

"Why was that?"

"Brad liked him, Brad trusted him, Juan worked hard, Juan had many talents—gardening, carpenter, electrician, sometimes almost a personal assistant to Brad."

"How long did Juan Suarez work for Brad?"

"Six or seven months."

"Did he work for you as well?"

"Not really. We had maids who worked inside the house. Juan was basically a superintendent of the work that went on outside. I knew what he did for Brad but I didn't direct him or supervise him."

"You said that Juan Suarez had the run of the house, correct?"

"He could come and go as he pleased."

"Did anyone else have the same access to the house? Did anyone else have the run of the house?"

"Just Juan."

"Was there a security system?"

"There was. It was recently installed. It relied, I was told, on heat sensors and other technologies."

"Was it operated by codes?"

"Yes, keypads in different areas of the house."

"Did Juan know the codes?"

"He did, he is a very smart man."

"He had the ability to shut down all or parts of the system, correct?"

"He did."

"How do you know that?"

"I saw him do it. In fact, I saw him giving instructions to Brad on how to do it."

When Margaret Harding paused the steady volleying of the questions and answers—it was exactly the right pace, Raquel knew, for leaving vivid tracks on the jurors' minds—Judge Conley unexpectedly said, "Let's take a ten minute recess. Ladies and gentlemen, I repeat the admonitions I've given you before. Don't discuss the case with one another, don't attempt to independently investigate the facts by going on Google or looking at any kind of media, and keep an open mind until *all* the evidence has been presented. For those of you taking notes, leave your notepads face down on your seats. See you in ten minutes."

During the break Raquel followed Juan, who was dressed in the sport jacket, white shirt, tie, and slacks that she bought for him, into the holding pen outside one of the rear doors to the courtroom. Juan was put in handcuffs as soon as all the jurors left the courtroom.

"We may not have much time, Juan. Harding doesn't have to tell us when she plans to stop asking questions. She could be finished soon after we walk back in there."

Juan, staring at Raquel and Theresa with an expression that conveyed complete calm, said, "And then you ask her questions?"

"That's right," Raquel said, feeling tense and impatient. "But I need you to tell me more than you have about what happened between you and Joan. All you've told me was that you were her boyfriend."

"I was."

"I need to know more about that. Understand me: there is no time left. I can't get her to come back two days from now, or a week from now. I can't ask her many questions now unless I know more about what happened. I need to destroy her."

"All that happened was that we did what men and women do. Mr. Richardson was away, always away."

Although they were separated by bars, they were so close to each other that Raquel could smell his breath, and it was in the odor of his fetid breath that for the first time Raquel detected Juan's fear. She needed to exploit that fear. "Joan Richardson is trying to keep you in jail for the rest of your life, Juan. She told the police that you killed Brad. She said you killed the dogs. She told them where you lived. She is not your friend, Juan. Now she's testifying against you. I don't think she's telling the truth. This is hard to understand, but Harding will ask Joan whether the two of you had sex, and Joan will say yes."

There was a look of surprise in Juan's eyes. "Why does she ask that?"

"Because Harding knows that I know. She had to give me the Grand Jury transcripts yesterday before Joan started testifying. I read that Joan at first denied knowing you as anything other than her yard worker. Then later Joan came and said you and she were lovers."

"Why?"

"Joan is a cold-hearted bitch, Juan. She lies and then when she knows she's been caught in a lie she pretends to tell the truth. That's what liars do. And it's good for Harding to bring out the fact that the two of you were lovers and ask her whether she regrets that and have her say she does and then move on."

"Joan told people about me and her?"

"Listen to me, Juan. You're smart, you're smarter than I am." She sounded exasperated. She recognized that she was more and more troubled by Juan and confused as to whether to believe he was Juan Suarez, Anibal Vaz, or someone else completely. She knew that to some extent she had been taken in by him, by his quiet demeanor, his patience, and his refusal to show any sign of fear. But she still believed, as she had believed from the morning she first saw him, that he hadn't killed Brad Richardson and that he hadn't beheaded the two dogs.

"I'm not smarter."

"Pay attention to me, Juan. It is not good for you that the jury, probably in fifteen minutes, will know that you were fucking Joan Richardson. Do you understand? There's no real evidence against you: no fingerprints, no bloody clothes, no knife, no one who saw what happened. You understand, Juan, don't you?"

He said, "I do," and she had no doubt that he understood.

"What they will have in a few minutes is a motive. No weapon, no witnesses, but a motive. And you're going to hear about it again and again."

Juan said, "I didn't hurt Mr. Richardson. I didn't hurt the dogs."

"Get this, Juan: that doesn't matter. It doesn't matter whether you did it or not. Juan Suarez, they're going to say, had a motive to kill—he imagined himself in love with a very beautiful, very rich American woman, and he believed she was in love with him. Juan Suarez was a man with many troubles in the world: he had no money, he could be deported, the police in New York were after him. Immigration could arrest him. How does he solve his problems? They'll tell the jury that he got it into his head that if he used his knowledge of the house, his knowledge of Brad Richardson's habits, his knowledge of where Joan Richardson was going to be, his knowledge of when the house would be empty, and if he left no weapon and picked a time of the day when Brad was alone, then he could do the perfect killing. They'll say Juan Suarez lived in a fantasy world where he believed that the fact he was having an affair with Joan Richardson meant that if Mr. Richardson was killed Juan Suarez and the beautiful Mrs. Richardson would live happily ever after."

"I never thought that, Raquel." And then, for the first time, Juan became as blunt as Raquel wanted him to be: "Joan Richardson liked to fuck, Raquel. I'm only 29, Raquel. I can fuck all day long.

Anywhere, anytime. Joan liked that. I'm not stupid, Raquel. I had no plans with her. Just to fuck her."

"Talk to me now, Juan. Who started this?"

"She did."

"Did she ever try to end it?"

"She didn't. I wanted to but I didn't want to. Why should I stop? She never said she wanted to stop. She liked what we did."

"Did she ever talk to you about Brad?"

"What do you mean, Raquel?"

"I mean, Juan, did she describe their life, what their marriage was like?"

"She said Brad should just live with one of his boyfriends and that he would be happier."

"Did she know he had boyfriends?"

"Sure, I knew, too. Once Joan was in bed with me. She said, Christ, that son of a bitch was just in here. She was talking about Mr. Richardson and another man, I don't remember his name. And then we really fucked, Raquel. That's what she wanted."

"Did she say anything else to you about Brad?"

"Not to me."

"To anyone else?"

"They argued, many times. She knows how to scream. I heard her say, *You butt fucker, let's break up.*"

"What did he say?"

"I didn't hear him. He never raises his voice."

"What else did you hear her say?"

"She said that she was going to use pictures of Mr. Richardson buying drugs. She took them when he didn't see it. She said she was going to give the pictures to television, newspapers, magazines."

"Did Brad Richardson use drugs?"

"Never saw that."

"Never?"

"Never."

"Did you sell drugs to Brad Richardson?"

"Sell? No."

"Give them to him?

"No."

"Did Joan Richardson use drugs?"

Juan paused. "Yes, the cocaine."

Suddenly the buzzer that signaled when Judge Conley was about to re-enter the courtroom sounded. One of the guards said, "It's show time, ladies and gents."

Juan stepped back while the guard opened the cell door and unlocked the handcuffs. Juan rubbed his own wrists. Raquel saw the deep indentations that the plastic handcuffs had made on his wrists in such a short time. She had one of those moments when she recognized that her client lived in a world of pain and fear unlike any she had ever known. Until that world-changing moment a year earlier when her doctor, a straightforward woman, said, "You've got cancer, Ms. Rematti." Even in the horrible months of chemotherapy when fear ran her life, she had never been locked for months in a cell from which there was no exit.

27.

MARGARET HARDING HAD NOT lost any traction during the break. "Mrs. Richardson, was there cash in the house?"

"Yes."

"Where?"

"In our bedroom, most of it. Brad wasn't careful about where he put money."

"Was any of the money in a safe?"

"Some of it. There was money in a safe. But Brad never locked the safe. In fact, he left the door open."

"Did Juan Suarez know where the cash was?

"He did."

"Where did the money come from?"

Puzzled, Joan asked, "Where did it come from?"

"There was cash in the house, Mrs. Richardson, wasn't that what you just told the jury?"

"Yes. Brad always had a great deal of cash in the places where we lived. But he carried only small amounts when he walked around. He never carried a credit card. Sometimes in restaurants I paid the check."

"Mrs. Richardson, I asked if you knew where the cash came from?"

"I don't know, Ms. Harding. He never told me. I never asked. He had no reason to tell me, I had no reason to ask."

"Who paid Juan Suarez?"

"I did."

"Why you?"

"Brad was an incredibly busy man. He ran a worldwide business, he wrote articles, he gave speeches. But he was terrible with cash. If he had paid Juan and the other workers, Brad would never have gotten the right amount. So I did it."

"How often?"

"Every week."

"In cash?"

"Yes."

"How much?"

"It varied, Ms. Harding. Sometimes two thousand dollars a week, sometimes four, depending on whether he did extra work for us. And sometimes Brad just handed me money to give to Juan, almost as a gift. Brad was generous, and he very much liked Juan."

"Why didn't you pay Mr. Suarez in a check?"

"He didn't have a bank account."

"Was there any other reason he was paid in cash?"

"He was an illegal alien. He told us he didn't have a Social Security number, he didn't have a driver's license, and he didn't have a bank account."

"You knew it was illegal to hire a person in his status?"

"I know that now. I didn't think about it then. He said he had a wife and two children, or that he lived with a woman and she had two children. We weren't trying to take advantage of anything. He was a hard worker. He was poor when he came to us. It just seemed natural to hire him and to pay him. Brad used to say *he* got paid for his work, so it seemed natural to pay Mr. Suarez for his work whether or not he was legal or illegal."

"And how did you know he didn't have a Social Security number or a driver's license?"

"He told us. You have to understand, he is a charming man, he can talk an oyster out of its shell."

As she was rising to her feet, Raquel said, "Move to strike that statement."

Judge Conley glanced at the jurors. "I instruct you to disregard the last answer."

Then Margaret Harding shifted the subject. "Did you know Mr. Suarez by any other name?"

Joan Richardson again glanced at the jurors. "Anibal."

"What was that name again?"

"Anibal. For some reason, once during a break while he was cleaning the pool, he just mentioned that his name was Anibal. But he said I could go on calling him Juan if I wanted to."

"Did he tell you his name was Anibal Vaz?"

"Not that I remember. Just the name Anibal. I didn't know whether it was his first or last name, or whether it was his name at all. I never heard the name before."

There was no transition, no skip of a beat, between that answer and the next question: "Did you have a sexual relationship with Mr. Suarez?"

There was a sudden audible stir in the courtroom. The reporters in the gallery became even more rapt. Joan Richardson felt that the lens of the television camera was drilling a hole through her forehead. "I did."

"For how long?"

"Weeks."

"Where?"

"At my house. And twice I brought him to my home in Manhattan."

"Where did you have sex with Mr. Suarez when you were at your house in East Hampton?"

"Many places, Ms. Harding. Kitchen, library, our bedroom."

"And when you were in your bedroom in East Hampton did Mr. Suarez see the cash?"

"He saw that. And Mr. Suarez said that Brad should keep the cash locked up."

"How much money did your husband have in the house on the day he died?"

"I knew he always kept at least two hundred thousand dollars, sometimes as much as five hundred thousand dollars. My husband was careless about money."

"How careless?"

"Brad and I were in the bedroom once, getting ready to drive back to the city. We had forgotten to pay Mr. Suarez that week. Brad was in a hurry. He called out to Juan to come into the room. When Mr. Suarez was in the room, Brad reached into the safe three times and took out many thousands of dollars, spreading the money on the bed. He said to Juan 'Take what you need, Juan.'"

"What did Mr. Suarez do?"

"What he always did. He picked up some of the cash, he put it in his pocket, and he said thank you."

"Did you say anything when that happened?"

"I always told Brad I thought he should be more careful."

"What did Mr. Richardson say?"

"That he trusted Juan."

"He trusted Mr. Suarez?"

"He did. I did, too."

Margaret Harding waited as Joan Richardson sipped water from a small Evian bottle. "Did Mr. Richardson know about your relationship with Mr. Suarez?"

"He did."

"How?"

"I told him."

"Why?"

"Ms. Harding, I wanted to see how he would react."

"How did he react?"

"He was upset."

"How do you know that?"

"He said he was, he said he couldn't believe Mr. Suarez would betray the trust."

"Was he angry, loud, excited?"

"Never. Brad Richardson was always quiet, determined, focused."

"What happened next?"

"Mr. Suarez was in the yard, raking leaves from a flower bed. Brad asked him to come into the house. He told Mr. Suarez that he was fired, not to come back. He handed Mr. Suarez several hundred dollar bills."

"Did Mr. Suarez ask why?"

"No, he knew why."

Raquel watched the jurors. None of them even glanced at her. They were focused on Joan Richardson. Juan Suarez, who on Raquel's instructions had not said a word, put his hand near her left ear, whispering, "Lies, Raquel. Those are all lies."

Raquel, without looking at him, raised her hand, the signal for him to stop.

"When," Margaret Harding resumed, "was Mr. Suarez fired?"

"The day before my husband died."

"How do you know that?"

"Brad made me watch it, and I did."

Raquel knew there were only a few fundamental truths about a trial. One truth was that you had to expect the unexpected, as she often told her students. It was adjusting to the unexpected, she said, that was one of the markers of a top trial lawyer. Being first in your class at Harvard Law School didn't equip you for the fast, erratic play of the courtroom. Like a basketball player, you needed quick and sure reactions.

And now the unexpected happened in the absolutely silent courtroom, somehow still resonating with the last few words Joan Richardson spoke. Judge Conley said, "We'll adjourn until tomorrow. Unfortunately, I have a commitment in another case. Please report to the courthouse no later than nine tomorrow. I believe Ms. Rematti will start her cross-examination when we get back."

For once in this trial, Raquel had been handed an unexpected gift—the time to craft a strategy overnight. *Expect the unexpected,* she whispered to Theresa Bui.

28.

RAQUEL REMATTI REGRETTED HER first question. "Mrs. Richardson, we've met before, haven't we?"

"Yes, Ms. Rematti. You've been at two or three of our parties. I think you even invited us to one of your parties in Manhattan when you published your book. We weren't able to come."

It wasn't often that Raquel stumbled in the starting blocks. Her first reaction was almost admiration for Joan Richardson. She was smart. No one could have prepared her for that answer.

"But we've never met to talk about Mr. Suarez or this case, have we?"

"No."

"The prosecutors—Ms. Harding—told you not to talk to me, isn't that right?"

"Not in so many words."

"But you met with the prosecutors, didn't you?"

"Yes."

"With Ms. Harding, right?"

"I did."

"With Detective Halsey?"

"Yes."

"With detectives Cohen and Cerullo?"

"Sometimes, not too often."

"In fact you met with Ms. Harding the day before the trial started, isn't that right?"

"I did."

"How many times did you meet with the prosecution?"

"I'm not sure; many."

"And you rehearsed your testimony, correct?"

"Not a rehearsal, Ms. Rematti. We discussed the facts."

"What do you know about facts? Mrs. Richardson. You lied even to them, isn't that right?"

"Sometimes. About insignificant things. I'm telling the truth now."

"We'll get to that, Mrs. Richardson."

Joan Richardson simply stared at her, contempt in her expression.

Raquel asked, "Before your husband died you came to know a man named Jimmy, isn't that right?"

Joan's expression didn't change, but Raquel had the innate recognition that Joan Richardson was surprised, even rattled. She answered, "I did."

"Did you ever know Jimmy's last name?"

"Never."

"And your husband knew Jimmy?"

"I think so."

"You think so? You saw Brad and Jimmy together, didn't you?"

"Yes."

"Many times?"

"I'm not certain. Many times? Several times."

"And did you see Jimmy with Brad five days before Brad died?"

"I think so."

"Four days before?"

"I could have. I'm not sure."

"Were you in the house the day before Brad died?"

"I was. That was the day Brad fired Juan."

"And was Jimmy in the house that day?"

"Yes."

Joan stared intently at Raquel. And Raquel gazed intently at her.

"Did you ever tell Margaret Harding about Jimmy?"

"No, I didn't see why I should."

"Did you ever tell Detective Halsey about Jimmy?"

"No."

"Why not?"

"Truly, Ms. Rematti, I was embarrassed by Brad's use of cocaine, and I didn't want cocaine to be part of his legacy."

At the prosecution table, Margaret Harding sat in complete stillness, staring at Joan Richardson.

"Did you ever speak with Brad about Jimmy?"

"I did. Jimmy was a pest, Ms. Rematti. He would come to the house without calling ahead, as far as I knew. And Brad never told me who he was. I wanted to have an open, welcoming house, yet I wanted to know who the people were who visited us."

"Did you ever see Brad hand cash to Jimmy?"

Finally the objection that Raquel had anticipated came. Margaret Harding, to her right, was on her feet.

And Judge Conley surprised Raquel: "Overruled. This is cross-examination. Ms. Rematti is entitled to leeway."

Raquel picked up her thread as though there had been no interruption. Testimony, she knew, should be as seamless, as uninterrupted, as possible. Trials were about stories. "Let me ask you again: Did you ever see Brad Richardson hand cash to Jimmy?"

"I did. Once or twice."

"And do you know why that happened?"

"I thought Jimmy might be delivering food."

"Mrs. Richardson, you never saw Jimmy carrying pizza when he arrived at the house, did you?"

"No."

"He wasn't delivering food, was he?"

"No."

"He didn't drive up in a Pizza Hut truck, did he?"

"No."

"He was delivering cocaine to your husband, wasn't he?"

"He was. I didn't like that. I asked Brad to stop. He used it recreationally."

"You never asked Jimmy to come to your house, did you?"

"Never."

"You thought he was evil, didn't you?"

"Evil? I'm not sure what you mean."

"You had no idea who Jimmy was, did you?"

"I was concerned that I didn't."

"He could come and go as he pleased, is that correct?"

"Whenever Brad was there."

"You didn't know where Jimmy lived, did you?"

"No. I didn't even know whether his name was Jimmy."

"Where did Brad and Jimmy meet when Jimmy came to the house?"

"In Brad's office."

"Did Jimmy ever go with Brad to any other room in the house?"

"Yes."

"Where?"

"Once or twice they went upstairs together. Brad usually let guests roam the house, as though it were an amusement park. That was his way."

"And Brad kept cash upstairs, didn't he?"

"I said that."

"When was the last time you saw Jimmy in your house with Brad?"

"He was in the house when I left for the city."

"And, Mrs. Richardson, that was the day before Brad was killed?"

"Yes."

"And Jimmy was delivering cocaine to Brad that day, isn't that right?"

Although her almost serene expression didn't change, Joan Richardson wanted this to end. It would end faster, she thought, if she started to answer these questions directly, quietly, tersely. She recognized that all of Raquel's questions were unerring: they tracked what she had actually seen, what she had in fact heard, and what she had said. Joan answered, "Yes, he was. Brad was buying cocaine again."

"Was Jimmy in the house when you told your husband you were having an affair with Juan Suarez?"

"Possibly."

"Not possibly, Mrs. Richardson. Answer the question *yes* or *no*."

"Yes."

"Did Jimmy hear Brad fire Juan Suarez?"

"Possibly. Jimmy was in the next room when it happened."

"Let me ask you this, Mrs. Richardson: When was the last time you spoke to your husband?"

"Just as I was leaving."

"Was Jimmy there?"

"Nearby."

"What did you say to Brad?"

"I said I was sick of him."

"And what did he say?"

"That he loved me, Ms. Rematti."

When Joan Richardson left the witness stand for the lunch break, Margaret Harding literally pulled her aside as she passed the prosecution table. There was anger in Harding's gaze. She waited while the reporters and spectators wandered out of the courtroom and the television cameras were turned off. As soon as Harding thought no one could overhear, she whispered, "What the hell did you think you were doing up there?"

Joan surprised herself. "Fuck off," she said. "I answered the questions she asked me. You told me I had to tell the truth, the whole truth, and nothing but the truth. So long as it is *your* truth."

"You never told us about Jimmy."

"I stopped thinking about him. Obnoxious little bastard, fawning around my husband. You asked me about cocaine. You never asked about cocaine dealers."

"We need to talk. Now."

"You know what? I'm not going to talk at all to you. I'm going outside to clear my head."

"There's a cold sleet falling outside, Mrs. Richardson. Are you really used to that kind of weather?"

There was gray sleet falling outside; the pavement was icy; and a dismal wet chill seemed to enter her skin. In the distance were black, wet trees and patches of gray snow on the ground among the trees. With good-natured but now quiet Davey in the front seat, she sat in the back of the car, recovered a pack of Camels she had bought at a convenience store that morning, and smoked. She cracked the window open, just as she had done when she and her friends were smoking on lunch break in high school.

Where is Hank? she wondered. "That bastard went into hiding," she said out loud. They were the only words she uttered in the car. Davey glanced at her in the rear view mirror. He said nothing.

Raquel's voice was soft, polite, almost deferential, as she started the afternoon session. "Mrs. Richardson, your husband was bisexual, wasn't he?"

Margaret Harding stood. Her voice sounded exasperated. "Objection."

Always with that schoolteacher's demeanor, Judge Conley said, "Overruled."

"Let me ask the question again," Raquel said, still softly. "Your husband was sexually active with men and women?"

"He was. I learned that after we'd been married for four or five years. It was what he did. I've learned to accept things, Ms. Rematti."

"Did you ever meet any of Brad's partners?"

"Pretty often, Ms. Rematti. Over the last two or three years we had no reason to hide things from each other."

"Did your husband have one of his friends at the house the day before he died?"

"He did."

"You left for New York at about five?"

"I did. Around that time. It was getting dark."

"Who was the friend?"

"Trevor Palmer."

"Who is that?"

Joan reached for the fresh bottle of Evian she had bought from a vending machine on her way to the courtroom. The crack of the plastic cap as she turned it resonated sharply throughout the room. It was the only sound as everyone waited for her to speak. "He was one of Brad's special friends. He was a songwriter."

Raquel focused only on the first sentence of that answer: "He was one of your husband's lovers?"

She sipped the water. "He was."

"What were they doing when you last saw them?"

"It was in the afternoon. We had had a glass of wine together in the kitchen. And then they went upstairs."

"What is upstairs?"

"Bedrooms, Ms. Rematti."

"Did they go upstairs before Jimmy arrived?"

"They did."

"How long were they upstairs?"

"We had the wine at lunch. Then they went upstairs. They came down at two or three."

"And then Jimmy arrived?"

"Yes."

"Did Jimmy see Trevor?"

"Yes."

"Did Trevor know Jimmy?"

"Trevor enjoyed Jimmy's company."

"What does that mean?"

"Trevor called Jimmy rough trade."

"Did Trevor tell you what 'rough trade' meant?"

"I already knew it, Ms. Rematti. So do you."

Someone in the gallery of the courtroom laughed. No one else did.

Raquel asked, "Was Trevor there when you left?"

"Trevor always stayed until I left. Yes, he was there. He and my husband always had unfinished business."

29.

KATHY SCHIAVONI FOR YEARS had spent vast amounts of time driving on virtually every road in East Hampton and Montauk. She knew this was the activity of a lonely person. She liked her solitude and loved walking on the gorgeous beaches that stretched for miles from Montauk to Southampton. She also particularly loved the two-lane, twisting roads, once horse and cattle paths, that led north and south off the Montauk Highway. Those narrow roads went through farmland toward the Atlantic. They were the arteries of this region, her home territory. Especially in Montauk, the air of the East End had that incandescent haze that radiated up from the Atlantic. The ocean was on both sides of the steadily narrowing peninsula that finally ended at the Montauk Lighthouse.

At night her headlights glowed in the ground fog, the eleven-foot-tall reeds gleaming at the edges of the roadside. She knew exactly where Raquel Rematti's house was. The house had been there for so long that it was almost an integral part of the landscape—a small seaside structure with faded wood, a shingled roof, and a deck overlooking the beach, just above the reedy dunes.

The house was at the end of a beach road that, for several hundred yards, was a compound of hard sand. There was a light on in the kitchen next to the deck. There were no other lights. In the fog, the single light was diffuse, soft, haloed. She wasn't certain anyone was in the house until she saw the two cars parked near a high bank of reeds: a BMW and a Mercedes.

Clutching a manila envelope close to her chest to keep it dry, Kathy climbed the long flight of worn wooden steps. There was an odor of salt water in the air. When she saw the black expanse of the Atlantic, she acknowledged to herself, as she had many times, that she wished she lived in a house exactly like this, rooted in a place that seemed almost a part of the shoreline and the ocean itself. She craved absolute, comforting solitude, each morning a renewal of life as the sun rose from the ocean and shed light on one of the easternmost areas of the country.

After Kathy knocked, Raquel was casual and unafraid even though she was in an isolated world. Raquel Rematti came to the sliding door on the deck. Although she had seen Kathy in the courtroom several times, she had no reason to know who she was: the gallery was crowded every day for the trial of Juan the Knife and this woman could have been a spectator or a reporter.

Without hesitating, Raquel slid the glass door open for this stranger. "Can I help you?"

Kathy said, "Ms. Rematti, I work for the Suffolk County DA. In the forensics lab. I need to talk to you."

"Come in."

30.

MARGARET HARDING HAD DONE what a genuinely experienced trial lawyer in a murder case would do. She waited. She listened attentively as Raquel asked questions and Joan Richardson gave answers. From time to time she made notes. For the most part she restrained herself from objecting.

As soon as Raquel said, "I have no more questions," Judge Conley turned to Margaret Harding. "Re-direct," she said.

No recess, no pause. Margaret rose quickly to her feet, asking, "Mrs. Richardson, was one of your husband's special friends Juan Suarez?"

"Do you mean special friends in the way Trevor Palmer was Brad's special friend?"

"Was Juan Suarez one of your husband's special friends, like Trevor Palmer?"

"He was."

"Did you ever see what they did as special friends?"

"I saw them together."

"And what did you see them doing?"

"I saw them hold hands. I saw them in rooms alone with each other."

"Did you see your husband and Mr. Suarez do anything else?"

"They swam naked in the pool together."

"And?"

"They went to New York together several times. They were close. Brad liked Juan a great deal."

"Did you ever ask Brad about his relationship with Juan?"

"Brad said Juan was a sweet man, very easy to be with. He'd often say how lucky we were to have found Juan."

"What else did he say?"

"How handsome Juan was. He asked me whether I thought Juan looked more like Antonio Banderas or Benicio Del Toro, the actors. More like the dashing Latin type or the dark, handsome brooding type."

"You told the jury yesterday, didn't you, that Brad fired Juan when he learned that you and Juan were lovers?"

"I did."

"Was Mr. Richardson doing anything with Mr. Suarez before Brad fired him?"

"We had some trees and branches that were hanging over the stone patio near the pool. It was fall. Juan was out there working. He was cutting down branches."

"Was he alone?"

"No, Brad was with him for about half an hour. Brad, who told me that he'd like to have a simpler life someday and do real work with his hands, sometimes watched Juan do things like masonry and gardening."

"What was Juan using to do his work on the branches?"

"A long blade that he called a machete."

"What was your husband doing?"

"Just watching for the most part. And then at one point Juan handed the machete to him and Brad swung at the branches. He missed, like a baseball batter hitting only air. They laughed together at that."

"How often had you seen Juan use that machete?"

"Many times. He used it when he was gardening to dig out roots, he used it on the shrubbery. We had lots of supplies and tools when Juan came to work for us. But the one thing he said was missing was a machete. And I remember that Brad and Juan went to the hardware store in Sag Harbor to buy a new machete for him just a few days after Juan started working for us."

"And did you ever see that machete after you saw your husband and Brad on the patio with it?"

"Never, Ms. Harding."

Raquel was shaken by what she heard Joan Richardson say. Joan had that thousand-yard stare Raquel had often seen in witnesses who had been on the stand for too long. She seemed no longer focused on what was happening in the courtroom; there was almost no forethought in the answers she gave. This made her unpredictable, dangerous.

Raquel also knew she had the complicated problem of wanting the jurors to believe much of what Joan Richardson had said—the presence of Trevor and Jimmy in Brad's life, his use of cocaine, his nonchalance about allowing people to know that there was cash in the house—and at the same time to disbelieve other parts of her testimony, such as Juan's use of a machete, his naked swimming with Brad, his unfettered run of the house. Raquel even thought that she should simply stop asking questions and let her leave the witness stand after Margaret Harding finished her terse redirect examination. But Raquel's experience was that this process was like a chess game in many ways, that each move demanded a counter-move, and that generally the player who stopped making moves was the one who had just lost. Losers had no more moves.

Raquel asked, "Mrs. Richardson, let's focus on the night Detective Halsey called you back to East Hampton. Are you there with me?"

She said, "I think so."

"Why don't you try thinking harder: Isn't it the fact that you re-call the night Detective Halsey called you back to East Hampton?"

"Yes."

"You testified that when Detective Halsey asked you who you thought did this the only name you mentioned was Juan Suarez. Do you remember that?"

For the first time Joan Richardson looked directly at Juan Suarez. He held Joan's gaze. "I remember," she said.

"And you also testified you saw people in the house the day before Brad died, correct?"

Joan Richardson shifted her gaze from Juan to Raquel. "There were."

"Jimmy?"

"Yes."

"And Jimmy was the coke dealer, correct?"

"He was, Ms. Rematti."

"And Jimmy knew where the cash was kept, correct?"

"He must have—Brad gave him cash upstairs."

"And you know that Brad used to take Jimmy upstairs and Jimmy came downstairs with cash, is that right?"

"I saw that. As I've said, we ran a pretty open house."

"And we know that Brad called Jimmy 'rough trade,' right?"

"He did."

"And we know that Trevor was there, correct?"

"For six months Trevor was there very often. He didn't seem to spend much time writing music. At least Jimmy was working, so to speak."

"And Trevor knew there was lots of cash in the house?"

"He must have. Brad often gave him cash for what Brad called walking-around money."

"But when Detective Halsey asked you who you thought did this the only name you mentioned was Juan Suarez, is that right?"

"It's the only name I thought of at the time."

"Let me see if I understand, Mrs. Richardson." Raquel's voice was very subdued, but utterly distinct. "The police asked you if you had any idea who killed your husband. And the only name you gave them was Juan Suarez."

"That's right. He was the man I thought murdered my husband."

"And you thought of his name not because you had any real information that Mr. Suarez killed your husband but because he had been your lover, right?"

"Not right."

"And you gave the police Mr. Suarez's name because you thought he was your husband's lover, right?"

"Not right, Ms. Rematti. Not even close. I gave them the name because I believed, and still believe, that Juan Suarez murdered my husband."

"But you didn't see him kill your husband, isn't that right?"

"I never said that."

"You never heard Juan Suarez threaten your husband, correct?"

"I never heard that."

"You never saw Juan Suarez hit or push your husband, correct?"

"No, I never saw that."

"Your husband never told you he feared Juan Suarez, correct?"

"No, he never said that." She sipped water. "But Brad did tell me that he was very surprised that Juan insisted on being paid for the drugs he provided to Brad. He thought that with all the money we paid Juan Suarez it was odd that Juan was such a high-priced drug dealer."

Raquel Rematti knew that she had to keep this quiet, unrelenting process going and that she could not react to Joan Richardson's words.

"You testified to the Grand Jury before Mr. Suarez was indicted, isn't that right?"

"I did."

"And you never once mentioned to the Grand Jury, in five hundred pages of testimony, that Juan Suarez sold drugs to your husband?"

"No one asked, Ms. Rematti. You just did."

"And you didn't tell the prosecution that, did you?"

"No."

"You get to decide what is important and what isn't, Ms. Richardson, isn't that right?"

"I haven't been able to decide anything in a long time."

"Do you know what the truth is?"

"Certainly. The truth is that your client killed my husband."

"And the jury should believe you, correct, Ms. Richardson?"

"I can't tell them what to do."

"And they should believe you even though you are a liar, right?"

"I'm telling the truth today."

Raquel's voice was not angry or loud: it was patient and driving even though she knew she was dealing with a difficult and defiant witness. Just three feet to Raquel's left was a large screen, in effect an oversize notepad, that rested on an easel; it had been used by Margaret Harding during her opening statement. With a Sharpie magic marker, Harding had written: *Follow the timeline, follow the money.* During the break after the openings, Raquel had moved the easel to the side so that the jurors couldn't see it. It was not good to let the jurors absorb, even unconsciously, the message written on the screen.

Almost seamlessly, like a magician eliding to the next magic, Raquel turned the easel toward the jury. She lifted the big page on which Harding had written her words. Raquel now had a clean sheet, a *tabula rasa* that was visible to Joan Richardson and the jury.

"Ms. Richardson," Raquel said, "do you see this screen?"

"Of course."

"What word am I writing at the top of the page?"

"The word *Lies*."

"Let's fill in the empty space under *Lies*. First, you lied when you told Detective Halsey that you were alone in your Fifth Avenue apartment on the day Brad Richardson was killed, correct?"

"I didn't tell him the truth."

"You lied?"

"I lied."

"So watch what I'm writing here, Mrs. Richardson: *Lie 1: Lied to police*. Can you read that?"

"Your handwriting isn't too clear. But, yes, I see it."

"And you lied to the Grand Jury when you told them you were alone that day. So we have *Lie 2: Lied to the Grand Jury*."

"I regretted that and I corrected it."

"And you were under oath both times, isn't that right?"

"It is."

"So which Joan Richardson should we believe? The liar who spoke the first lie? Or the liar who said the second lie?"

"I corrected the lie."

"You are under oath today, aren't you?"

"Yes."

"And the jury should believe that you've been telling the truth now."

"That's correct."

"And that's because you took an oath in front of them? An oath to tell the truth, the whole truth, and nothing but the truth?"

Raquel held up her right hand, as if she, too, were swearing.

"Yes, certainly."

"Was there something different about the oath when you testified to the Grand Jury? Which part of the oath did the clerk leave out when he asked you to swear to tell the truth, the whole truth, and nothing but the truth?"

"It was the same oath, Ms. Rematti."

"Yet you lied to those people, yes or no?"

"Most of what I said was the truth."

"Tell us. How is it that the jurors facing you today are supposed to know when you speak the truth and when you don't? Do you have some sort of signal?"

"Objection," Margaret Harding said, knowing what the judge's response would be.

Judge Conley spoke into her microphone without looking at Harding: "Overruled. This is cross-examination. You'll have the opportunity for re-direct, Ms. Harding."

Raquel, still at the easel and with the big magic marker in her hand, said, "Let's get back to the lies we know about. Before the Grand Jury you never mentioned the name Jimmy, the drug dealer, did you?"

"No."

Raquel said as she wrote *Lie 3: No Jimmy*, "And you told Ms. Harding yesterday that you didn't mention Jimmy because you were concerned about Brad's reputation, is that right?"

"That's right."

"His reputation? You care about his reputation? And yet you've told the world that Brad Richardson was a drug user, that he was bisexual, that he had boy toys like Trevor Palmer to whom he gave what you called 'walking-around money,' that he had an affair with Mr. Suarez, that he kept hundreds of thousands of dollars on display in his bedroom, and that he spent his time with drug hustlers and rough trade. And you want this jury to believe that at the Grand Jury, when you were under oath to tell the truth, the whole truth, and nothing but the truth, you were concerned that if you mentioned Jimmy the world would know Brad Richardson used cocaine?"

"That was my concern."

"Wasn't your concern that you didn't want to place too many people in the house with Brad Richardson in the twenty-four hours before his death?"

"That isn't so."

"Really, Ms. Richardson? Isn't it true that if anyone reads the five hundred pages of your Grand Jury testimony the only person you mention being in the house in the forty-eight hours before your husband was killed was Juan Suarez? Isn't that true?"

"I didn't remember anyone else."

"And you didn't remember Jimmy?"

"Apparently I didn't."

"And you didn't remember Trevor Palmer?"

"It's hard for me ever to think about Trevor Palmer."

"But you didn't mention him to the Grand Jurors, correct?"

"If you say so, Ms. Rematti."

"If I say so? Let's take a look at page 326 of your Grand Jury testimony. Mr. Oz asked you: 'Who did you see in the house in the two days before Mr. Richardson was killed?' Do you remember your answer? 'Only Juan Suarez.' If you need it, I'll give you a copy of the transcript."

"I don't need it."

"And that was a lie, wasn't it?"

"It was. It wasn't the whole truth."

Raquel walked away from the easel, but made sure that the list of lies she had written on the big white page faced the jury. At the podium, Raquel said, "Ms. Harding asked you about the Borzois, the dogs. They were killed when your husband was killed, correct?"

"Obviously the same person who murdered Brad killed the Borzois as well. They did nothing to attack the man who killed Brad. Their teeth had no traces of blood or clothing. Only Juan knew the dogs so well that they wouldn't have tried to attack. They're hunting dogs, after all."

Raquel decided not to engage Joan Richardson's blatant, angry effort to damage Juan. She asked, "Do you remember testifying that taking care of the Borzois was part of Juan's job, part of what he was paid to do?"

"That was part of his job."

"Did you ever see Juan play with the dogs?"

"I did."

"Did you see Juan feed the dogs?"

"I did."

"Did you see Juan groom the dogs?"

"Yes."

"Did you ever see Juan hit the dogs?"

"No."

"Mistreat them?"

"No, never."

Raquel turned slightly to look at the jurors. She let ten seconds pass. "And you lied to the Grand Jurors about who you were with on the day your husband died, isn't that right?"

"I shouldn't have. I wanted to protect someone."

"And that person was your other lover, Senator Rawls, correct?"

"I didn't think it was anybody's business."

"You also lied to Detective Halsey, didn't you?"

"Yes."

"And you lied to the prosecutors, didn't you?"

"At first."

"And you lied to the Grand Jurors?"

"I shouldn't have. It was meaningless, it was stupid. I was afraid and confused."

"And finally, Ms. Richardson, listen to me carefully. There was another man in the house in the days before your husband died?"

"I told you, Ms. Rematti, there were always many people in the house, both the day before Brad died and many other days before that."

"And one of them was named Oscar Caliente, isn't that right?"

"Brad said he was new to East Hampton, a polo player from Argentina who wanted to buy a horse farm. He knew people Brad knew who were involved with horses and the August polo shows in Southampton. Oscar Caliente, who Brad said was renting one of those old mansions on the beach in Southampton, wanted to be introduced to the horse people Brad knew."

"You met Oscar Caliente, didn't you?"

"At the house."

"When?"

"Not long before Brad died."

Raquel paused, stepping away from the podium and standing alone in the well of the courtroom without pencils, easels, or props of any kind. Raquel—tall, composed, and a master of these scenes—looked steadily at the fourteen anonymous jurors seated in two rows, one higher than the other, a kind of choir. "Ms. Richardson, you didn't see Juan Suarez kill your husband, did you?"

"No."

"You didn't see Juan Suarez steal money, did you?"

"No."

"You were 120 miles away when Brad Richardson was killed, isn't that right?"

"Yes."

"You never saw the weapon used to kill Brad Richardson, did you?"

"No."

"And you never saw the weapon used to kill the Borzois, correct?"

"Never."

In unison, like the choir they resembled, all the jurors had been looking back and forth from Raquel Rematti to Joan Richardson as the questions were asked and the answers given. At that moment, after Joan Richardson said "Never," they were looking again at Raquel.

"No further questions," Raquel said.

When Raquel sat at the defense table between Juan Suarez and Theresa Bui, the judge, in one of those frequent interludes that happen after a lawyer finishes a long series of questions, turned off her microphone and whispered to one of her clerks. As they waited, with Joan Richardson plainly angry and impatient, still on the stand, and the jurors staring into space ahead of them, Theresa leaned forward toward Raquel, whispering, "That was amazing."

Raquel, who knew that people Theresa's age and younger used the words *amazing* or *awesome* to describe anything they liked, whispered, "Thanks, but take it one step at a time. Amazing or not, it doesn't matter until there's a verdict."

A feverish sweat shined on Raquel's face. She was exhausted and in pain. When Theresa saw that there were even droplets of sweat on Raquel's upper lip, she put the edge of her hand next to the edge of Raquel's elegant, long-fingered hand. It radiated sick heat.

Overcoming the stillness in the courtroom, Judge Conley switched on the sound system. "Ms. Harding, do you expect to have re-re-direct examination?"

Margaret Harding stood. "One or two hours."

"In light of that," Judge Conley said as she turned to the jurors, "we'll break until tomorrow morning."

As the jurors were being led out of the courtroom through the side door reserved for them, Juan Suarez said to Raquel, "You did something very wrong, Raquel. Bad."

They were still standing. Raquel glanced at him without speaking. She had never before heard this tone in Juan's voice: it was harsh, furious, even threatening, so altered that it was scary, as if another person were speaking through him. "You should not have said the name Oscar Caliente to anyone. I told you that."

31.

CENTRAL PARK WAS ABSOLUTELY black when Joan Richardson rose from the back seat of the car to the sheltering cone of the umbrella the doorman Frank held over her head. Streams of rain fell in rivulets from the eight points of the umbrella. A cold trickle struck the back of her neck. As he kept the umbrella above her on the short walk from the car to the awning, Frank said, "Nice to have you back, Mrs. Richardson." Doormen, who knew everything, also liked to appear impervious to everything. She was certain that Frank had followed every word she said during the televised trial, yet his tone was the same as if he were welcoming her home from a vacation.

As soon as she reached the awning, Joan took out her cell phone, pressed the button for Hank Rawls's number, and put the sleek instrument to her ear. This was the tenth call she had placed to him since leaving Riverhead. His cell was turned off. As she waited, she looked out from under the dripping awning into the massed black tree trunks and branches of Central Park. Cold rain blew through the street lights on Fifth Avenue. Yellow taxis created a constant hissing noise as they sped down the avenue, tossing wings of rain water from their tires.

At the seventh ring, just before his message was about to start, Hank Rawls answered. "Joan?"

She had been certain she'd lash out angrily at him, or treat him icily, because of his vanishing act. Instead, she was deeply relieved to hear his voice. "God, Hank, I'm so glad you answered."

"Things suddenly got crazy for me."

"Are you upstairs?" For months the doormen had just waved Senator Rawls in. He had his own key to the apartment. She added, "I'll be right up."

"Joan, I'm in Miami. I've been here a few days. I got a call out of nowhere for a role. Donald Sutherland cancelled a short part at the last minute, and, if you can believe it, they called me."

She didn't believe him. She sensed throughout her body an anxiety more profound than anything that had happened since the night she received the call from Bo Halsey. Even though she was actually trembling, she stepped out from under the awning, which had radiant heaters under the canopy that cast warming light down onto the sidewalk, into the sleety darkness. She didn't want anyone to hear her. "I really need to lie down with you, to hug you," she said.

"I saw pieces of the trial on TV, sweetie. You were a real trooper. But it must have been painful for you."

"Hank, I really want you to come home."

"We're in the middle of this. Another two or three days."

"I'll fly down. I can leave tonight. Where are you staying?"

"Joan, I'm working my tail off. I'll be on the set for the next two days. I won't have time to see you."

She stared into the alluring comfortable glow created by the lights from the awning. To her left the monumental Fifth Avenue building rose into the mist and sleet; the stone surface of the building was streaked with wet stains. When she focused on the conversation that was now unfolding, she remembered the very few times when a man had spoken so evasively to her. She had only been dumped twice in her life, once, twenty years earlier, by the young George Clooney. Two years before she had married Brad Richardson, the scary-looking Salman Rushdie had dumped her with his convoluted locutions. It sounded like a philosophy lecture. She had cut him off. "Just do it," she had said.

But tonight, wanting not to hear what she imagined she was about to hear, she said, "I don't mind staying in the hotel room while you're out, Hank. I could read Trollope again." This was painful to her. She felt desperate.

"Joan, I really need to concentrate on what I'm doing. For some reason, I really don't want Fred Thompson to be the only ex-Senator to make millions on television."

Joan thought of saying, "I can give you millions," but she sensed that would be like a lash, one that would hurt her more than it would hurt Hank and might give him a reason to utter angry, decisive, irretrievable words. She asked, "Is there a woman with you?"

"That'd never happen, sweetie. All I need is a few days."

"It's all right," she said, as quietly as she could in a world where there was noise all around her—the sibilant rain, the rushing tires on the pavement of Fifth Avenue, the sound of slamming taxi doors.

Joan closed the lid on her cell phone. She was crying. She wiped the rain from her forehead and cheeks. Smiling for the doormen, she walked under the awning and into the lobby.

Hank Rawls, who was in New York and not Miami, never had to tell Joan Richardson that Rain Chatterjee, a gorgeous, 32-year-old Pakistani woman educated at Oxford and now a weekend anchor at CNN, was in his apartment, as she had been for three days. Hank Rawls never had to tell Joan Richardson that because he never saw her again.

32.

DETECTIVE HALSEY WAS ONE of those crisp, no-nonsense cops who made great witnesses because they were laconic, informative, and impossible to ruffle. Almost all of his answers were *yes* or *no*; when he had to say more, his sentences were terse, the modern version of Sergeant Joe Friday. Generally, as Raquel Rematti knew, it was best to get witnesses like Halsey off the stand as quickly as possible and not to linger on cross-examination. Through Margaret Harding's own crisp questioning, Halsey had spent his two hours of direct examination describing the emergency call that led him to the seaside estate in East Hampton, his entry into the office where Brad's body and the bodies of the two Borzois were already covered under the tarpaulin-like sheets, the arrival of Joan Richardson, and his sending of two detectives upstairs after Joan told him that Brad kept cash in the bedroom.

And he testified that the two detectives, Cerullo and Cohen, came downstairs with nothing. Bo Halsey didn't testify that several weeks earlier Ang Tien had shown him a clear video that unmistakably depicted Cohen and Cerullo carrying brick-like stacks of cash out of the Richardsons' bedroom.

Raquel Rematti asked, "Detective Halsey, let's just be clear: there were no eyewitnesses to the killing of Brad Richardson, correct?"

Halsey leaned forward to the microphone slightly, just as he had in all his answers to Margaret Harding's questions. His shaved head glinted. He looked at the jurors each time he answered a question: years earlier he had learned that jurors found witnesses who looked at them were trustworthy. He said, "None."

"And there were none of Mr. Suarez's fingerprints in Mr. Richardson's office, were there?"

"That's right."

"And there was no DNA from Mr. Suarez at the crime scene, was there?"

"None."

"And no weapon was found in Mr. Suarez's possession?"

"None."

"And no cash was found in Mr. Suarez's possession, right?"

"None."

"And the only reason you sent Detectives Cerullo and Cohen to look for cash was because Mrs. Richardson told you there might be cash in the bedroom, isn't that right?"

"Not right. She told me there *was* cash in the bedroom. Well over two hundred thousand dollars. She didn't say it might be there. She said it was."

"And Cerullo and Cohen reported to you that there was no cash, is that right?"

Detective Halsey again leaned forward to the microphone and, looking at the jury, said, "The cash was gone. That's in their report."

"Let me understand: the only reason you, as the lead investigator, believe that Mr. Suarez stole more than two hundred thousand dollars is because Mrs. Richardson told you there was cash in the bedroom, isn't that right?"

"Not right, counselor. Point one, she said it was there. Point two, it was gone."

"And you didn't ask Jimmy if he saw cash there the day before Brad was killed, the day Mrs. Richardson said Jimmy was in the house, is that right?"

"We never heard of Jimmy, counselor."

"When did you hear about Jimmy?"

"Two weeks ago."

"Did you look for him?"

"We did."

"Did you find him?"

"We did."

"Did you speak to him?"

"Not much."

"What did he say?"

"He said he was in a drug rehab in Arizona trying to recover from crack addition during the month Mr. Richardson was killed. The records at the place, which is very expensive, show he was there. He said he was a drug user, not a drug dealer."

"Did he say he knew Brad Richardson?"

"He said he did."

"Did he say he visited the Richardson home?"

"He did."

"Why?"

"Mr. Richardson paid him, he said, two thousand dollars a pop—his words—for oral sex."

"Did Jimmy say there was cash in the bedroom?"

"He said if there was he never saw it."

"And you never asked Trevor Palmer if he saw cash in the bedroom, right?"

"Never heard of him either until two weeks ago. When we interviewed him, he said he thought there might have been cash there, but he said he wasn't sure."

"So this could be phantom money, Detective Halsey?"

Margaret Harding rose to her feet. To Raquel's surprise Judge Conley said, "Overruled," before Harding could even object.

Halsey was an experienced witness. He knew he had to answer the question as though no objection had been made. "I don't know what phantom money means, Ms. Rematti."

"Money that never existed?"

"Mrs. Richardson said it had been there. And when my officers looked it wasn't there. Is that phantom money?"

It was time, Raquel knew, to wind down the cross-examination.

33.

AT THE END OF Bo Halsey's testimony, Ang Tien, who had been sitting in the back row of the gallery, walked out into the crystalline late winter afternoon. He'd waited to hear Bo Halsey's testimony, hoping Halsey would describe the surveillance tape. That hadn't happened.

Ang Tien had twenty of his business cards in his pockets. He moved among the reporters standing near the glistening television panel trucks. He handed out his cards. Deferentially he asked every man and woman holding a microphone or a notepad for their business cards. All of the dozen or so reporters he approached either handed him a business card or, after he explained he had important information about the trial, wrote their names and email addresses on pieces of paper. They were hungry for information, and even though they didn't know the young Asian man with spiky black hair who looked like a computer-obsessed nerd, they didn't hesitate to give him their contact information and take his cards. He could be anyone—a friend of a juror, someone who knew Juan Suarez, or just one of the law junkies who haunted courtrooms.

That night Ang Tien created an untraceable email address for himself. He typed "Bedroom in the Richardson House on Murder Day" in the subject line—he knew the subject line had to have a message that the reporters couldn't ignore—and in the body of the email he wrote: "Law enforcement officials taking cash from the Richardson bedroom." Then, without hesitation, he pressed the *Send* key to distribute the video to the reporters. He then posted it on YouTube. His screen flashed that the message had been sent.

He leaned backward in his chair, raising his arms above his head. Suddenly lifted from him were the anxiety, resentment, and anger he had felt for weeks while Bo Halsey never again spoke to him about the tapes of Cerullo and Cohen methodically carrying cash from the bedroom to the bathroom. Ang Tien shouted and pumped his hands in the air.

Less than two hours later a CNN anchor introduced another story at the start of the seven o'clock news: "A bizarre twist in the trial of the man accused of killing billionaire hedge fund owner Brad Richardson in ritzy East Hampton. CNN has received through anonymous sources a tape of two police officers taking cash found in the Richardson bedroom. Here is part of the tape, taken several hours after Richardson was murdered, police say, with a machete."

The high-resolution tape, enhanced by Ang Tien's wizard skills, captured the faces of Cerullo and Cohen and their quick, furtive movements. The tape also captured them as they continuously looked around the room for the kinds of small security cameras they obviously expected to see. There was even an occasional murmur of voices, almost of grunts, but that was far less distinct.

As soon as the tape ended a young reporter—Asian, sleek, articulate, attractive—said, "Our sources have definitively identified the men on the tape as law enforcement officers named Dick Cerullo and Dave Cohen, described as experienced detectives with years of experience in the NYPD and the Suffolk County Sheriff's Office. Interestingly, their names were mentioned today at the trial by seasoned lead detective Bo Halsey as the two officers he had sent on the night of the murder to look for more than two hundred thousand dollars in cash that Brad Richardson allegedly kept in his bedroom. Halsey said at the trial that the two officers came back from the assignment with no cash."

The screen suddenly turned into a tape of Bo Halsey that afternoon walking from the courthouse. He wore sunglasses. He looked like the veteran soldier—tall, strong, his head completely shaved—he in fact was.

The reporter continued, "The illegal Mexican immigrant on trial for the murder of the billionaire is also accused of stealing well over two hundred thousand dollars in cash from the bedroom where the law enforcement officers were filmed. The lead detective, Halsey, was reached a few minutes ago. He said he had never seen the tape before. It was, he said, news to him. He also said that any further questions had to be referred to the prosecutors. The lead prosecutor, Margaret Harding, hasn't yet returned messages left for her."

Raquel's cell phone rang as she was having dinner with Theresa at the American Hotel in Sag Harbor. They were in the room with the ancient bar and the fireplace, which was lit. The carefully carved tin ceiling glowed with the candlelight from the tables and the fire. In the wine at Raquel's table a deep glow filled the glasses.

"Hello," Raquel said when her cell phone screen lit up with the caller ID *New York Times*.

It was Jennifer Hoover, a reporter from the *Times* who had Raquel on what she called her go-to list. She said, "Raquel, where are you?"

"We're at the American Hotel. In Sag Harbor."

"Do they have a television set?"

"No, and I hope they never do. They do have a moose head high on the wall with a cigarette dangling from his lips."

"Let me tell you what the entire country has been looking at for the last half hour. Maybe I can get your reaction. I'd like to get my article into the online edition pronto."

"I never heard you breathless before, Jennifer. What's happening?"

"An hour ago someone sent out emails and posted on YouTube a video of two Suffolk County detectives."

"Tell me more."

"In it the cops are carrying stacks of cash out of Brad Richardson's bedroom."

"What?"

"It was a surveillance tape taken on the day he was killed. The two cops are the ones Bo Halsey mentioned today as the guys who came back empty-handed from the search for the cash. Obviously they found it, and they kept it."

Raquel paused, holding her breath. "Jennifer, I think all I can say now is that if the tape depicts two rogue policemen stealing cash that Juan Suarez is alleged to have stolen then this situation is outrageous, particularly if the prosecutors knew about the existence of this tape."

"Did you ever see it?"

"Of course not."

"What do you plan to do?"

"Jennifer, why don't you just write that we'll take all necessary steps to vindicate Mr. Suarez's rights, or something like that. That's for the record. But between us, off the record, you were wonderful to call me. This is the best news I've heard in a very, very long time. I'll give you the first word on anything that develops from this."

As they had on many nights during the trial, Raquel and Theresa drove to the seaside house in Montauk when they left Sag Harbor, almost deserted at this time of the year and profoundly attractive. The drive to the house took less than forty-five minutes. The Montauk Highway, essentially a two-lane street after it passed through East Hampton, had almost no traffic.

Raquel was bone-weary, as she had been on most nights for the last two weeks. She hadn't called her doctor for the simple reason that she was afraid about what she might hear. Raquel was not convinced—or she didn't want to believe—that the cancer had recurred because she didn't have the pain through her entire body that had first alerted her a year ago to the possibility that she might be sick. But for the last two weeks the pain and lassitude, and the deep-down, secret fear, had destroyed her sleep.

Raquel loved to drive her black Porsche—another of the few toys she had given herself when she recovered—but on this night as on many others she let Theresa drive. In multiple ways Theresa had witnessed Raquel's rapid transformation. She saw how blanched Raquel's vibrant, dark face was by the end of each day. And she also saw Raquel's daily strength as she rallied during each trial day to be alert and strong until the jury left the room to go home. At that point, Raquel would sit with her head resting on her hands in the private, usually empty room reserved for lawyers next to the courtroom.

On the quiet drive they listened to the local NPR station with *All Things Considered* set at low volume. The familiar, subdued cadence of Robert Siegel's cultured voice, a throwback to the days of baritone-voiced broadcasters like Edward R. Murrow and Walter Cronkite—seemed to soothe Raquel. She and Theresa both smiled when a ninety-second summary of the day's trial was broadcast—even NPR regularly covered the trial.

As usual, Theresa prepared supper; it consisted mainly of heating food they regularly picked up from a stop at the fancy Citrella store in East Hampton. She set the food on the table. Raquel, who poured one glass of wine for each of them, ordinarily put the dishes in the washer.

Each night Raquel used the small guest bedroom. It was closer to the sound of the sea than her own bedroom. She believed the rhythm of the waves might ease her into fitful moments of sleep. Theresa always seemed uncomfortable with the idea of using Raquel's far larger, well-decorated bedroom, but Raquel quietly insisted on it.

Not long after they started regularly using the Montauk house they started embracing before Raquel left for the small bedroom. It was Raquel who initiated the embraces. They lasted for thirty seconds, sometimes a minute. At first uneasy about them, Theresa soon became comfortable. Raquel obviously derived something comforting from them.

Tonight, at the end of the embrace, they pressed their cheeks together, almost kissing. Raquel said, "Thank you, my sweet friend."

Raquel, wrenched up from another fitful sleep, had no doubt that the odd *pop-pop-pop* sounds she heard were rifle shots. As always, she was naked when she was in bed. She jumped to her feet and, naked, sprinted toward her bedroom.

As soon as she entered the room she saw that the floor-to-ceiling window that overlooked the beach was shattered. She turned on the lights. Tiny shards of glass glinted over the bed and floor. Panting, shouting *Theresa, Theresa*, she glanced all around the devastated room.

Theresa Bui's body was slumped against a wall. The bullets had struck her head. Blood drenched her jet-black hair.

Raquel, oblivious to the shards of glass under her bare feet, ran to the body and knelt, praying, beside it. She instinctively knew that the sniper thought the person he had killed in Raquel's bedroom was Raquel herself.

34.

THE TRIAL RESUMED FIVE days later. When Raquel drove into the parking lot, it seemed to her that thousands of reporters and spectators were gathered there to see her. Although she had refused police protection, three cruisers followed her from Montauk to Riverhead. When the cruisers pulled into a protective triangle around her car as she parked, and as several policemen formed a protective corridor for her to walk to the building, she was grateful that Richie Lupo had ignored her polite "No, thank you" when he had called over the weekend to offer her the protection and to say he was "sorry" about the loss of Theresa Bui.

It was early. Ordinarily the jury was led into the courtroom at nine-thirty but Judge Conley had asked that the lawyers report to her chambers at eight. The austere, unattractive building was locked at that time because it officially opened to the public at nine. Once Raquel entered the building, two court security officers led her to the judge's chambers.

Helen Conley was, as always, bland. Not wearing her black robe, she sat quietly behind her large desk; her hands were folded like a parochial school girl waiting for class to start. Margaret Harding and a court reporter were already there.

As Raquel took a seat at the long conference table directly in front of the judge's desk, she was surprised when Helen Conley said,

"Ms. Rematti, before we go on the record, I want to express my deep sympathy for what happened to Ms. Bui. It's terribly, terribly disturbing. And it was obvious to me from where I've sat every day at this trial, facing the two of you, that there was a bond between you."

"Thank you, Judge," Raquel said. "This has been very hard on me and, more importantly, on her family. She was an only child. There was a tremendous attachment between her parents and her. It's heart-breaking to see them."

"Where do they live?"

"In Chinatown."

"What are the funeral arrangements?"

"Theresa was raised in Chinatown, but born in Taiwan. She has already been flown back there for burial."

"When you speak to her parents, please convey our condolences. She was well-liked and well-regarded here."

Margaret Harding said, "Yes, Raquel, please do the same for us. We got to know her over the last three or so years. She was a terrific young lawyer."

And then, as if on some unseen cue, Judge Conley said to the court reporter: "Ready to proceed."

He settled into position above his machine, like a dancer poised to start. "Yes, Your Honor," he said.

As though dictating, Helen Conley said, "This is an *in camera* session in the case of the People of the State of New York against Juan Suarez. Present in my chambers are Margaret Harding for the People, and Raquel Rematti for defendant."

Conley glanced down briefly at an index card in front of her. She had written down the subjects she wanted to cover. She was a careful person. "This session is being held for two reasons. The first is to discuss the impact of the death five days ago of one of the defense attorneys. The other is to address an email the Court received yesterday from Ms. Rematti requesting that Detective Bo Halsey, who testified last week for the prosecution, be recalled to the stand and re-examined by Ms. Rematti in light of the public disclosure of a video that purports to describe, according to Ms. Rematti's letter, two Suffolk County police detectives apparently carrying something from the bedroom of Brad Richardson, the victim."

Margaret Harding said, "The People are prepared to address both issues."

Raquel said, "I can simplify the first."

Conley looked surprised. "Go ahead."

"I am not seeking a mistrial. The defense will proceed with the trial. I do ask that you interview the jurors as soon as possible to determine whether one or more feels that his or her ability to be fair is compromised by the murder. I think we can assume they all know about it. I also think we can assume that they will say they can be fair and rule on the basis of the evidence at trial and nothing else."

Conley turned to Margaret Harding. "Do you want to comment?"

"Certainly. This is not what we expected. We anticipated a motion for a mistrial. If the defense waives that, we want to go forward."

Conley was an efficient woman. "So, that resolves that issue. I'll interview each of the jurors separately. If I conclude they can be fair, we'll go forward with the trial at ten today. If any one of them presents a problem, we have four alternate jurors. Anything further on this subject?"

"No," Raquel said.

Relieved, Margaret Harding said, "No." Since she had expected Raquel Rematti to urge a mistrial, she wondered whether the legendary lawyer seated across the table had some intuitive sense that the trial was evolving in her favor.

"What we're about to discuss," Conley said, "will be sealed, as will all of this conference. No one is going to discuss with the press or anyone other than your client, Ms. Rematti, what happens here."

Raquel never allowed her personal emotions—such as the flash of annoyance she felt now or the chilly change in the atmosphere of the room—to interfere with the work she had to do.

Conley said, "Ordinarily what happens outside of the courtroom is no concern of mine. But in this case it does concern me when I see a broadcast that certainly suggests that there is information, important information, that I'm not aware of."

Raquel waited through the pause. It was important not to volunteer anything until she had a sense of this plain woman's direction. She waited just long enough for Margaret Harding to say, "We knew nothing about this video, Your Honor."

"That's not what concerns me right now, Ms. Harding."

While the judge paused again, Raquel again waited. An essential rule: when there's no need to speak, keep your mouth shut.

"What concerns me right now is how to secure the source, the original, of this video. It's obvious to me that the authenticity, the completeness, of this is important, very important. Ms. Harding, what's the source of this video?"

"Our computer people are working on that right now."

"But at this critical moment, as we sit here with a jury about to arrive to start the third week of this trial, you don't seem to know whether this video is authentic?"

"Not yet," Margaret Harding said.

"If not yet, when?"

"I'm just not certain."

For the first time Raquel saw an expression other than calm indifference on the judge's face: she raised her eyebrows above the black frame of her glasses.

"When we finish do you think you can ask Mr. Lupo what his office is doing? And by the mid-morning break I'd like to get some kind of report on this—where this tape has been, is it complete, who has had access to it? That kind of thing."

"I just want to make clear, Judge," Margaret Harding said, "that we never had this tape."

"You know, Ms. Harding, I try not to decide anything until I know what the facts are. But at the moment I don't know what you mean when you say *we* didn't have the tape. You just told me you didn't see it until this morning. And *we* is a very large concept, isn't it? It's not just you. You have a large office, or I should say Mr. Lupo does. Is the detective who testified last week part of the *we?*"

Margaret Harding gave Conley a narrow-eyed, withering look, the scorn of the beautiful for the plain. She said nothing.

Conley turned to Raquel. It was, she realized, the first time Conley had ever looked directly at her. "And is there anything you want to say, Ms. Rematti?"

"I appreciate your sensitivity in handling this, Judge."

"I'm not looking for compliments, Ms. Rematti."

But Conley seemed, somehow, to like these words from this famous woman. She looked flattered. But quickly she reverted to form: "I'm trying to deal, Ms. Rematti, with a situation that's very troubling to me, too. I find it's best to take things in steps. So my question to you is: Do you want anything done now, before we go any further?"

"Certainly, Judge. As I said in my email, I want Detective Halsey recalled to the stand. And I want to ask the detective when he first saw that tape. Or when he was first aware of it. Or when it was first mentioned to him."

Margaret Harding interrupted Raquel. "We are prepared to dismiss the charges relating to larceny and burglary."

Judge Conley had no visible reaction. She waited for Raquel.

Harding's words caught Raquel off guard. She immediately recognized that this unexpected statement was very skillful. If Harding dropped the charge to which the video related, then Harding could argue the video was not relevant. Raquel said, "That doesn't remedy the problem, Your Honor. I understand that the government wouldn't want the jurors to see the tape in this courtroom, and that to prevent that from happening, Ms. Harding is willing to drop the theft charges. But the tape has greater importance, Judge. If other people—in this case the police—were doing things that Mr. Suarez is accused of doing then the jurors are entitled, at this stage, to see the tape to evaluate whether Mr. Suarez did other things."

"I can't prevent the government from dismissing part of its charges, Ms. Rematti."

Raquel had an only uncertain grasp of how to deal with this judge. There were times during the trial when she was surprised by her willingness to sustain her objections, to listen to her arguments, and to make small rulings that were helpful. There were also times when Conley's parochialism—her grandfather had been a county supervisor, her father a judge, she had benefitted from the nepotism of an engrained political party in the county—led her to allow Margaret Harding to ask questions that were certainly irrelevant but damaging to Juan. Yet Conley was savvy. She was worried about reversals: she wanted a promotion, and a reversal in the most high-profile criminal case in the country since the Casey Anthony and George Zimmerman trials wouldn't help her.

Raquel said, "I know you don't have any control, Judge, over whether Ms. Harding drops the theft charges, just as you had no control over what charges Ms. Harding brought in the first place —"

"Ms. Rematti, it's not Ms. Harding who brought these charges. It was the Grand Jury."

Raquel shrugged off the fourth-grade teacher's reprimand, just as she shrugged off the impulse to say that a Grand Jury would indict the Pope if the DA asked for it. "But this tape is essential for reasons that relate to the murder charges."

"You said that before, Ms. Rematti, and I'm not sure you're right. In fact, it seems to me the tape could be irrelevant. The fact that, even assuming the tape is authentic, other people were stealing money on the same day as the murder does not mean that another person was in the house that day committing a murder."

"That's for the jury to decide, Judge. But without the tape the jurors don't have the ability to decide one way or the other whether the fact that other people were stealing cash leads to a reasonable doubt that Mr. Suarez committed the murder."

"Ms. Rematti, there is another problem with this tape. I have a sense that the end of the case is fast coming on. Whether it's relevant or not, whether or not it tends to exonerate your client on the murder count—and at the moment I don't necessarily see that it does—I have no idea whether it's authentic. I'd never let a jury see any piece of evidence where there's an obvious question as to whether it's authentic or a fabrication."

"Mr. Suarez is entitled to a fair trial. Suspending a murder trial for a day or two to test the authenticity of the tape is more important than the possibility of an innocent man's conviction."

Judge Conley gave Raquel an icy glance and then turned to Margaret Harding. "Ms. Harding, you've been uncharacteristically quiet. Is there anything you want to tell me?"

"We're not looking at a one- or two-day break, Judge. My office is unlikely to know in what format this video existed. Even when we do find that, we may not have the electronic forensics people who can do the kind of analysis we would do on a traditional recording device. It will take time, and resources the government may need even more time to locate, to find out how the tape was recorded, where, who set it up, who was responsible for maintaining its integrity, where the recording has been all these months, who released it, and whether it was or wasn't altered. We live in the age of electronic animation, the Pixar era."

"Pixar?" Raquel said. "A man's life is in the balance, and we're talking about Pixar?"

Conley ignored her. "I'd like to hear some sort of presentation late this afternoon, Ms. Harding, where the best expert you've currently got can answer some of the questions you've just raised."

"I don't know whether we even have the capacity with the assets we have now to do that by this afternoon."

"That," Judge Conley said, "is your problem."

And, before calling an end to the conference, she said to Raquel, "It's only fair to alert you now that I'm not inclined to require Detective Halsey to return to the stand for further cross-examination by you regarding this video. I just heard that the state is dropping the theft charges. Even if it's authentic, the video has little or no relevance to the murder charge."

This time Raquel Rematti couldn't control herself. "That is so profoundly unfair. It negates any likelihood that Mr. Suarez will have a fair trial."

Conley stood up. She said, "I won't tolerate being spoken to like that by any lawyer, including you, Ms. Rematti. I want an apology now or I'll call a hearing after the trial to hold you in contempt."

Raquel stood, too. "I'd welcome that."

Juan Suarez was in the holding cell outside the courtroom. Raquel hadn't seen him since the day the trial recessed, a day when Theresa Bui was still alive, vital, and filled with the promise of the young. Raquel said, "Juan, there are two things I want to talk to you about before we go back into the courtroom."

"What?"

"The first is that there was a film that somebody sent out showing that two cops, not you, stole the cash in Brad's bedroom."

"You know I never stole anything, Raquel."

What, Raquel thought, do I really know about this man? "The theft charges have been dropped," she said. "You're not charged with stealing anymore. The jury won't be asked to decide whether or not you took the money."

"I never had any money. I only had money I worked for."

They were face to face, whispering even though the guards were inattentive. "But understand, Juan, there are still the killing charges."

"I didn't kill Mr. Richardson."

Raquel Rematti had learned over the years that even the guilty could frankly, earnestly, and disarmingly stare into her eyes while saying, *I'm innocent.* For her it was an illusion that people who lie can't look you straight in the eye. And it was an illusion, too, that an evasive, nervous person was lying. Continuing to look at Juan's unwavering, earnest eyes, she decided to say nothing.

"I never lied to you, Raquel."

"And there's something more I need to tell you, Juan."

Strangely impassive, not speaking, he waited.

"Theresa was killed last Friday night. Murdered by a sniper."

"I know that," he said, his voice oddly fluent, as though he always had the capacity to speak English far better than he had.

"How?"

"Prisoners watch television, they talk all the time."

"I know how much you liked Theresa."

"I did, Raquel." But suddenly the eyes with which he now stared at her, the expression on his face, and the stance of his body, were transformed into hostility.

Raquel Rematti, who had spent years dealing with dangerous men and never once was afraid of them, was now afraid.

"You killed her. You spoke about Oscar Caliente. And now see what happened."

35.

Bo Halsey lived in a ranch house where he was raised in the Springs area of East Hampton. Still covered with dense woods, Springs was where Jackson Pollock and Willem de Kooning had lived. It was where Pollock had driven his car into a tree at ninety miles an hour. Bo knew their names and had seen pictures of the paintings. Awed tourists sometimes knocked on his door for directions to the artists' shingled weather-beaten houses. For Bo, the blessing of the area was not that these inexplicably famous men had once lived there but that the bay waters were less than a mile from his house, the waters where fish were abundant every day of the year.

When he heard the knock on his door as he cooked a breakfast of eggs and bacon, he thought that tourists had come to the house for directions.

There were no tourists this morning. The men at the door were Vic Santangello and Paul Arena, two FBI agents who had worked from time to time with Bo.

Bo Halsey knew exactly why they were there.

"Hey, guys, come on in. I just made some coffee."

Santangello and Arena followed him into the kitchen. Just outside the big window two deer stood completely still. The woods in Springs were filled with deer. "When I was a kid," Bo said as he pointed to the coffee, which he still made in an old Pyrex percolator his mother had used years ago, "I loved to see the deer. It was like Christmas all the time. Rudolph the Red-Nosed Reindeer. Now there are so many of them they look like rats on long legs to me."

"Bo," Santangello said, "I gotta get this out because we really hate doing this."

"It's part of being on the job, Vic. We're supposed to hate doing the things we do. It's lousy work no matter how you look at it."

Arena said, "They want to talk to you. There are two fucking U.S. Attorneys waiting for you in Riverhead. You gotta come with us."

"My, my. U.S. Attorneys? When did the feds get involved in this?"

"When that gook who works for you went to the Justice Department and said you were a racist who suppressed evidence in order to convict a Mexican."

"Since when," Bo said, "was that a crime?"

"The Italian broad took him to our bosses in the city. They think the DA out here can't really investigate one of his own people."

"And that would be me, right?"

"Appears to be," Arena said.

"Sorry about this, Bo," Santangello said, genuine apology in his voice.

"No problem, guys."

36.

"AND TELL ME AGAIN," Judge Conley said, "why you think I should let the jury hear this woman." She glanced at her notepad, searching for the name. "Kathy Schiavoni?"

There was an uncharacteristic urgency as Raquel Rematti spoke, "We know she conducted all the forensics tests on evidence taken from the Richardson bedroom."

Margaret Harding, standing next to Raquel but looking only at the judge, said, "We've presented our case, Judge. The prosecution has rested. At no point did we find it necessary to put on forensics evidence. We've conceded that Mr. Suarez's fingerprints and DNA were not in the office where the killing took place. We know that his fingerprints are all over the kitchen and other areas of the house where he would have worked. We didn't use that evidence because we were trying to be careful in what we presented. We want a fair trial for this defendant as much as Ms. Rematti does."

"And I know," Raquel said, "that the next thing Ms. Harding will say is that, since the state presented no forensics evidence, we don't have a right to present any."

Raquel recognized that Judge Conley was again deliberately working in this conversation, just as she had two days earlier with the tape, to navigate a way through the maze to exclude more evidence, now the testimony of Kathy Schiavoni that there were semen stains on the sheets in the Richardson bedroom that had no known source, the semen of an unidentified man.

Conley tried a new approach: "Let's assume, Ms. Rematti, that it doesn't matter that the state elected not to use a fingerprint or DNA expert, and that you are entitled to put on any witness you think would assist your client. What's the relevance of whether there were any stains at all on the sheets? This is not a rape case, it's a murder case, isn't it?"

Raquel said, "And I have information from a forensic scientist employed by Ms. Harding's office that there is an unknown source of semen undoubtedly placed there by an unknown man at some point within twenty-four hours of the killing."

Through her thick, unfashionable glasses, Conley looked at Raquel. "I know you've said that, Ms. Rematti. But isn't that information tenuous, remote, possibly misleading to the jury? Whatever your views may be, I've given your client a fair trial, but I don't have to give him the opportunity to present any evidence he wants to present if it's not relevant to the case. What is relevant is that his semen is on the sheets, but the state decided not to use that DNA evidence. What is the conceivable relevance of the fact that there are also semen stains of an unidentified man? It can be said, can't it, that Ms. Harding did your client a favor by not presenting evidence that we know gives the identity of one set of semen stains—Juan Suarez?"

"We appreciate all the favors we are blessed with," Raquel said, "but Mr. Suarez is entitled to present his own evidence, not just evidence that responds to what the state has put on."

"Ms. Rematti, I was trying to avoid making comments on strategy, particularly for a lawyer of your experience. But if I let you put on Ms. Schiavoni to testify about her findings aren't we opening the door to Ms. Harding putting on rebuttal evidence that Mr. Suarez's semen was there?"

"Of course, but where's the damage? The jury knows that Mr. Suarez and Joan Richardson were lovers."

"I'm not concerned with who sustains what damage as a result of evidence. The fact that evidence is not good for a particular side's case doesn't make it legitimate or illegitimate evidence. You may remember, Ms. Rematti, even though you've shared with me your view that your client has not had a fair trial, that I excluded the evidence that your client assaulted a man in New York with a long knife. Although that would have been compelling evidence for the state, I didn't allow it. I said on the record that its prejudicial impact outweighed its probative value. Maybe you forgot that?"

Knowing that she was losing the opportunity to call Kathy Schiavoni, Raquel used a gambit: "Ms. Schiavoni would also testify that Ms. Harding knew about the results, knew that there was the semen of an unknown person, another man who must have had access to the house. And that Ms. Harding deliberately decided not to pursue it. I know Ms. Harding didn't once tell us about this."

"So what, Ms. Rematti? Another person who had access to the house? Apparently half of East Hampton had access to the house. It seems there were people who had lots of private access to Brad Richardson and Joan Richardson and their bedroom. This is not a trial about adultery or homosexuality."

Raquel felt a sense of futility. "And, again, Judge, Ms. Harding and her office knew there was exculpatory evidence and never gave it to us. We learned about it through Ms. Schiavoni voluntarily coming forward to tell me this evidence existed but was never developed or revealed."

"Judge," Margaret Harding said, "I've tried to maintain a professional relationship with Ms. Rematti. But now this is getting personal. I have no obligation to provide the defense with irrelevant evidence, only evidence that might exonerate her client. She's suggesting that I did or failed to do something I had an ethical obligation to do. She's calling into question my ethics."

"The lady doth protest too much, methinks," Raquel said, regretting as she spoke the quote from Shakespeare.

"Ms. Rematti," Helen Conley said, "stop that. It's been a very difficult, wrenching trial to everyone. Don't start poisoning the well. Your client is on trial. Ms. Harding isn't. If she's done something wrong, she'll have to answer for it either with a reversal of the conviction or before the disciplinary committee, or both. Her conduct has no bearing on this case now, unless you want to move for a mistrial. If I grant that, then we can go through all this process again."

Raquel's mind raced. Was there enough evidence in the case Margaret Harding had presented to convict Juan Suarez beyond a reasonable doubt? Or would these jurors—most of them retired from government jobs as clerks, assessors, and the county public works department—ever understand what reasonable doubt meant or were they hard-wired in their isolated world on the East End of Long Island to convict? And, Raquel thought, what about me? I've been over-invested in this man. Do I really want a mistrial? Do I really want to go all over this again?

Move on, Raquel Rematti said to herself, *move on.*

"We're not asking for a mistrial, Judge."

Kathy Schiavoni was so angry that there was a tremor in her hands as she and Raquel Rematti stood at the microphones on the concrete steps of the courthouse after Helen Conley ruled that Kathy wouldn't be allowed to testify.

She stood just to Raquel's left, a shy woman with bushy hair worn in the style of the late seventies. Raquel spoke into the cluster of microphones. "We were prepared today to offer the testimony of a forensic specialist employed by the District Attorney's office. Her name is Kathy Schiavoni, and she is here with me. She is a whistleblower. She performed most of the forensic examination on materials at the Richardson home. Among the things she reviewed, and she would have testified to this today if her testimony had not been ruled out of the case, was that she examined sheets that were found on the bed in the Richardson home on the day of Brad Richardson's death."

As Raquel spoke, her cold breath slipping out into the bright air, Kathy Schiavoni stared, almost defiantly, into the lens of a CNN camera held aloft by a cameraman.

Raquel continued: "She found semen stains on the sheets from two identifiable men. One was Brad Richardson. The other was my client, Juan Suarez. The third semen stain was from an unknown man. Ms. Schiavoni would have testified, but was prevented from doing so, that she brought those results to the District Attorney's office. She expected that further search warrants would be issued to obtain evidence from men such as Senator Rawls to locate a match for the unknown semen. The prosecution refused Kathy Schiavoni's request for those warrants. And Ms. Schiavoni would have also testified that, when she sought to re-examine the sheets, they were missing from the evidence locker maintained and strictly controlled by the DA's office."

Raquel paused briefly while a jet roared overhead, leaving a vapor trail across the acutely blue winter sky as it headed out and over the Atlantic. When the sound could no longer submerge her voice, Raquel said: "Bravely, when Ms. Schiavoni realized she wouldn't be able to complete her report and certainly would not be called as a witness by the prosecution, she approached me to disclose the results of her work. While she can't be called as a witness for my client's defense, I wanted to acknowledge, publicly, that she stepped forward to do what was obviously right—let the public know crucial information was suppressed by the state about the events surrounding the death of Brad Richardson. Her information, while no longer able to assist Juan Suarez, reveals not only her integrity but also the obvious lack of integrity that has afflicted this prosecution."

One of the reporters, Gloria Arroyo, wearing a baseball cap on which the word "Fox" was woven, asked, "Raquel, is there any information about the missing man?"

"None. That was precisely what Ms. Schiavoni wanted to learn."

Her blonde face squinting in the harsh sunlight, Gloria asked Kathy, "Ms. Schiavoni, who did you show your report to in the DA's office?"

Kathy Schiavoni stepped slightly to her right, toward the microphones, as Raquel moved to make room for her. Her voice was defiant. Kathy had her chance. "I gave the report to Margaret Harding."

37.

Bo Halsey actually smiled as he sat across the scratched wooden table from Gary Upchurch and Vanessa Strong, who tersely had introduced themselves as Assistant United States Attorneys leading a criminal investigation. They were in their mid-thirties. Santangello and Arena stood behind them. Halsey had often used this bleak and windowless room as the place where he interrogated men and women.

"Hey, guys, I guess I'm under arrest," Halsey said.

Upchurch responded, "To be honest with you, Mr. Halsey, you should be aware of the fact that you are the target of a federal criminal investigation that was initiated when the video was released. We have reliable information that you saw this video months ago and instructed someone who worked for you to hide it. So you're the target of a federal criminal investigation for obstruction of justice."

"Hot shit."

"You don't have to speak with us today. You know that, don't you?"

"Do you think I need a twelve-year-old to tell me that?"

Upchurch glanced at Vanessa Strong. He didn't respond to Halsey. Instead, he gave a signal to Santangello to open a laptop and turn the screen toward Bo. On the small screen the scene of Cerullo and Cohen, who stumbled around almost like comic characters in a silent movie, was played from start to finish, a span of no more than three minutes. At several points they were crawling on the floor, rear ends up in the air like clowns. At other points they were glancing furtively around the room in search of cameras. And, through most of the video, they were carrying packets of cash.

The video already had more than a million hits on YouTube.

"When did you first see this?" asked Vanessa Strong, an attractive black woman with blonde-streaked dreadlocks.

Halsey was still grinning. "Wrong question, fella. It's not when, it's if. Never saw this Keystone Cops routine until it came up on the Internet."

"Are you sure?" Upchurch asked.

"Does the sun come up in the east?"

"Maybe," Strong said, "you should think about that. Lying to federal agents, even if you're not under oath, is a crime."

"You know what I know? A gook with spiky hair has told you he showed me this. He's lying."

"Why would he do that?" Upchurch asked.

"Why would flies buzz around shit? Have you ever heard that people who work for you are either at your feet, kissing them, or at your throat, trying to strangle you? Maybe he's got grievances because I have more hair than he does."

Vanessa Strong said, "Maybe you should think about your answer again. Take your time."

"Let me tell you something: all I'm thinking about is why you would waste *your* time treating me like this. Do you think that anybody is going to believe him? I've been around a long, long time. Nobody but nobody has ever said I lifted a pencil from the office and took it home."

"Ang Tien took a lie detector test yesterday," Upchurch said.

"Let me guess? He passed."

"How would you like to help yourself," Strong said, "and take a lie detector test?"

Halsey repeated words that he had often heard when he was interrogating people in this room. "How'd you like to take a good flying fuck for yourself?"

38.

It was two in the afternoon when Judge Conley suddenly emerged from the rear door of the courtroom. At the words "All rise," everyone in the crowded courtroom stood until she said, "Be seated."

Escorted by three guards, Juan Suarez quickly emerged from the holding cell. Raquel Rematti noticed that there wasn't a trace of anxiety or confusion in his expression. He smiled at Raquel when he sat.

Since Raquel expected that the jurors had a question—they had only deliberated for a day—she was surprised when Conley announced, "We have a verdict."

For Raquel, that was too sudden. Usually a fast verdict meant a conviction. She put her hand on Juan's shoulder as the jury filed into the box.

"Ladies and gentlemen," Judge Conley said, "I understand you have a verdict?"

A 72-year-old woman with silver hair, a retired school teacher who had been picked as the foreperson, said in a voice remarkably similar to the judge's, "We do."

Not one of the jurors had glanced at Raquel or even in the direction of the defense table since entering the courtroom. They stared at the courtroom deputy as he took a slip of paper, the verdict form, from the hand of the foreperson. He carried the paper, folded, to the judge. Her face absolutely expressionless, she glanced at it for no more than a second and handed it back to the deputy.

Judge Conley then looked toward the spectators, many of them reporters. Conley, speaking directly into her microphone, conscious that her words were being broadcast around the world, said: "I want to make it clear that when the verdict is announced there will not be a sound, there will not be a reaction, from anyone in this courtroom."

Raquel Rematti, despite the many times over more than twenty years that she had been in precisely this situation, just as a verdict was about to be announced, felt the blood throbbing in her temples.

And then the silver-haired lady spoke the word: *Guilty.*

39.

WHEN RAQUEL REMATTI EMERGED from the courthouse to the stone plaza, she found what she expected: dozens of cameras and boisterous reporters. It was chaos, like a demonstration veering out of control.

She stopped behind the microphones. It was another clear winter day. When the sound of the crowd subsided slightly, she said into the microphones clustered around her, "Today's guilty verdict is the result of a deeply flawed prosecution and a trial in which the jurors were deprived of essential information. It is a shameful result. It is a prosecution that had its source in a blatant rush to judgment. It was directed not just at Juan Suarez but in effect at an entire community of men and women whose only offense is that they came to America, as all of our ancestors did, for a better life."

Julie Harrison, a reporter from NBC who once had dinner with Raquel, asked, "Will there be an appeal?"

"Certainly. Throughout my career I have had confidence in our criminal justice system. Many jury convictions in high-profile cases are reversed."

Harrison asked, "What issues can you raise?"

"Many," Raquel said, "and they stem from the first hours after the tragic killing of Brad Richardson. First, with no concrete evidence—no eyewitnesses, no tell-tale traces of anything at the crime scene—they hunted down Juan Suarez. They did this solely on the say-so of Joan Richardson. The rich, powerful, profoundly troubled, and lying Joan Richardson. The prosecution never looked for another person. And, in fact, as you saw in the courtroom, the DA's office succeeded in doing all it could to prevent the jury from hearing about all the other people who surrounded Brad Richardson at the time of his death."

Another voice, deeper in the crowd, asked, "What else?"

"The government's staggering misconduct, and the court's willingness to condone it. We know that Juan Suarez did not steal anything, we know that two rogue detectives did, and we know that the jury was prevented in the courtroom from hearing anything about that.

"We also know that an honorable woman, a person of integrity, came forward to tell us extremely troubling information about how her forensic work was thwarted and then was silenced. I understand that even now she is the victim of retaliation, placed on involuntary leave without pay.

"This trial is Alabama justice in the 1930s, not a fair trial in the America of the twenty-first century."

Raquel Rematti knew that her critical words, broadcast to the world, would end in disciplinary proceedings that could result in revoking her law license. Lawyers lived in a feudal regime: they weren't supposed to say what they truly believed about prosecutors or judges, they were expected to keep in line with an unwritten set of standards controlling what it was permissible to say about the system. There were serious costs to violating the code of silence.

Raquel wasn't concerned about these costs.

Another voice rang out: "Where is your client now?"

"He is being returned to the detention center in Riverhead where he has been held in deplorable conditions for months."

"Can you say something about that? Why deplorable?"

"Not only has his treatment been harsh, he has been assaulted by prisoners acting, we believe, at the direction of a Mexican drug lord, Oscar Caliente, whose inexplicable contacts with Brad Richardson I was not allowed to explore. The prison staff did nothing to stop the deadly attack. And then they prepared a report that was not just a whitewash. It was a fabrication."

"What was your client's reaction to the verdict?"

No one in all her years of practice had ever asked that question. "Thank you, I want to address that. Prosecutors, judges, the public—and you in the media—never see criminal defendants as men and women, as people who have feelings, fears, hopes, thoughts, love for their children and others. Instead you see all of them as evil-doers."

She stopped briefly when someone, a heckler, shouted, "Come on, lady, cut the bullshit."

"Juan Suarez is human. When he heard the verdict, he was very disappointed, he continues to assert his own innocence—and I fully agree with him—on the accusation that he killed Brad Richardson. But Juan Suarez is also a stoic. He's never once raged at the racism that brought about this prosecution. He's never once complained about the unfairness of the trial. He is now what he always has been: patient, decent, and respectful."

Raquel Rematti began to turn away from the microphones when someone asked, "Can you comment about Theresa Bui, the woman who was killed at your house?"

"Theresa was a remarkable woman—intelligent, caring, attractive in every imaginable way. She was also growing into a great lawyer. She enriched my life. Now that this trial is over, I'm going to join her lovely family and join in their grief."

"There's information that you were the target, not Theresa. Is that so?"

Raquel was already making her way through the dense crowd. Two microphones followed her. "If that's so, then it would have been far better if I was the one who died."

"What steps are you taking to protect yourself?"

Struggling steadily through the press of men and women, Raquel Rematti thought about the months of her cancer. She said: "I always pray for God's will."

40.

A CHAIN LINK FENCE with razor wire on top encircled the landfill on the edge of the Sag Harbor-Bridgehampton Turnpike. In the twenty years since the landfill was closed the fence had steadily decayed. There was a rip in the mesh through which anyone could pass.

Billy Jones and Robert Hedges, both of them kids from the long-time colony of blacks who lived along the old road, often went through the rip in the curtain of fence. They were both thirteen. The rip was large enough not only for them but also for the worn mountain bikes they had waited all winter to ride. There had been a string of warm, spring-like days. After school they took long trips around Bridgehampton and Sag Harbor. At some point on each of those trips they went through the hole in the fence. The landfill was like a private preserve for them, a playground. They were able to smoke there.

After all the years of dormancy, the landfill sometimes gave up its secrets, just as in warm weather it gave up a sweet aroma of rot. Metal cans, broken glass, shattered plastic toys somehow appeared on the surface. Rain, moisture, snow, dirt, and time made anything Billy and Robert found completely useless, but the boys still felt like treasure hunters when they discovered something.

The landfill was a small mountain of dirt and grass draped over a steadily decomposing mound of garbage and debris that had accumulated from 1920 to the early 1990s. In any kind of sunlight, even in winter and early spring, the area of the landfill became warm. Its decaying debris was a heat source: snow melted more quickly over it than anywhere else.

Loose dogs often made their way through the fence to the landfill, attracted by the scent of decades of waste. Each time Billy and Robert went into the landfill they found new holes left behind by the dogs. Sometimes the boys kicked dirt back into the holes, and at other times they widened the holes.

Billy was the one who saw the ripped plastic bag that had been pulled part of the way out of a hole. The boys clawed and kicked and dug around the bag. It came apart. They reached inside it.

Inside was a large yellow rain poncho and a long knife. There were big brown stains on the poncho and the knife. These were the most interesting things the boys had ever seen this stale landfill give up. The poncho looked cool to them—it was still intact, as they saw when they stretched it between them. And the long, curved knife was even cooler than the poncho. They rolled the poncho around the long knife and took them home.

41.

SHOCK AND AWE.

Bo Halsey had done it so often himself that it long ago became a routine part of his work: the appearance, just after dawn, of the police at your door, shouting, *Police, open up.* People were vulnerable when they were sleeping, or just awake, disoriented. And, when they saw five or six strangers, sometimes holding guns, they were afraid. Arresting people at dawn infused them with terror, with a sense of the enormous power of a government that had suddenly turned on them.

But Bo Halsey couldn't be shocked or awed. He had already been awake and had breakfast and coffee when at dawn he heard the three cars and two SUVs pull up on his lawn. He knew what was happening.

He opened the front door before the phalanx of men could cross the lawn and knock. He wasn't surprised to see Santangello and Arena in the lead: their bosses knew that the two agents liked Halsey and they had to prove that they could do their jobs without letting emotions such as loyalty and friendship interfere.

"What is it," Bo said, "you guys never heard of a cell phone? You could've called."

Vic Santangello said, "I know, but the fucking kids made us come out here this way."

"Must've been because I talked fresh to them, right?"

"Something like that," Arena said. "You were fresh, Bo. It was fun to watch. Can we come in?"

"Hey, my door's always open. I don't even use locks."

Santangello and Arena stepped inside. The others remained on the porch. The kitchen had not been renovated in years. It had brown cabinets, a linoleum floor, and a yellow refrigerator. It was neat and orderly.

Arena said, "I have to say this, Bo. You're under arrest. I have to read you your Miranda rights."

"I have the right to remain silent. Anything and everything I say can be used against me. I have the right to have a lawyer represent me."

Arena repeated those words.

Bo Halsey laughed, crossing his wrists. Arena snapped on the plastic handcuffs, loosely. As Bo began to lead the way to the door, Santangello said, "Slow down. We have a search warrant."

"Not a problem," Bo Halsey said. "The sheets from the fucking Joan Richardson bedroom are in the basement next to the oil tank."

Vic Santangello shouted at the other men who stood like phantoms in the semi-dark on the porch. "Get back to the vehicles, get back." Since Vic was the senior guy, the other men receded, not speaking.

Arena was already on the stairs leading to the basement. Halsey and Santangello heard the uncertain footsteps. "Man," Santangello said, "we've known each other a long time. Just between us—I swear this is just between us—what the fuck were you up to with the video and these sheets?"

"Just between us girls, this was the last and biggest job of my life. I did lots of work, made lots of decisions. There was no way I was going to let a kid with a videotape and a sad girl with sheets mess up my conviction. It worked."

"No," Santangello said, "it really didn't."

42.

Raquel Rematti was in her office when the call came at two in the afternoon. She had done nothing since mid-morning as the waves of relief and peace, the quiet ecstasy of safety, passed over her. Her day started with that early morning dread she had so often experienced in the last year. After she ate breakfast and dressed herself in her most expensive business clothes, she had taken a taxi, through heavy traffic, to Columbia Presbyterian Hospital on the East Side. Although she tried to read the *Times* on her black Kindle during the wrenching half-hour ride, her attention barely registered the headlines. She finally gave up and just stared at the congested traffic on York Avenue, always chaotic, the only two-way avenue in the city.

Zain Anil, an Indian-born woman who had been her main doctor for the last year, had developed real affection and respect for Raquel Rematti. Only 42, Dr. Anil managed all of Raquel's treatment, coordinating a small army of surgeons, radiologists, oncologists, and technicians who were involved in the complicated process of saving Raquel's life.

Raquel made Dr. Anil's life easy. She never complained, she never resisted, she was never in denial. She never cried. She also made no arbitrary demands on Dr. Anil's time or attention. She was respectful of the needs of other patients.

The doctor was a prompt, orderly, and efficient professional. When she delivered bad news, she didn't sugarcoat it. When she had good news, she didn't clap her hands. She was kind and orderly and even.

As soon as Raquel arrived and seated herself at the chair in front of Dr. Anil's desk in her cramped office, Zain said, "I have good news, Raquel. What you have is Lyme disease, not a recurrence of cancer. You're free of it. But you're one of the dozens of people I've seen who have houses in the Hamptons. The area is overrun with deer. There must be millions, or billions, of deer-borne tics out there. You were bitten. The symptoms of the Lyme disease—soreness, body pain—sometimes mimic the feelings that cancer survivors have."

"Thank you, Zain, thank you."

"You've put yourself through hell for the last six weeks. You could have told us and we would have relieved your nightmare."

"I was afraid, Zain," Raquel said. "And I had work to do."

"I know. You can rest now. You're exhausted. Antibiotics will cure you."

Raquel Rematti, thinking *I'm cured, I get to live*, put her hands over her face and cried.

She was still floating in that profound sense of relief when the call came in from Margaret Harding. She hadn't spoken to Harding since the end of the trial. She had seen some of the television broadcasts in which Margaret, who looked even better on television than she did in person, claimed victory. She had appeared on many interviews; she was a guest on CBS, NBC, CNN and other stations. She was obviously in her element and wanted more, more. There was one level at which Raquel couldn't blame her for this—Raquel was enough of a warrior in this business of warriors to understand that *to the victor belong the spoils*. There was another level at which she recoiled at the sight and sound of Margaret Harding.

Raquel said to Roger when he told her Margaret Harding was on the line, "Tell her I'm busy."

Roger said, "It's extremely important, or so she says."

"Maybe she's been nominated to the Supreme Court," Raquel said.

"Or maybe she's Miss New York in the next Miss America pageant."

Raquel decided to take the call. She pressed the key for the speakerphone. Margaret Harding's now too-familiar voice filled the office. She got right to the point. "Two weeks ago, two boys playing in a landfill in Sag Harbor found a poncho and machete. The poncho and the blade were rich with the DNA of Brad Richardson."

Completely alert, Raquel had a sense of the direction this was taking. But, as she always did at the times when she wanted to learn things, she waited for more.

"We've determined," Margaret Harding said, "that the only other DNA—and there is a rich amount of DNA—is the DNA of a guy named Jimmy Ortega. There is absolutely no DNA of Juan Suarez."

Raquel stood up and walked to the wide windows overlooking Park Avenue. On the median strip dividing the uptown and downtown traffic, the faintest traces of green and other spring colors were starting to emerge in the flowerbeds. The median stretched in a straight line as far uptown as she could see. Again she said nothing.

As if reading from a script, Margaret Harding said, "The FBI labs and our own forensics experts have determined that it is the machete that killed Brad Richardson and the Borzois. The killer could not have been your client."

Raquel was elated but controlled as she said, "Margaret, I appreciate your honesty in making this call."

Margaret Harding interrupted: "Honesty has nothing to do with it."

Raquel ignored the tone of her words. "If you can give me the DNA report, I'll prepare a motion to vacate the verdict."

"No need for that. In fifteen minutes our office and the United States Attorney's Office are issuing a press release saying that your client has been exonerated. We've already notified Judge Conley. Later today she will sign an order vacating the conviction and dismissing the indictment. Your client will be taken to JFK and deported to Mexico."

Raquel decided she didn't need to speak. There was nothing to say. She hit the *End* button on her phone and, staring at the beautiful avenue, she cried again.

43.

THE METROPOLITAN DETENTION CENTER was on the waterfront in Brooklyn. Raquel drove carefully under the elevated Brooklyn-Queens Expressway, through arches that created dark shadows even on a day as bright as this. Beyond the immense prison—the newest building along the waterfront—strikingly tall cranes stood against the crystalline sky. The air was as clear as on that Tuesday when the planes hit the towers of the World Trade Center. In the years when the towers were still standing they were visible, three miles away, from the open, windswept parking lot. Now the new tower, completed just months earlier and far more beautiful than the destroyed rectangular towers, soared above Manhattan's sharp-edged skyline. To the left was the immense span of the Verrazano-Narrows Bridge.

Raquel had made many trips to the MDC over the years. She and the other lawyers who regularly represented clients awaiting trial in the federal courts in Manhattan and Brooklyn often called the prison their "store," the place where the clients were. Most of the prisoners in the maximum security facility were accused of drug-running. Many were street gang members. Some were Wall Street types charged with insider-trading and fraud; they were scared out of their skins by the other prisoners. And some of the prisoners—none of whom Raquel had yet represented, although she often thought that she would volunteer to do so—were called "Islamic terrorists." This was Guantanamo Bay North.

Intricate procedures governed visits to prisoners at the MDC. Access to Juan Suarez at the far more lax state prison in Riverhead took less than fifteen minutes. Here, in this warehouse-like prison, Raquel had never been able to reach an inmate in less than an hour, often longer. Passing through the security was like peeling an onion; there were layers on layers of bars and guards, scanners and friskings.

For the first time in a year, Raquel had been living in a state of peaceful ecstasy brought on by her liberating meeting with Dr. Anil. She felt that she was reconstructing her life. Once a woman with many friends, she'd allowed those friends to drift away as she went into isolation at the moment a doctor had told her she had stage 2 breast cancer. She gave up clients and suspended her beloved teaching at Columbia. Only her secretary, Roger, knew all the details about the chemotherapy, radiation, and surgery. When she lost her hair, she stayed in her apartment. Roger constantly sent her text messages about the dangers of isolation. But she saw herself as hunkering down, in battle mode, a dedicated soldier.

But it was different now. Raquel—taught by Theresa Bui about the happiness and feeling of community that friends could bring—was reaching out to people. She had joined a support group for cancer patients and survivors. She let the dean of the faculty at Columbia know she would return. She'd even had two television appearances on CBS for the first time in more than a year.

Raquel had done something else in the last five weeks. She had a small group of retired FBI agents now working in retirement as private investigators. Freed from the Bureau, they were also free to use techniques and means of access that as agents they couldn't use. Raquel was never sure how they went about their business. She welcomed the results, not the process. Over the last several weeks she spent more than thirty thousand dollars to get the results.

And now she wanted to use those results.

After she had finally passed through all of MDC's security stations, Raquel waited less than five minutes in the stuffy visiting room before Juan Suarez suddenly emerged from a sliding iron door like an actor from behind a curtain. Dressed in the trim blue uniform of a federal prisoner rather than a baggy green state uniform, he looked relaxed. He was smiling. Kept in rigorous solitary confinement, Juan had no idea what had happened in the five weeks since they had last seen each other in the holding cell in the Riverhead courtroom after the verdict.

Although Raquel hadn't intended to do it, she rose to her feet when Juan reached out to embrace her. She recalled how angry and how altered Juan had become from time to time in the closing days of the trial; it was unsettling to recall that his voice could change in an instant from the faltering, often charming Spanish accent to a voice that seemed fluent in English.

"Raquel," he said as he sat at the plastic table, "I've missed you. And I worry that you forgot about me. Or that you are mad with me."

"No. There was a whole backlog of things I had to do after the trial. I helped Theresa's parents arrange for a memorial service."

"I think about Theresa."

"There were hundreds of people at the memorial. People from her childhood in Chinatown, people she knew in college and law school, her friends in the city. The service helped her parents and family, it made the grief a little lighter."

Juan said, "I loved her."

There it was, she realized, that sincere charm whose presence had led her to look forward to the weekly visits, many of them not even necessary, in Riverhead. Juan Suarez was one of those rare people who gave energy to any room he was in, even a prison conference room. *I loved her*, he had just said about Theresa. And Raquel forced herself to think, *Be careful, girl*.

"How is life here?" she asked.

"Not bad, not good. I can only get out of the cell fifteen minutes a day. But they let me have *Don Quixote*. I'm almost finished. Then I'll ask for another book. Maybe they give it to me."

Raquel said, "Actually, Juan, you don't need to worry about whether they'll give you another book here. You won't be here very much longer."

"What are you telling me?"

"You're going to be taken to JFK soon and put on a plane to leave the country."

"I don't understand."

"Your conviction has been thrown out. You're being deported to Mexico, where you will be set free."

Juan Suarez folded his hands on the table in front of him and lowered his forehead onto them, a gesture of prayer. He murmured in a low voice in Spanish.

"Do you want to know why?" Raquel asked after a minute.

"Sure, please."

"Two kids playing in the landfill near your house in Sag Harbor found a poncho and long knife buried in the ground. The FBI and the state labs tested them. None of your blood and DNA was on the poncho or the knife."

"*Gracia de Dios.*"

"Do you want to know what else has happened?"

He nodded, his hands folded at his lips. "What?"

"The FBI has arrested the three detectives—Halsey, Cohen, and Cerullo—who testified against you. Halsey for obstructing justice and lying during his testimony at the trial, Cerullo and Cohen for stealing the cash in the Richardson bedroom."

Juan said, "Those are bad men."

Raquel Rematti had made this trip to prison not just to tell Juan Suarez that he was about to be set free. She had another purpose. She said, "How do you know that?"

"Sure they are."

"Don't you know them?"

Juan became very still. "What?"

"You met Cerullo and Cohen, didn't you?"

"I saw them when they came to court."

"You didn't know them before?"

"Before? No. Why do you ask?"

"And do you want to know about Jimmy?"

"The coke dealer?"

"He was indicted for killing Brad. His DNA was on the machete and poncho. Since he was arrested five years ago on another charge, his DNA was taken and stored, and it matches the DNA on the weapon."

As she had expected, Juan simply stared at her.

"But, Juan, they can't find Jimmy."

"Why not? They found me."

"You knew Jimmy, didn't you?"

"Sure, Raquel, I saw him around the house all the time. Mrs. Richardson hated him. Mr. Richardson liked him."

Raquel Rematti leaned forward, her elbows resting on the table and her index fingers touching her chin. "You know that we'll never see each other again. You'll get back to Mexico and be free."

"Who knows, Raquel? Maybe I'll come back."

"Let me ask you this, Juan: You didn't know Jimmy just through seeing him at Brad's house, right?"

"I don't understand."

"You've said that many, many times to me."

"What?"

"That you don't understand."

"There's been a lot that I don't understand."

Raquel, now very concentrated, said, "You and Jimmy worked for Oscar Caliente, right?"

"I told you, Raquel. I worked for Oscar in the city, and then he forced me do some work on the island. I didn't want to, but I did. And one of Oscar's drivers, Jocko, told me that Jimmy was working for Oscar, too. So, yes, I know that Jimmy worked for Oscar."

"People force you to do a lot of things, don't they, Juan?"

"Sometimes. I was afraid of Oscar. I told you that. I'm still afraid of him."

"Were you afraid of Brad Richardson?"

Raquel saw that Juan's charm was dissolving. "Why are you asking me that?"

"You owe me some answers, Juan."

"Raquel, I've always given you answers."

"Where's Jimmy?" she asked.

"I don't know where he is." In his voice now was that disturbing edge she had heard before, the voice of someone who knew how to scream and command. As he grew more intense, more focused, his English became more fluent, the accent dissipating. "Why are you asking? Where are you going with this?" He was moody, combative.

"Juan, nothing can touch you now. You can never be charged with anything relating to Brad's death. And I can't say anything to anyone about what you tell me about anything you've done. I'm still your lawyer, you're my client. In a way, I'm your partner. You could tell me you blew up the World Trade Center and I could not repeat that. You understand that, don't you?"

"I've always trusted you, Raquel."

Raquel knew she was alone with Juan Suarez in a small room with an iron floor, concrete walls, an iron ceiling, and a locked door. She also knew because her investigators had told her Juan Suarez was a man with infinite rage: they had visited the two men he attacked in East Harlem and brought back pictures of the lacerating wounds Juan had inflicted in seconds. And she knew that the hoodlum in the prison yard who attacked Juan had all the cartilage in his throat broken, also in a second.

Raquel said, "You know Jimmy is dead, don't you?"

Juan came closer, his arms stretched across the table toward Raquel. Quietly he said, "We took Jimmy on one of those boats with a small kitchen and a small bedroom out into the ocean. We left from the marina in Sag Harbor. Oscar was with us."

"Was this after Jimmy killed Brad Richardson?"

"Jimmy didn't kill Brad Richardson," Juan Suarez said. "I did."

Raquel stared at Juan's black eyes. He stared at her. The isolated room was absolutely still. The iron door was locked.

"Why?"

"I introduced Oscar to Brad. Oscar told Brad and everyone else that he wanted to buy polo horses. Brad liked meeting people. Oscar said he owned horse ranches in Argentina and needed polo horses. Oscar can pretend to be anyone."

"And you can, too, isn't that right, Juan. Or is it Anibal?"

He ignored the question. "Oscar got mad at Mr. Richardson."

"Why?"

"Mr. Richardson couldn't keep his hands off anyone."

"What else?" Raquel asked. "Oscar Caliente is too smart to have Brad Richardson killed because Brad tried to kiss him."

"Brad knows hundreds of people all over the world. A friend in Argentina told him that there was no Oscar Caliente there who bought and sold ponies for millions."

"And Brad told Oscar that?"

"Yes. Brad didn't know how to be careful."

"And Oscar felt disrespected?"

"He did."

"And Oscar had expected to get money from Brad for a horse deal?"

"Sure."

"How do you know that?"

"Brad told me. Oscar, too."

"And then Brad walked away from the deal?"

"He did."

"But he expected Oscar to still hold hands?"

"Brad was a nice man, Raquel. I've always told you that. But he didn't understand other people. He thought everything was a game."

"And Oscar?"

"Oscar has people killed, Raquel, because he likes to."

Raquel felt the onset of a fever of anger in all her body. "He had Theresa killed, didn't he?"

"No, he had you killed. He wanted you. I told you to leave him alone. You didn't. You need to think about that, Raquel."

She didn't respond to that. It was too painful.

"Oscar told you to kill Brad?"

"He knew I learned to do that in Mexico."

"And you did it?"

"Yes."

"And you took Jimmy out on the boat and killed him."

"We did."

"You are an animal."

"You haven't lived my life, Raquel. I've survived."

Raquel was tempted to ask how he felt about the people he had hurt to enable him to survive. But she wanted facts, not justifications, and besides no criminal in her experience had ever accepted responsibility. It was always the same litany: denial, excuse, crazy rationales.

"Tell me this: Did Oscar say why he wanted Jimmy to vanish?"

"He said he didn't trust him."

"And Oscar didn't trust you either, did he?"

"We put Jimmy's blood on a new poncho while we were still on the boat. We burned the poncho I wore. But first I took the blood from Brad and the blood from Jimmy and put it on the new poncho."

"And the blood from the Borzois, right?"

"Yes, Raquel."

"And you cleaned the machete?"

"I did."

"And you put Jimmy's blood on the machete?"

"Yes."

"And you brought the poncho and machete back to the marina in Sag Harbor?"

Juan's smile was cold. "Be careful, Raquel. You know too much."

"I'll worry about myself." Raquel was rigid. "You were supposed to put the poncho and knife in Jimmy's apartment in Hampton Bays?"

"You need to be careful."

"Jocko was going to drive you out there the next day?"

"Who told you all this?"

"You put the poncho and knife in the abandoned dump to hide them overnight, didn't you?"

"You know, Raquel, that Oscar is in Mexico. He will come back here. He has lots of disguises."

"But the police came for you before Jocko, isn't that right?"

"Sure, they came first."

"Oscar was mad at you?"

"Oscar is always mad."

Raquel's hands were clenched. "Where did you put the money?"

"What money?"

"Come on, it's time to stop it. You stole money from Brad's office, didn't you? The cash upstairs wasn't the only money, was it?"

"Raquel, Oscar is still out there. He won't forget you when I tell him you know all this."

"You're threatening me."

"No, Raquel, this time I'm telling you the truth."

The iron door slid open. It was time for the random headcount that brought an abrupt end to all visits.

He smiled as he left the room. "I love you, Raquel." And then he vanished behind the closing gate, leaving for some place in the world where Raquel Rematti would never see him again.

She drove to Brooklyn Heights. She walked on the high promenade that overlooked everything that was glorious about New York: the glittering harbor, the century-old span of the Brooklyn Bridge, the clean, gleaming skyline. White gulls floated on invisible waves of wind.

In the breeze and bright air, Raquel Rematti felt that she was cleansed.

CPSIA information can be obtained at www.ICGtesting.com
Printed in the USA
LVOW08s0602140116

469958LV00008B/14/P